M000045947

DARK RAINBOW

QUEER EROTIC HORROR

Taste the Rainbow!

[signature]

EDITED BY
ANDREW ROBERTSON

Dark Rainbow© Andrew Robertson 2018

All Rights Reserved. No part of this book may be reproduced or transmitted in any form or by any means, electronic or mechanical, including photocopying, without permission in writing from the publisher.
This is a work of fiction. Names, characters, places, and incidents are the product of the author's imagination or are used fictitiously. Any resemblance to actual events, locales, or persons, living or dead, is coincidental.

All stories published with permission of the authors who hold individual copyrights.
For more information contact:
Riverdale Avenue Books
5676 Riverdale Avenue
Riverdale, NY 10471

www.riverdaleavebooks.com

Design by www.formatting4U.com
Cover art by Scott Carpenter

Digital ISBN: 9781626014848
Paperback ISBN: 9781626014831

First Edition October 2018

Table of Contents

Introduction

I've always been drawn to horror, darkness, outsiders and underground culture. Like a moth, the undeniable flame of everything and everyone that is weird, dark, feared and even despised lures me in.

I was about ten the first time a black and white horror film lit up the TV at my parents' house. It was Tod Browning's vampiric masterpiece starring Bela Lugosi as Count Dracula based on Bram Stoker's legendary novel. Dracula was clearly a monster, but there was so much more. He was irresistible, handsome, powerful and nearly immortal. Growing up knowing that you are queer and feeling society's judgment being cast on you before you even come out makes power like that so very attractive. The next day I was at the local hobby shop purchasing a glow-in-the-dark model of that same character, soon to be followed by Frankenstein, and the Wolfman.

I would sit on my bed in the dark, watching the green glow cast by those models like a magic mist in the corner of the room, wondering what my future could hold, and when I would finally get to be a vampire too.

When it comes to horror, I think that many queer people have a special place in their heart for all the freaks and weirdos that populate the screen during a midnight madness screening. That goes for both the heroes and the villains. Some of us feel disjointed, like a half-assembled Frankenstein's monster waiting for something to complete us. Others long to turn into a bat and fly away to something better. Some of us just want revenge, cause growing up as a queer in this world is never easy. Maybe you long to become your bully's nightmare, like a rainbow-striped Freddy Krueger, or to be an immortal and untouchable vampire god, like Lestat.

As the years passed, I discovered films like *Frankenhooker, A Nightmare on Elm Street, Doctor Gore* and *Friday the 13th*, before my all-time favorite, Clive Barker's carnal horror masterpiece *Hellraiser*. Soon after came the 1980s erotic experimental films of Richard Kern, which challenged the viewer in ways I had never experienced before. Did I feel almost guilty watching them? Well, we are all guilty.

My personal library grew to include books by Anne Rice, Anaïs Nin, Lydia Lunch, Stephen King, Tricia Warden, Evelyn Lau and Henry Miller, and my personal soundtrack came via albums by Siouxsie and the Banshees, Throbbing Gristle, Coil, The Cramps, Skinny Puppy and Ministry.

One of the threads that tied all those works together was the darkness that they brought to the light…that the line between sex and violence, lust and love, queer and straight, horror and delight were often blurred. At times, they became the same thing, and that is as uncomfortable as it is attractive. That is also the thread that binds the stories in this anthology.

This book is by no means a comprehensive study

of what it means to be queer, or meant to define erotic horror in that context. In these pages are imaginative, dark and unsettling works that explore these themes under a queer lens, and dare to weave those often contradictory threads together. Queer erotic horror is a nascent genre, and my aim with this collection is to give the reader 15 unique tales to help that genre grow.

I hope you enjoy what you discover at the end of this dark rainbow.

—Andrew Robertson
October 2018

Pip and Estella
Valerie Alexander

Some men fall in love so easily. It robs me of the sport of it. I can't be a champion of heartbreak if these men succumb too rapidly. My date tonight falls in one swoop when I unhook my bra in his car.

"You're so beautiful, Estella."

I used to think rich men would be harder to seduce but all men seem susceptible to the same witchcraft: my mouth, the Southern moon, my open-legged splendor on their laps. Which is perhaps why my date makes a strangled noise and comes out with, "You're my dream girl."

Of course I am, I want to say to him, *I'm Estella Havisham, I was raised to be your dream and your destruction too.* But then I think, *Where's my dream?*

I've seduced construction workers, the high school baseball coach, some of the rougher studs at the local bar. All were for practice, none of them interested me. But now I am 19 and time is of the essence. The Havisham family funds are running dry, and so I practice my wiles on richer men. Learning their thinking, their vulnerabilities: practice for even wealthier, future victims and finally a very rich husband.

I kiss my date goodnight in his car at the end of my driveway, between the cypress trees. "I have to go."

"Can I come in?"

"No, my mother's home. She doesn't like men in the house."

He begins talking about me meeting his parents tomorrow night. He's already so besotted that he's willing to ignore the town rumors about *those crazy Havisham women out in that decaying mansion*. No doubt everyone has warned him. No doubt they've shared the rumors about my mother's insanity and the occasional men who go missing. Probably he accepts that my mother is a lost cause but thinks that he can salvage me like a beautiful feral kitten.

All the men think that. Maybe not in so many words when I'm pulling up my skirt, but they all follow me down the same path of ruin. Even though I never feel anything for them.

* * *

The house is lit with candles when I come in. My mother comes floating through the living room in a tattered silk peignoir. In the darkened room, she looks almost like the supermodel goddess she was 20 years ago.

Her makeup-smeared eyes stare at me. "Who was that one?"

"Tom. The new D.A."

She laughs a low guttural laugh of satisfaction. "That's my Estella." She assesses my eyes, my hair, my legs. "I taught you well, didn't I?"

She drifts through the wreckage piled between the overstuffed sofas—the old copies of *Vogue*, the dusty crystal globlets, the framed painting of a tiger, the dead potted trees. The racks of chiffon beaded dresses. An enormous stuffed black panther hung with costume jewelry looms over the pearls scattered across the floor for the kittens to chase. To her, it's a museum of preservation. To me it's a mausoleum.

"It's time for breakfast." She disappears down the dark hall.

Only one meal is served in this house, and it is served in the dead of the night. Salmon benedict with roasted potatoes, bacon, muffins, coffee, juice: the wedding breakfast menu my mother devised 20 years ago for a ceremony that never was.

I'm pulling the muffins from the oven when the wheels roll up the hallway. My mother pushes the chair up to the table and smiles. "A mimosa for me, darling. Your father's joining us for breakfast today."

The brownish withered thing at the head of the table slumps slightly in his wheeled throne. My father's broad shoulders have collapsed in the tailored suit, which has held up well for two decades. But the body within seems to hunch in on itself, no longer muscled or six-foot-three. His hands are mere stubbed claws curling on the tablecloth, his dessicated face puckered in a permanent, moon-sad 'O.'

"Hi, Daddy." I put an empty glass before him, a mimosa before my mother.

She eats vigorously, dispensing advice between bites. "Your D.A. may be intelligent, Estella, but he's a crude animal like any man," she says. "Remember, nature made men physically stronger but made us more

3

beautiful. It is our duty to break them so they can't commit the arrogance and cruelty they would otherwise."

"I know, Mom."

She muses on the rich victims ahead of me, the men who will spoil me with their fortunes. When I was a child, my mother would reminisce about her modeling days, when she traveled the world at 15 to be photographed by day and passed around by businessmen at night. But in recent years she's focused on providing guidance intended to hone my predatory powers so I can stalk that ultimate quarry: a very wealthy husband.

"It's good that you don't feel anything for these men, Estella. You can stay detached. A billionaire is the real game. And you'll deserve every penny, because a beautiful wife is the ultimate gift."

My mother smiles at my mummified father, as if he did take her for his beautiful wife instead of rejecting her the night she told him of her pregnancy. As she speculates on which CEO or heir I might marry, her eyes glow. Her fortyish face is unravaged by time; she sleeps by day, walks the house at night, and hasn't been exposed to the sun in almost 20 years. Her once-famous face still has the cheekbones and lips that got her on magazine covers once. But her eyes shine like green moons of insanity.

After breakfast I clear the dishes and she brings my father's corpse into the living room for their nightly, one-sided conversation. A Brahms violino concerto has just begun to unwind its initial sweet notes out the windows as I go out the veranda doors, past the garden of tuberoses and hydrangeas, down to the small hexagonal summerhouse to watch the stars

4

which, my mother named me after, to enforce my mission of staying beautiful and unattainable forever.

Maybe it's the faint ache of the violin floating over the swamp night noises, but melancholy pierces me until I fetch the special powder from inside the summerhouse—a mix of mugwort, mustard seed, wormwood and pipsissewa. The local swamp witch makes it for me, just as she made my mother the mummification powder all those years ago.

I sprinkle it at the foot of the yew tree. Here is where I buried the brownish toe I snapped off my father's mummy, so I could always conjure him forth.

He rises up, a businessman turned into a wispy specter no more substantial than mist. "Hi, Daddy," I say for the second time that night.

"Estella." He sounds so pitiful. "What trouble have you stirred up now?"

"I just wanted to say hello. I miss you."

"Why can't you let me rest? Every time you summon me, you force me to suffer because I know you're still her pawn."

My father's ghost is always doleful, always bitter toward my mother. But he's the only sane conversation to be had out here in this swamp kingdom of dripping Spanish moss and old *Vogue* magazines. The swamp witch isn't one for socializing and she's usually busy with her rituals besides.

"I'm not her pawn, Dad. And I'll be leaving soon to get married." There aren't any truly rich men around here. And someone has to make some money, with all of her jewels long since sold off and her modeling money almost gone. "I'll be going to Los Angeles, maybe, or New York."

"Don't marry without love," he insists. "You haven't been in love yet. Once you have, you'll know better."

"I'm not going to fall in love, Dad. She trained me better than that."

"Estella, you have to get away from her," he says. "But first send me home. I can't rest with my corpse in that house. Bury me up north, in Connecticut with the rest of my family."

This is the point of the night when I remember that my father didn't want me to be his family. That he's the married man who dumped my 19-year-old mother when she told him she was pregnant.

"I'm your family too," I say. "And I don't know if we'd still be able to have these visits with your remains so far away."

"Estella..." He continues to whine, but my attention is caught by headlights traveling up the road, through the cypress trees. No one lives out here but us. Long past midnight, it's too late for any deliveries, any visitors. So I creep back through the garden to see a man approaching our delapidated antebellum mansion. It's Aaron, the software engineer I practiced on last week. Just a few nights ago he confronted me in town and demanded I stop ignoring him.

He walks up the porch steps and rings the bell. I watch from the dark.

"I'm not leaving until she talks to me," he tells my mother when she answers. "Estella owes me. She *promised* me."

(That isn't true but I know it feels like a promise: my opening arms, my smitten eyes and all those faked orgasms that convinced them I was falling in love also.)

"Estella is done with you." My mother looks triumphant.

Aaron pushes the door open and stalks past her. "Estella?"

Oh no. *Oh no, oh no, oh no*. But it's too late. His scream rips through the night and by the time I've run inside he's on the kitchen floor, a wet gurgling noise in his throat while my mother stabs him in the stomach again and again. His brown eyes meet mine in helplessness and disbelief. *But you're good*, his eyes say, *you're special* and I wish he could live long enough to grasp that he mistook which of us was the mouse and which was the cat.

His eyes go empty. My mother looks up at me in her red-soaked pegnoir.

"They always *intrude*," she says. She's trembling with indignation. "Why do they do that? They leave when you want them to stay and they intrude when you want them to leave."

"Mom.*"* I'm struggling not to vomit. A foul smell has filled the kitchen and Aaron's dead eyes are still on me. Murder smells horrible, no one tells you that in advance. "You can't keep doing this. The police are going to figure it out."

She considers the size of him. "You'll have to take him in pieces."

My stomach lurches. "I can't."

"Oh, Estella. So sensitive and delicate." There's a note of contempt in her voice. "Apparently I have to do everything."

Together we drag his body down the veranda steps and onto the grass. I bring her the electric saw and go inside, plugging my ears. But nothing

7

completely blots out the enthusiastic roar of dismemberment. When the saw goes quiet, I bring her rags from a trunk of old clothes. Then it's back down to the mosquitos and the cypress, the thick pungent stench of swamp water filling my nose. It's barely visible in the dark but I find the swamp witch's house and knock on her door.

She looks at my bloody bundles. "Again?" is all she says.

She calls the alligators as she calls the owls, the snakes, the cats. Speaking the language of animals isn't witchcraft, she says, but a forgotten art. The gators rise to the swamp surface, their eyes gleaming, as she unwraps the severed limbs and tosses them forward like so many treats.

My father's ghost flickers next to me, a phantasm glowing in the swamp darkness. "Look what you've done," he says. "How many men will the two of you kill?"

Other corpses flash through my mind, the baseball player's head rolling across the foyer, the dentist's chest ripped open with an axe in the driveway. "I killed no one. She did it."

The swamp witch frowns and dismisses my father with a wave of her hand; she dislikes his whining. She's told me before that she believes the dead are meant to serve and obey. "I understand your mother's bitterness," she says. "But there's more to life than hurting men and marrying money, Estella. Give real love a chance."

It's hard to take life advice from a woman who's chosen to live alone in a swamp. But I humor her. "Real love? Men bore me."

The swamp witch produces a twisted root from her pocket. In the faint starlight filtering through the cypress, it looks like a spindly hand. "Then look for who you do love." She traces the root across my face and then drops it into my hands.

I head back home in the moonlight to collect Aaron's torso.

* * *

The next night the cops come out, faintly annoyed that they've had to visit us yet again. They stand out in the yard because they know my mother doesn't like them in the house. The insect zapper turns their faces golden in the humid Southern night.

"Aaron's friends say he was talking about you a lot," says the oldest cop. "His car was found up the road. Any idea how it got there?"

"Well, he was spying on me, obviously," I say. "I was on a date last night, he was probably trying to see who I was with."

One cop asks wearily if Aaron had gotten violent with me. I watch one of the kittens disembowel a mouse on the porch and say no. He was just a pest.

"Is your mother around? We'd like to talk to her."

Please no, not that, but I retrieve her from her boudoir of cosmetics and delusion, and she comes out in a brocade robe of emerald green and jade. Black mule slippers with one broken heel taped together. "Gentlemen," she says seductively.

"Ms. Havisham."

They ask if she's seen Aaron and her enormous green eyes are liquid insanity as she says, "Oh, the boy that was hounding my daughter. I can't tell one from another."

A cop makes a good suggestion: shrubbery so my obsessive ex-boyfriends can't see from the road into the windows. One calls his friend Joe the landscaper and asks if he can come pronto to protect the beautiful and hunted Estella Havisham. He can't, he says, but his assistant Pip can be there tomorrow.

* * *

A new man is a fresh conquest. In the afternoon sunlight I watch a dark-haired boy climb out of a battered truck. I go out in my white cotton dress to give him a head tilt and dazzling smile. "I'm Estella. Thanks for coming."

Then Pip turns and I realize she's a girl. She's my age, about 19 and tall, with tanned muscled arms. She's cute in a punk rock way, with lots of tattoos and a face that's suspicious and adorable at the same time

She looks me up and down like she's never seen anything like me before. "Why are all you dressed up?" she says finally, with the air of someone who's taken a long time to think of something to say.

"I'm not. I like wearing dresses in the summer."

I don't know how to charm women, even handsome butch girls like this. An unusual energy is surging through me, followed by confusion: should I vamp it up or play the initiator? "Come on, I'll show you where we want the shrubbery."

Pip tells me her story as she works, how she's going to school in the fall but came here to help out while Joe recovers from a heart procedure. I express interest, bring her glasses of sweet tea. I only flash her once, at the end of the day. "Accidentally" of course, by bending way over a ceramic pot and giving her a full look at my pussy. When I straighten up, she's rooted to the grass, face flushed.

But we're still on the front lawn and that won't do. "I should show you the summer house. Come on."

I beckon her through the wild garden, where the shadows of evening are stretching across the grass and cooling the air. She frowns but follows me to the summer house, where I've spent so many afternoons reading and playing with the kittens.

This is the first girl I've had here. The first person at all I've allowed this far onto the property, for who could I allow to see our splendid degradation? I pick a rhododendron and sniff it before staring into her eyes in the fading light of sunset.

"I think Joe said you had a boyfriend..." Pip says in a strangled voice.

"I've had lots of boyfriends. But none of them have ever interested me like you."

Pip pulls off her T-shirt, leans naked and trembling against the wall of the summer house. She's so beautiful with her half-moon breasts over that flat brown stomach, that I see now the error of my ways in seducing all those men by moonlight, that nothing can compete with a naked girl lit in the rosy nimbus of sunset. Her brown eyes turn feral in its glow, her dark hair already damp and rumpled and the silver rings through her pierced nipples mine for the tugging. As my fingers move over her tattoos, her legs start shaking.

So this is what it's like to really want someone, to

11

feel lust rising up my spine. I slide my hands down her back. Her muscles are hard from years of real labor and her ass is firm in my grip. Still in my white dress, I go on my knees and take down her jeans, looking up at her so innocently, even though no truly innocent girl would eat her cunt before we've even kissed.

The heat and smell of her make me dizzy. My tongue swims over her the way I would want it and though I can't play the expert with her as I can with other lovers, she melts under my mouth. She sinks down to the grass and pets my hair, groaning, whispering "Oh Jesus" and all those other things I've heard before, but in her voice they sound like prayers to the goddess kneeling between her legs.

The taste of sweet girl honey in my mouth. Her pussy clings to my fingers and I suck her clit until she begins shaking for real. And then her softness begins to squeeze me and a tangy new taste floods my tongue.

Pip brings me up to her face and we kiss. Then I straddle her in my grass-strained dress and play with her nipple rings. "I don't know what to do."

The words come out of their own volition. I'm more surprised to hear them than she is. But Pip smiles and says, "You don't have to do anything—let me take care of you."

She feels my pussy until I pull off my dress and show her what she's been touching. "You're the most beautiful girl I've ever seen," she mutters in anguish and while I've heard that before, it feels new this time. Like being naked on a cool spring morning can feel like being born again.

Pip takes her time feeling every part of me, my knees, the nape of my neck, even my toes come in for her exam. The sun is extinguished and a deep twilight shrouds the garden in blue fog until all we can see are our pale bodies as I mount her hips.

Slowly I push my cunt against hers, rocking just enough to savor it for myself. It might be so long until I have someone like this again. A girl this tough and sweet and beautiful, where filling my hands with her tits feels like attaining a long-awaited gift. Her wet clit rubbing on mine feels so good I want to cry. I fuck her very slowly, no tricks or techniques tonight. I want to feel everything.

But then Pip grunts and grabs my upper arms suddenly, flipping me into the dirt. She pushes me face down into the earth and holds me there by nape of my neck. "Spread."

It's so unexpectedly rude and commanding of her that lust rockets through me and I open my legs as wide as I can. She releases my neck and turns her attention to my thighs. With one thumb, she strokes my pussy, then plunges inside. It's the oddest feeling, her thumb moving inside me as I can feel her eyes move over my ass, my split cunt. This is my least beautiful position, I've always felt, but I let her look because this is someone I either don't always need to be beautiful for or someone who finds me beautiful no matter what. Or both. I bury my face in the ground and breathe in the smell of earth and flowers as her fingers thrusts in and out of me. Then without warning she yanks me backward, pulling my bottom half up. She buries her face in my pussy, licking me roughly and biting my thighs.

I claw at the ground and scream. Pip masterfully takes control of my entire body, her fingers working inside me as she sucks my clit. Panic surges through me as I feel all control desert me. I'm lost, my own body betraying me as she reaps an orgasm from me, pulling it out like a hummingbird sucking out pollen from a flower. I've never felt anyone take my heart and my orgasm like that before, and I'm bewildered as she flips me over again.

She sits back on her haunches and pulls me onto her lap. I wrap my legs around her, struggling to hang on as she slides her fingers inside me and begins to fuck me hard, bouncing me on her lap. She's fucking me deep and fast and hard, those lean hips of hers moving in a blur. She pounds me so hard that it's like heartbreaker Estella gets driven right out of me and all that's left is the howling, ecstatic animal at my core. It's like a religious conversion, a wave of sweat and joy breaking from my scalp and sweeping down my body as we fuck. And that's how we come, me bucking in Pip's lap with her teeth in my neck, both of us covered with dirt and sweat and coming on each other in a sticky hot glory.

We collapse onto the ground. Night has covered the Southern countryside with its foggy symphony of crickets and swamp music. Gradually we get up, Pip looking like I've just created the world and delivered it to her, but I twist around the edge of the summer house and look up at the main house. Its massive antebellum decay looms in the night.

"Looks like no one's home…" Pip says.

"My mother's in there."

"All the lights are off."

"She likes the dark."

I slide my hands up her chest, cupping her breasts. "Will you sleep out here with me tonight? In the summer house?"

It's too romantic, the crickets, the summer night, just the two of us in our bungalow in Paradise. Pip plucks a bluish-lavender sprig of hydrangea and tucks it into my tangled hair. I almost feel bad at the misconceptions this girl is growing inside her trusting heart. But I deserve a treat, don't I? Breaking men is real work, and no one appreciates the sacrifices I've made for my mother. Just once I should have someone for my own satisfaction, and not as practice for capturing a smitten multimillionaire.

Pip pulls me onto the summer house couch and we go to sleep.

* * *

So now I know about butch girls, how they're all ink and muscle but melt like kittens. So tender, so hard, Pip pulling me against her in the night and muttering "Will you," as we begin to fuck again. Sleepy at first, her skin warm against mine as we grind against each other slowly, in that somnabulistic lethargy that makes every inch and breath so excruciatingly real. Then we get more energetic until I hang off the couch and put my hands on the dusty floor and open my legs so she can wheelbarrow me, licking me and ramming me without mercy. Her fingers are rhythmic and ruthless, making me think I've found the dark mystery I've never found in my other practice victims. When she drags her nails down my spine, I come and come, screaming and soaking the dusty floor.

* * *

15

I've broken hearts like a stiletto stabbed through a frozen lake. The color of my love is pale blue. I'm from the moon.

All the things I want to say to Pip as the sun creeps into the summerhouse, streaking the damp leaves moldering on the floor.

The birds are loud. My stomach growls. I know my mother's asleep by now, so I pull on my grass-stained white dress and lead Pip back up to the house. Her tools are still in the grass.

"Stay out here and I'll get our checkbook."

Inside the dim penumbra of the house, the sweet smell of candle wax hangs in the air. In the library, where I manage our accounts, I fetch the checkbook from the rosewood secretary. But when I bring the check out, Pip is standing in the living room with a stunned face. "Someone like you can't possibly live here." She turns slowly, scanning the piles of magazines and clothes, the scattered jewelry.

Why did she have to ruin it? "You have to leave. Now."

She looks at the framed magazine covers of my mother, the iron sconces on the walls and the dried wax beneath them on the carpet.

"Where's your father?" She sounds stupefied.

"Vanished off the face of the earth." I hand her the check.

"He didn't pay child support?"

Hard to pay anything when you've been stabbed in your sleep, but I don't say that. This is a house of murder and we keep the secrets of the house from outsiders.

Pip turns to me with a resolute face. "I'm going to rescue you."

A wave of cold humiliation sweeps over me. Pip pities me. She thinks I'm a pathetic girl living in a hoarder's house. "You'd better hope someone rescues you from me first."

She doesn't hear it. She looks around again, then back at me with determined pride. "I have a scholarship to Berkeley this fall. Come with me."

A cruel retort forms on my lips but then something new, something unknown, softens me. "Look," I say. "You can't be here. Come back tonight. I'll meet you at the summerhouse."

Pip looks at the grandfather clock, the cracked gilt-framed mirror. But then she nods and kisses me goodbye, and vanishes into the sunlight.

* * *

The sun sets, the toads begin and then it's another night in the loneliest swamp in the South.

Upstairs I put old records on the turntable, turn on the lamps. A black lace dress and pearls, 20 minutes with my makeup brushes, and I'm an assassin again. From my velvet jewelry case I retrieve another toe from my father, this one kept in a silver locket. I sprinkle the necromantic powder on it and he rises up like a mirage.

"You're wearing me out," he begs. "Oh, Estella, just bury me. Even if you can't send me home, give me my rest."

His shade is so bitter here in my lavish indigo bedroom, amidst the high heels and mirrors and old records. "Hush, Daddy," I say. The needle travels across the groove and then the scratchy next song

17

begins. "And anyway, I have good news tonight. I'm in love and I'll be leaving. Just like you wanted."

"Bury me first," he pleads. "Please, Estella, send me home."

"The things you say." I twirl the toe locket around his phantom head. "Aren't I your family? Isn't your home with me?" And, I realize now, the present situation is best; my mother will need his corpse here for company after I depart. And he'll be my only family once I've left with Pip, I'll still want these visits with his spirit.

So this is how ghosts weep: soundlessly, their eyes crumpling and their mouths in a silent wail of endless grief. But the sound of a truck door slamming distracts me.

"Estella!"

I fly out to my bedroom balcony. There she is on the grass in a white tank top and jeans, still ignorant of the house of horrors looming over her.

"Stay there. I'll come down."

But to my alarm, Pip heads for the door.

Oh no. My mother could rise at any moment and it could be the machete, the baseball bat, the axe. I stumble on the stairs in my heels and the record playing from my bedroom is all I hear as I move through the dark and ruined first floor rooms. The front door is open to the night, the crickets. The song ends upstairs. From somewhere there's a door opening, a rustling. I circle the ruins of magazines and evening gowns and then there's a spill of light: the door to my father's study is open.

Heart thumping, I move to the doorframe to see them together, Pip and the withered brown king of the mansion: my mummified father.

She stands frozen in this room of half-rotted velvet sofas and filthy drapes. She extends one hand and tentatively touches my father's withered face.

"Pip," I say. "Meet my father."

Pip takes one step back. "What the fuck is this?"

"Don't—" I beg but she charges past me, knocking over my father's chair.

And now pieces of destiny fall like dominoes. My mother's footsteps upstairs, her scream of outrage at hearing an outsider's voice in our house. The sound of her pounding down the stairs, knife in her hand, her face a smeared mask of makeup and fury. But Pip is already outside and sliding into her truck.

Her tires squeal out of the driveway. I watch her go, my only escape, as my mother stabs the knife into the door over and over in impotent rage.

"You," she pants. "You stupid, trusting girl." She shakes her head, sobbing but also laughing. "You fell for a female. A broke landscaper. She can't take care of us like a rich man can!"

Then she calms herself. "You'll learn," she says. "You'll still be my legacy. Because they're animals, Estella. You'll remember that and you'll take everything from them."

She walks so tiredly up the stairs. Maybe she's returning to her vanity to put on lipstick, a new evening gown for the police.

Instead the smell of smoke curls down the staircase. I try to liberate my father's withered corpse from the chair and drag it out to the patio but the wallpaper is burning and finally I run. The harsh smell of the burning house fills my nostrils. I've just reached the thick embrace of the swamp when the sound of engines come down the road.

Shouts of jubilation and violence: the townspeople are already at our house, screaming their suspicions as to where local men have been disappearing to.

I listen to the sirens of the police. The firemen are shouting at the townspeople to *get back, let us handle it, the women might still be in there*. Through the trees I can see the smoke billowing into the sky.

The swamp witch appears next to me, with a jar in her hand. "I don't expect I'll see you again," she says. "So in honor of your mother's madness, consider this a going-away gift. You'll need it; like her, you can't be alone."

* * *

The tech genius who becomes my husband falls in love with my celestial coldness. He takes me away from my gothic Southern tragedy (my murderous mother's funeral, my innocent sobs) to become his Silicon Valley bride indulged by his millions. But within a year of purchasing my beautiful mystery, my husband grows bored with my coolness just as he loses interest in his villa in Phuket, the Tibetan mastiff he had flown in from a European breeder. I don't take much when we divorce—stock, jewelry, a house in Pacific Heights, the dog. A trunk packed with a few powders and ointments and one grass-stained white cotton dress.

* * *

The fog comes in thick the night of my 31st birthday. From my front steps I listen to the distant fog horns as the silvery mist of dusk deepens into night.

I've requested a gift tonight and now the soft *thwap* of footsteps approaches the iron gate.

Pip at 30 is still dark and sexy, more imposing. We look at each other through the iron bars.

She hands me a collection of hydrangea blooms, their bluish-lavender petals glowing in the night. "Happy birthday."

It's been so long and I've thought of how this would go so many times since tracking her down. "Thank you for answering my email."

A small smile twists her lips. "You're still as beautiful as ever, Estella."

"It never got me anything I needed, unless that's why you've come here tonight."

She laughs uncomfortably. "I did want to see you. But I can't stay, Estella. I'm married now and I don't like lying to my wife..."

I unzip my black dress and let it fall, not caring if any neighbors can see me through the fog. Reaching up, I hold the top of the iron spikes, which lifts my nipples out of my black lace bustier. Pip reaches through the bars and traces my skin with just one finger, as if verifying I'm real.

This is the last time I'll play the unattainable goddess. I'm not in it tonight to torture my prey but rather to end my career of heartbreak with the only person who's ever mattered. Her fingers on my stomach remind me what it was like, being touched as the new and flawless dreamgirl. It's been so many years since I faded to beloved bride, then ignored wife, then reclusive divorcee. But tonight I feel beautiful in the fog and the dark, cool flowers under my feet. Tonight tells me love is mine at last.

I press up against the gate. "Don't stop. I've been missing you ever since that night."

Pip pulls down my underwear and touches me through the bars, her fingers possessing that same tactile magic as before. It's been so long and I've thought of her so many times that a churning storm roars through me. But I grit my teeth and let her torture me slowly, sliding her fingers in my pussy, drawing out that same flood of need she did before. I open my legs wider until we're fucking through the bars, slow and deliberate at first, each deep thrust pushing us back together. And then the last vestiges of her mistrust dissolve and she groans. Her fingers work me with all the power and inevitability of our reunion until I come in a throbbing wet mess.

I open the gate. "I just need to feel you in my arms one more time."

Pip hesitates. "One time," she says finally. "But then it has to be like tonight never happened."

"One time," I say, if one time can be eternity. And then because melting her is still what I do best, the last vestiges of her marital guilt dissolve and she follows me into my house.

"Just this once," she repeats. She thinks she's leaving after this. She doesn't know that this *once* is our wedding vow as I lead her to the bedroom, leading her to a knife and the swamp witch's jar of mummification powder, and into immortality.

Goldilocks and her Undead Bear
Julianne Snow

The mouth worked its way down the hard shaft, the tongue stroking frantically, taking it deep down the back of its throat. Gums work the turgid flesh, bringing moans of pleasure from the man almost driven to his knees with the force of the suction. The unrelenting pressure of the tongue and constant pulling on his cock quickly bring him to orgasm, the noise of the greedy giver sucking down his cum both satisfying and somewhat disturbing all at once.

Using all his strength to extricate his penis from the always hungry mouth, Howard Goldman turned and brought the silky edges of his eggplant colored robe together, cinching the belt around his waist.

"It's almost time to go on, my Bear," he said, his voice taking on the slightly higher timbre of his alter ego. "Maybe tonight I'll start with Gloria's *I Will Survive*?"

* * *

Her svelte sequined body swayed to the heart pumping rhythm of Stevie's *Edge of Seventeen* as she sang for the audience of her adoring fans. She expertly moved around the stage, not wasting a moment of emotion in the power ballad, her hips moving in time with her struts, her arms enveloping the surging squeals of the crowd, silently willing her Bears to keep out of her way.

Their act was a hit in all the downtown drag clubs. Goldilocks and her Three Bears played shows to sold-out, standing room only crowds almost every night. Goldy loved it: the attention, the praise, and mostly the hard cock she could get anytime she wanted it. That was one of the many bonuses of being a sought-after drag queen—not only could she pay the rent on time, but she was never alone when she didn't want to be.

Tall with the androgynous features that captivated many, Goldy was blessed. She had her Bears—Abraham, Gavin, and young Dave—to back her up on stage and a wealth of patrons who wanted nothing more than to support her and give in to her every whim. To say she was a diva put it mildly.

...just like the white winged dove sings a song...

A shrill cry cut the music pounding through the club like a knife, so loud even Goldy heard it over the playback in her ears. She stumbled to a stop high atop her six-inch platform satin stilettos in the marvelous shade of lilac that matched the sequined corset contorting her body into a more feminine outline. The blush pink and sky-blue tutu completed her current ensemble.

As Goldy struggled to see past the hot stage lighting shining down on her, the crowd surged forward as if it were trying to get away from something. Screams split the room as the music died completely, the hollowness of dead air alive with the sounds of terror.

"What the fuck…" she said into the still live microphone as she was joined on the edge of the stage by Abe, Gavin and Dave.

They all struggled to see the source of the commotion in the darkened recesses of the floor and when the house lights came on, the sudden bright lights and Goldy's shock almost knocked her over.

"Oh, hell no!" she wailed, turning on the platformed balls of her feet and strutting her way off stage. "Tell me I did not just see what I saw!"

Gasping while holding onto the edge of the crushed velvet curtains hanging in the wings, Goldy looked back into the crowd and couldn't believe what she did in fact see. Pure violence radiated from everywhere—people attacking others, biting them, blood everywhere.

"Goldy, we need to leave. C'mon!" Abe pulled at her arm so forcefully he almost pulled her off her heels. His desperation spread from his fingertips into the flesh of Goldy's arm.

She pulled away suddenly, her gaze spinning to rest on his face. "Have you seen what's going on out there?"

As if to emphasize her words, a low guttural growl came from her left just before a searing pain invaded her senses. Looking to her left, she saw a bloodied woman lift her head from the shredded mess that used to be the sequin and studded evening gloves she wore as part of her costume. While the broken teeth of the woman had made a mess of the satin and studs, it didn't look like her alabaster skin beneath the fabric had been affected. Screaming, Goldy tried to rip

25

her arm from the woman's grasp but found she was up against inhuman strength.

The bloodied woman's face crumpled just before her body crumbled to the ground, the black stiletto from Goldy's next number firmly entrenched in her skull. The terrifying countenance she adopted in death a stark contrast to the stillness of her body. As she stared, Goldy could see the blackened veins running up the neck of the woman, the spiderweb of the infection, or drug reaction, whatever it was, creeping across her slack face.

"It's officially time to get out of here," Gavin said, his eyes searching for makeshift weapons among the props backstage. Spying the axe behind the glass of the fire suppression system, he used a nearby folding chair to smash it and grab the wooden handle. Turning back to the group, he moved forward, toward the door that led out the back alley.

Tottering high atop her heels, Goldy moved toward the door, carefully sidestepping the broken woman on the floor. She beckoned for the boys to follow her, grabbing the remaining black stiletto for her own weapon as she passed by.

"We can go to my loft," Goldy said. "We should be safe there."

Not waiting to see if any of them had something to say to the contrary, Goldy burst kamikaze-like through the door into the alley. Stopping short before fully exiting the club, she came face to face with a contorted visage being chased by something far more terrifying. The body tried to squirm past her, all hands arms, and elbows. With nowhere to go, the young man is stopped short, the frantic arms of the ghoul chasing him, dragging him backward to its open mouth. With a scream and an arterial spray, the young man went down with the monster atop him.

Goldy and her Bears ran through the alley, knowing they had very little time to escape. It was mostly clear as many of the patrons had been chased out of the club through the front doors. Knocking aside the grabbing hands of the few zombies outside, Goldy and her Bears navigated the length of the alley without too much interference, turning left at the first cross street to make their way to Goldy's loft which thankfully wasn't too far away.

* * *

Getting to the loft had been easier than expected—the streets were still clear and if they encountered one of the inflicted, they were easy enough to swat away as they ran. A few times Goldy had tripped over her own feet, almost breaking an ankle in the process, but Abe and Gavin were able to keep her on her feet and moving in the right direction. Dave had fallen a little farther behind the group, his ankle appearing to bother him for some reason, but managed to keep up. Once inside, they assessed their situation, turning on the television for the news coverage.

...it appears the dead have come back to life in a Romero-esque version of reality. No one knows what is responsible at this time, but the nation's top scientists are on the case. Police have begun to mitigate exposure but only time will tell how far the damage will extend, but encourage everyone to stay indoors, and wait for further updates from officials. With the

carnage on our city streets, we all hope a cure is soon on the horizon. For KXDW News, I'm Lester Charres. Stay tuned to this station for additional coverage and updates as they become available…

"If I hadn't seen it with my own eyes, I wouldn't have believed it," Gavin stated as he stalked to the window to look out into the street.

"I need a drink!" Goldy stated as she dropped onto her plush shag couch. It was obvious she expected someone else to get it for her. "Dave? Would you be a Bear and get it for me?"

Dave got up with some discomfort, limping across to the kitchenette.

"What's wrong with you?" Abe asked, following Dave across the room with his gaze.

"I'll be fine. I just cut my ankle on something in the alley," he replied.

"Lemme see," Gavin said as he turned on the light in the kitchenette. After examining Dave's ankle, he looked across the room to Goldy and Abe. "This isn't a cut."

"What the fuck do you mean it's not a cut?" Goldy said into the pillow she'd been holding. "What is it then?"

"A bite," was the answer given by Gavin.

* * *

"It's for your own good, Dave, trust us." With Dave securely tied to the sturdiest chair in Goldy's loft, the threat was minimized for the moment. Abe continued, "I'm sure there will be a cure soon so once they have that, we can make you better."

"He's not going to get better," Goldy hissed to Gavin. Even she could already see the streaks of sepsis radiating across the exposed flesh of his body. "What are we going to do?"

As Dave deteriorated, the three talked into the morning, constantly checking the windows and the news outlets for any updates. Nothing was forthcoming and with no real idea of what to do, they were at a loss of how to handle Dave's condition.

"Should we take him to the hospital?"

"Goldy, you heard what the newscaster said. We have to stay indoors and wait until the authorities tell us it's okay to go outsider again," Abe answered.

"Goldy's right, Abe. Dave needs more help that we can give him here. I say we risk it." Gavin's gaze swung over to Dave as he sat tied to the chair. "Shit! Something's wrong!"

Both Goldy and Abe turned to look at Dave and saw him slouched down in his bonds, not moving at all. As they all watched, Dave lifted his head suddenly, his eyes glazed like a Krispy Kreme doughnut.

"Holy shit!"

What used to be Dave gnashed its teeth, pulling against the bindings that secured him to the chair. It was focused solely on its need to get to them, but luckily Abe had tied him down tightly, his fetish for bondage coming in handy. They took a step back all the same, no one wanting to be too close to the monster in their midst.

"What do we do now?" Gavin asked.

"What did they say to do on the television? Do we kill it?" Goldy responded.

"It? That's Dave!"

"It's not Dave anymore, Gavin." Abe stated calmly. "And the television said to call the Police if you managed to capture one."

"We can't just turn Dave over to the Police," Goldy said. "What if *they* kill him?"

"It's not Dave anymore and you saw what these things are capable of, Goldy. We have to call the Police and let them deal with it." Abe was insistent.

"Excellent point. We can call when it's not so hectic for them out there," Goldy said, her mood resigned. "Since he's tied up, we should be okay until then."

* * *

For four long days they waited as the city fought for control. The news outlets reported both the highs and the lows of the situation for the captive audience in Goldy's loft. The forced confinement played wildly on their emotions, causing them to fight amongst themselves, and the presence of the monster that was once Dave weighed even more heavily on them. With the apartment starting to smell, mainly from the rotting corpse sat in the middle of it, the news it was safe to go home and back to the daily grind of normal life was met with relief.

Both Gavin and Abe were anxious to get out and check on their family and friends. In their haste to leave, they left the issue of Dave's reanimated body solely on Goldy's incapable shoulders. After they'd left, she'd stared at the monster, watching its mouth move in the rhythmic motion of mastication. The issues of the past few days had caused Goldy to crack just a bit—not so much you'd notice, but her mind had fractured from the things she'd seen. She simply couldn't reconcile what she knew of Dave with what she saw before her, tied to the chair in her living room.

"What am I going to do with you Dave?" Goldy asked, knowing she wouldn't get an answer. Her mind worked overtime, trying to figure out what to do. She knew deep down she should call the Police, but she'd always liked Dave. In time, she'd hoped she'd have been able to talk him into her bed and once that veil had been broken, there was no telling where they would have ended up.

If Goldy were being honest with herself, she'd have admitted she liked Dave. Like really liked him.

"What am I going to do…"

* * *

The worst thing had been removing Dave the Monster's teeth. Its hunger was insatiable and every time Goldy stuck the pliers into Dave's mouth, it fought her, thinking they were food and trying in vain to bite off a finger.

Luckily its teeth had loosened enough with the decomposition they came out easily but that hadn't made their extraction easier. The process had been a battle between the physical exertion of pulling out all Dave's teeth and the emotional toll of what she was doing. Not to mention why…

But she couldn't have turned Dave over just to be killed. Or worse, to be experimented on. No, it was better Dave, or the monster that was once Dave, stay with her forever.

31

At least until it got too difficult to keep it. Or until the smell got too much to handle.

Goldy converted the spare room in her loft into its room. With reinforced shackles built into the walls and sound-proofing installed to keep the noise in, the room was ready. She'd already moved Dave, and yes, she'd taken to calling him that again because it was easier, into his new space, telling herself he'd be happy with her.

She almost didn't mind the greyish tinge to his skin or the milkiness of his eyes. To her he was still Dave—her young clumsy little Bear who danced behind her—albeit an undead little bear.

Opening her robe, she stepped closer to Dave, her semi-hard cock dangling in front of the undead Bear's slack face. Goldy leaned forward, taunting Dave with his member sexily, knowing that in a few seconds his cock would be in that toothless, dead mouth.

Zombies give the best head so long as they don't lose theirs.

Think of Me
Lindsay King-Miller

The worst is when Sasha and Taylor are fucking and Sasha is thinking about me. She tries to stop, but the harder she tries to push me out of her head, the more space she makes for me there.

She thinks about the way I fucked her—things she still hasn't worked up the courage to ask Taylor for. Things she could only do with me, because there was never any question who was the more damaged one in our relationship. Taylor is very pretty and college-educated and normal in that all-American tennis-scholarship lesbian kind of way, and Sasha doesn't want to scare her off, so she thinks about me and the good ways I used to hurt her.

This of course leads to thinking about the bad ways I hurt her, and there are so many of those. She's rocking her hips to the motion of Taylor's fingers but the rhythm in her mind is me banging my head against our bedroom wall. An image of my body the way she found it, slumped over in the bathtub, flashes through her head in the moment before she comes. Guilt and grief and rage and shame and lust all at once. She hates it, and I hate it too, but I can't look away. I don't even have eyes to close.

* * *

I was halfway through the ceiling when Sasha found my body. Would it be different if she'd come in just a few minutes later? Maybe there would have been a point of no return, a point at which everything that made me Jess was so scattered, there was no gathering it back together. Maybe I would have been nothing, which is another way of saying, maybe I would have been *free*.

But the first breath Sasha took when she saw me dead was like a magnet, pulling the metallic scraps of me back from whatever they were dissolving into. Before she even screamed, I was Jess again, except that I wasn't in my body. It hurt, and it hasn't stopped hurting.

The more Sasha thinks about me, the more I am. I feel whatever she feels about me. It's ingenious as a punishment: I get to experience every second of sorrow, anger and loneliness that I've caused her. The night after my funeral, she lay on the couch, unable to bear our bedroom without me, and cried so hard she gave herself a nosebleed. I was every drop of blood as it hit the floor.

I don't remember dying, but I remember wanting to. This is like that, but more so.

* * *

Taylor wants to marry Sasha, the real way, with white dresses and a license from the state. On paper, Sasha isn't a widow. When we were together she still hadn't changed her name and gender on her driver's license, and she wasn't going to get married under her dead name, the one no one who loved her ever said out loud.

We had a bunch of our friends over and I wore a Bikini Kill shirt and a red tutu, and Sasha wore a white negligee and a tiara from the Halloween store, and we both cut our fingertips with this one witchy girl's ceremonial knife and bled into a glass of three-buck Chuck. Then we took turns drinking it until it was empty. The last sip, I swigged then spit into Sasha's open mouth.

"I promise to love you until I die," I said, and put this ring on her finger that I got at a thrift store, heavy steel coiled like a snake, with yellow glass eyes. Later that night she rocked the snake's head against my clit, her fingers deep inside me, whispering "You're mine, you're mine, you're mine." I used to introduce her as 'my wife.' Her name wasn't mentioned in my obituary.

She still wears the ring. I feel it on the memory of my own third finger, heavier than it could possibly be—psychic weight. It rubs me raw, like it was made of heavy rope, burning away the skin I don't have.

The ring Taylor gave Sasha has a small sapphire, her birthstone. It's real gold. She wears that one on her right hand, the engagement ring finger. When Taylor proposed to Sasha, she touched my ring gently. Bile and guilt burned the back of Sasha's throat. "I'll never ask you to take this off," Taylor said.

Sasha cried and kissed her. I tasted stomach acid. "Please forget me," I said, but nobody heard.

* * *

She used to ask me to bite her during sex. I was always careful, never broke the skin. I can feel the tension curled up inside her, like a lizard about to outgrow its egg. Taylor is so careful with her. She's read some thinkpieces about how to respectfully fuck a trans woman.

At the beginning there was a lot of "Is it okay if I touch you here? What do you call this?" At the beginning Sasha was relieved because Taylor was so unlike me. She was safe. But now safe makes Sasha crazy. She masturbates in the shower before Taylor is awake, biting the inside of her own arm to hide the gasp when she comes. Taylor never asks about the teeth marks.

When Sasha's not thinking about me, I'm somewhere else. There's space between the molecules of me, and the world moves through it and I don't mind. I'm still Jess, but only barely. Maybe this is what going into the light feels like.

But every time Sasha comes, she calls me back.

* * *

Sasha lost her receptionist job after I died because she didn't talk for three months. She'd pick up the phone and just listen. People found it creepy. Now she makes coffee, mostly for college kids having study groups. When she's bored she thinks about me, and about which of the college kids are going to fuck each other, or already have.

Sometimes I try to move things. I can feel what Sasha feels so strong it's like I'm sharing her body, so I try to flex her muscles, to touch something because I want to, not because she does.

36

If she'd just left a note, Sasha thinks, and I flinch. She thinks it would all be easier if I'd told her why, if she could look at the words "It's not your fault" in my handwriting.

She's making a grocery list on her phone. I feel for the border between her hand and mine, try to visualize it dissolving. A message from the beyond will be comforting, right? It will soothe her, it will release me, at least for a moment.

It feels like pins and needles, and also like Novocaine, and also sort of like slipping my tongue into her mouth, but not in a sexy way. Like trying to kiss someone who's asleep. It's trespassing. I wait out the surge of revulsion that pulses through me, or through Sasha, it's hard to tell. Does she know I'm here?

I flex her finger, stretch toward the I on her keypad. Her hand spasms and her phone drops to the floor.

She shakes me off. I'm still inside her, but out of place. The view through her eyes is wrong, like I'm staring through the shattered glass of her phone screen.

* * *

She has a dream about the time she found me in the bathroom, tears and snot on my face, meticulously pulling hairs out of my head, my hairline at the back of my neck red and raw. That was right before I shaved the bottom half of my head. It hurts more to feel Sasha remembering it than it hurt to actually do it.

Taylor rolls over, half awake—she doesn't have to get up for work for another two hours—kisses Sasha good morning, but Sasha doesn't, or I don't, kiss back. Sharing a body with Sasha is impossibly lonely.

"Everything okay?" Taylor asks.

"I had a dream about Jess," Sasha says, twisting my ring around her finger. It scrapes.

"I'm so sorry, babe," Taylor says, stroking Sasha's hair. The only one who wants Sasha to forget me more than Taylor does is me.

But the weight of Taylor's hand on Sasha's shoulder is dulled by the thin sheen of me. Sasha sighs, whispers, "Get some more sleep," and rolls out of bed.

I try to say, "It wasn't your fault" so she can hear me. Over and over, while she's brushing her teeth, getting on the bus, putting on her apron for her shift. I try to place the thought gently in her mind, then I try to scratch it in with my fingernails. Whenever I try to get her attention she stands still, her gaze wandering.

I thought I knew what unbearable meant when I was alive, but now there's no way to scream or bleed or puke out the rage I feel. I don't have fists, but the best I can explain what I'm doing is that I beat my fists against the inside of Sasha's head, begging her to let me out.

Sasha's heart hiccups. Her breath snags. She stumbles, freezes, grabs whatever she can reach to keep from falling. Scalding hot steam pours out of the espresso machine and her hand, my hand, it's on fire, the skin murderously red, Taylor's engagement ring cutting a line across the furious flesh as it starts to swell.

* * *

Taylor picks Sasha up from the emergency room and drives her home, the bent and twisted ring in a plastic sandwich bag where the nurse put it after cutting it off.

"I'm sorry," Sasha says, her left hand tapping on her knee, her right in a mitten of burn pads. She's going to have a scar.

Taylor must have been thinking about the ring already because she instantly knows that's what Sasha is talking about. "It's okay, babe," she says. "We'll get it reset."

* * *

The coffeeshop gives Sasha a week off, but she doesn't go back on the eighth day. Her hand itches like a motherfucker where it's healing. That's what she tells Taylor, and her boss over the phone, but really she doesn't want to go back there because it reminds her of me.

How can it remind her of me? She knows it doesn't make sense—she didn't start working there until I was already dead, we never even went there together—but she thinks about me too much when she's there. Maybe it's the smell of coffee, the sense memory of the strong pots I used to brew in the morning after staying up all night, drank black and too hot. The way my burned tongue tasted when I kissed her. Taylor buys bottled cold brew at the grocery store, with almond milk already mixed in.

When we met, Sasha was tending bar downtown. Maybe she can get that job back, she thinks. Which is stupid, if her goal is to avoid reminders at me. We used to fuck in that bathroom while she was on the clock. Still, she's going to put on a nice skirt and head over there while Taylor's at the office, see if they have anything open.

In the shower, Sasha struggles to manage her razor with her left hand, her right still swollen and clumsy. She nicks herself behind the knee, a tiny cut that stings more than it bleeds. I used to tell her she didn't have to shave her legs. "It's patriarchal bullshit," I said. "There's nothing inherently masculine about body hair. We're fucking mammals."

"If *you* don't shave your legs, you get called a dyke," she used to respond. "If *I* don't, I get called sir. It's not the same thing." Taylor never tries to convince her not to shave her legs.

The drop of blood behind Sasha's knee, though, it bothers her. She runs her finger over it, comes away pink. She rubs the cut like you'd rub a place a fly had landed on you, to make sure it's gone, that you're clean. Razor blades make her think of me, though the only thing I shaved in all the time we were together was the back of my head that once.

Sasha's been trying all this time not to wonder what it was like for me, why I kept cutting myself, going deeper and deeper until I fell down that bloody hole and never crawled back out. Did it feel good? Was it like the biting, but more so? The kind of good pain that hits right where you need it to, that so-bad-it's good sting like peeling off a scab?

She kind of wants to put the razor down, to slide her hand between her thighs, but that's sick, she tells herself, that's fucking unforgivable, to be turned on thinking about what your wife felt when she died.

Besides, she doesn't jerk off with her left hand, has never been able to.

It happens because her mind wandered, she tells herself later, because she was thinking about me and got upset, but I feel the moment she decides. She means to do it. I try to fill her hands with my hands, hold her back, but she digs the razor in and yanks it up—three deep parallel lines, one for each blade of the razor, diagonally across her smooth, round calf.

I want to cry, to scream, at least to look away, but I can't because Sasha doesn't. She stays in the shower staring down at her leg, at the red paisley patterns of blood against tile, until the water runs cold.

* * *

Sasha doesn't go anywhere that day, doesn't ask for her bartending job back or even pick up groceries. Taylor comes home to find her watching TV in her sweatpants, though it's a hot day.

"I missed you," Sasha says, and pulls Taylor into the bedroom. The window shade is closed and the room is dim, enough that Taylor doesn't notice the lines on Sasha's legs when she's pulling her pants off.

They haven't fucked since before Sasha hurt her hand, and Taylor is the least polite she's ever been, grabbing Sasha by the hair and kissing her greedily. They're both only partly undressed, Sasha's bra still on, Taylor's business-casual skirt up around her hips. Sasha kneels on the floor, Taylor's thighs around her head. With her injured hand, she grabs Taylor's hip, anchoring herself. With the other, she guides Taylor's hands back into her hair.

41

"Don't be gentle," Sasha says, and Taylor isn't, and they don't say anything else for a long time, and I shouldn't be here, but Sasha's left hand is between her own legs, patient, precise, waiting until Taylor is starting to quake and buck under her tongue before she lets herself go. They come at the same moment, and it crashes over me like being drowned. Sasha's not left-handed, but I am.

* * *

While she's sleeping, her mind adrift, her body feels lighter. I can shrug it on more easily. It doesn't take more than a few tries, even with the ache in her right hand, to pull my cheap snake tchotchke off her left ring finger. I drop it behind the bed. She doesn't need to be reminded of me whenever she looks at her own hand. She doesn't need to wonder whether her hands could do what mine did.

* * *

It takes Sasha a few seconds after she wakes up to realize why she's panicking, but the panicking itself starts before she opens her eyes.

"Where's my ring?" It's a whisper and a shout.

"Babe, it's the middle of the night," Taylor murmurs, rolling over to nuzzle against Sasha's tense back.

"Where's my wedding ring?" Sasha insists, shaking Taylor off and sitting up, feeling around in the bed, under pillows and sheets.

"I don't know," Taylor says, sitting up too. "Did you take it off last night?"

Sasha shakes her head. Now she's on the floor, running her hands over the carpet. Her desperation is a sickening plummet. If I had a stomach it would be in knots. "I didn't take it off. I don't take it off. I never take it off," she says like a chant, like a prayer.

Taylor knows better than to say anything about the other ring, the one they cut off Sasha's finger and she hasn't gotten around to replacing, but Sasha knows—or at least, she thinks she knows, and I feel it with all the fire and ferocity of a revelation—that she wants to. She reads it in the arch of Taylor's eyebrow.

"What?" Sasha snarls.

Taylor's hands go up defensively. "I didn't say anything."

Exhaustion, confusion, panic, and this persistent unease—like coming home to find all your things an inch removed from where you left them—are bubbling into something toxic inside Sasha. I try to blend into her, like I did while she was sleeping, to take a few deep breaths and calm down. But she feels me doing it. She doesn't know what it is, just that for a terrifying moment her body is not fully under her control, and it only feeds her rage.

"Oh my God," Sasha says. "Did you take it? Did you take my wedding ring?"

"What?" Taylor's eyes go wide. She's genuinely hurt. "Why would I do that?"

"Because you're jealous," Sasha says, and every word burns on its way out, like vomit. "You're jealous of Jess. You hate that I was married before I met you."

"That's bullshit, Sasha," Taylor says. She doesn't sound angry, just sad. "I would never try to take Jess away from you. You know that's bullshit."

43

"Then where's my fucking ring?" I feel it, the terrible hopelessness: if Taylor didn't take it, that means she took the ring off herself—without even noticing she was doing it. That would mean she's forgetting about me. She has to blame Taylor for the missing ring, she already blames herself for so much.

Taylor stands up and turns on a lamp. "I don't know, but we can find it," she says. "Is it on the nightstand?"

"No," Sasha wails, and buries her head in her hands. The sobs shred her body, Taylor reaching out to touch her but never quite making contact. I can't watch anymore, so I put on Sasha's body and leave the room with it. She doesn't help me, but she doesn't fight me either.

* * *

I'm more and more of myself every day. I take up more space inside Sasha, and I feel more of her pain. She doesn't understand what's going on. In her sleep, I dug out the ring from behind the bed and left it on her pillow, a peace offering, but it scared her more.

She wonders if she's going crazy. She's ashamed to talk about it to Taylor, who is gentle with her in a frightened way, like Sasha is a sick kitten who also might explode.

Sasha writes me letters. She apologizes for not saving me. She begs me for forgiveness. She doesn't know that I'm reading through her eyes; she's having this conversation with the version of me who exists in her imagination, the avatar of her guilt.

I feel her fingers around the pen. I flex them. I write the letter "I."

Sasha screams, or I scream. There's only so much pain you can hold while you're alive, because death is always the trapdoor at the very bottom of the worst thing you can imagine. This pain has no analogy to the human body I used to have; it's bigger than my body could ever have felt.

Sasha only feels a flicker of it, but it's enough to make her drop her pen and curl into a ball on the floor, tears and snot running down her face. She heaves and heaves until vomit is coming out of her nose. Taylor runs into the doorway and stands there staring, but doesn't come closer.

* * *

Sasha's dreams are hideous, so I try to stay awake, floating at the top of her mind. I'm possessing her, and I don't want to be, but I don't know how to stop.

I sit up in bed, suddenly, so abrupt that I'm afraid I've woken Taylor. But she doesn't move. I wear Sasha's body clumsily—I don't know if it's because I'm out of practice driving one of these, or because hers fits so differently than mine used to. I have to get out.

Sasha's skin feels swollen, like an overinflated balloon. Feverish and hot. Too dry. I'm pressed up against the underside of her and there's not enough air in here.

She wakes in the middle of a panic attack, my first since I died, her first ever. We stumble into the bathroom, splash water on her face. I don't know which of us is in control. She feels feral, hunched over the sink, her hair in her eyes. I have to get out. It's definitely my hand, the left one, reaching for the razor blade.

It's me digging the blade into Sasha's right wrist. She's angry and terrified, but she isn't trying to stop me. Maybe this is a kindness I can offer her.

I've barely broken the skin when Taylor's grabbing Sasha's wrist, holding on hard, twisting until I drop the razor. The twinge in Sasha's arm is barely anything. What hurts is the rush of shame that slices through Sasha when she sees the look on Taylor's face. Sasha hates being pitied.

"Why?" Taylor says, and her face looks like she's been crying for hours, although no tears are falling.

"It's not me," Sasha says. She doesn't know any other way to explain it. "I'm not me."

I realize with a shock of horror what I might have done, what I almost did. What if Sasha's death didn't mean my freedom at all, didn't mean the end of Jess, but just linked me to Taylor with another chain of grief?

There's nothing I can do. I'm trapped.

"Don't do that," Taylor whispers, her arms wrapped around herself like she wants to be holding onto Sasha. "Don't ever do that. How could you, after her?"

Sasha says, "I didn't," but even she isn't sure whether she's telling the truth. I'm slamming myself against the inside of Sasha's brain, one last desperate rush for escape. If Taylor knows I'm here, maybe she can find a way to make me leave.

Am I here at all? Am I just a way of naming the feelings that are impossible for Sasha's heart to hold, the grief that's too big for her body?

The blood on my right wrist—Sasha's wrist—our wrist—it looks black in the darkness of the bathroom as we reach for Taylor. Taylor turns and kisses the cut, and now there's blood on her lips. She doesn't let go of our arm as we move closer, kneeling face-to-face with her on the floor. One of us presses Sasha's right wrist harder into Taylor's mouth.

She hesitates, her eyes flickering to Sasha's. Who does she see there? Then Taylor's eyes flutter closed and she sinks her teeth into the soft underside of Sasha's inner arm.

I press my thigh between Taylor's legs, and she moans. She lifts her head and kisses me, blood on her lips. Sasha loves her and doesn't want to hurt her. I bite her bottom lip until I draw more blood. Taylor kisses us harder, her fingernails digging into my back, sliding up underneath Sasha's shirt. She's trying to reassure herself of Sasha's body, to convince herself that it's still here.

I grab a fistful of Taylor's hair in my left hand, yank her head back so she's looking me in the eyes. She gasps in pain, but the way she's still leaning toward me, it's not just pain. "I love you," she says, and she says it to me, whichever me that is. "Don't leave."

"I'm here," Sasha says, holding her, "and I'm not going anywhere," I add. Which of us says "I'm sorry?" Does anyone? Or do the words just hang in the air like the smell of sweat?

The razor blade is lying on the floor. I reach for it with my right hand, then use my left to pull Sasha's shirt over her head. We put the razor in Taylor's hand. We kiss her. Without words, we tell her where to hurt us.

47

Odd Man Out
Derek Clendening

"Of course, we've done this before," Patrick said. "So, we won't be going into it blind. We can show you the ropes."

"You'll have to." Mack wrung his hands.

"Don't be nervous. Ben and I won't push you along any faster than you're ready to move. I promise."

"If you don't mind my asking, how many times have you done this?"

"Just once. Daniel was his name. It lasted a while, and the lifestyle didn't turn him off per se. New opportunities came his way, opportunities that didn't include us, so he moved on. No hard feelings."

Mack nodded.

So far, the lie had worked. Fabrication in motion, he touched Ben's hand underneath the table to acknowledge it.

This was your idea, Ben would tell him. If he backed off, or the deal fell through, Ben would remind him that he'd courted Mack.

Patrick had expected the question even at the fancy Italian restaurant where they'd treated Mack. *Who wouldn't ask?* He thought. *How often can*

*anyone, especially someone as inexperienced as Mack,
join the love of an established couple?*

Yet the question seemed obvious.

He'd spotted Mack at the gym. The lean, early
20-something stood before the mirror curling
dumbbells, but never grunted or flexed. His eyes
always shifted away like he couldn't admire his own
body like the other gym rats. Patrick wondered if the
young man appreciated his own smooth face, brown
hair with matching eyes and dimpled cheeks.

If he couldn't appreciate those features, others
could.

The young man made Patrick lick his lips, driving
him to learn his name. They never crossed paths in the
locker room, but conversation sparked each time they
followed one another on a bike or treadmill. Deeper
conversations blossomed when they met at a used
bookstore, which led to asking him out, and
introducing him to Ben.

Dating led to kissing and kissing led to groping,
but Mack had never visited their bedroom. Invitations
struck roses into Mack's cheeks. His smile teemed
with flattery, but he wouldn't succumb. For all Patrick
knew, Mack could be one of those guys who required
commitment before shedding his clothes and sharing
himself with another . . . or several others at once.

Even in the restaurant, his fingers curled at the
mention of kink.

"I'm sorry if this sounds weird," Mack said. "But
how does a relationship like this work?"

"No rules," Patrick said. "We'll march to the beat
of our own drummer and make our own rules."

"That makes sense. Until now, we've been

sharing laughs and having a good time with no labels. But, if we take the next step..."

"We like to think of ourselves as free spirits," Ben said. "A relationship with us can go any direction we want. If something feels right then it probably is, so we go with the flow."

"Okay." Mack considered this. "But I feel like there could be a lot of pitfalls."

"Such as?"

"I don't know, just... problems."

Patrick released his breath. If he couldn't think of a reason, he would kill his point, letting Mack off the hook. No more lies or spins to draw him into their fold, he decided.

"There will always be an odd man out," Mack said. "You know, when it's all said and done? How can there not be?"

Patrick shrugged. "I think I know where you're going with this."

"Two's company, three's a crowd, right?"

"Right. And that's just a saying."

"But it's a saying for a reason, isn't it?"

Mild and bashful as Mack seemed, Patrick found him sharp as a whip. He could serve up another lie, but the stench of bullshit would overwhelm them. He would leave the ball in Mack's court.

"Say in six months," Mack said, "you two don't want me to live with you anymore. What happens then?"

"That could happen," Patrick said. "In theory."

"And let's say you and I fall so deeply in love with each other that we ditch Ben. That could happen, couldn't it?"

Others hadn't asked such questions but, of course, the others could no longer vouch for them. Patrick hated to let this one slip away, but he couldn't blow their cover.

Mack said, "I would want you to know, if I move in with you guys, that I'd want us all to love each other equally. I'd hate to see jealousy tear us apart. You guys have been too good to me."

"We wouldn't extend this invitation to just anyone," Ben said. "You're special, Mack."

"I know. You're special, too. That's why I want to be sure this arrangement will work."

"Of course it will."

"Can I have time to think about this?"

"Of course."

Mack called the next day, accepting their offer. Patrick dreamed of Mack at the gym, and how his rippling muscle gleamed in the light. The thought drew saliva into his mouth.

He licked his lips.

And then Patrick remembered the pact he and Ben had made upon their arrival in town.

Decent people keep their promises, he told himself. *Bad people spit on theirs. Good people don't tell lies, especially to gullible dopes. Boy, you're two-for-two.*

The more he dreamed of Mack, the more he struggled with his promise. But he would keep trying if it killed him.

After all, it was his idea.

* * *

"You remember your promise, right?" Patrick asked.

Ben nodded but avoided eye contact. Patrick grabbed his wrist and towed him into the hall.

"Let's make sure we really are on the same page before getting in too deep.

"With how long he takes in the bathroom," Ben said." We should have plenty of time to sort things out. Besides, aren't we in deep enough already?"

"I know, but we can handle this if we keep our word."

"Fine, have it your way."

Mack wanted to shower, shave and present himself nicely for their first encounter, a gesture Patrick appreciated, and Ben scorned. Patrick's fingertips froze as their past crept up on him. When he considered the bones they'd picked clean, and how their desires had overcome their intentions, he meant to hold Ben to his promise.

"Quit looking all worried," Ben said. "He'll think something's wrong."

"Something *is* wrong."

"Not if you control yourself. I told you everything will be fine, and I meant it. Now, get in there and show Mack why getting together with us is the best decision he's ever made."

Patrick shuffled into the bedroom where Mack toweled leftover shaving cream off his face. He looked as stunning in a T-shirt and jeans as in a suit. Patrick met his chocolate eyes and summoned him forward, wordlessly.

Arms open, Mack fell deep into Patrick's embrace, their lips melting together. Mack's chest heaved against his and Patrick squeezed him tight. Mack's prick poked his leg, driving Patrick to tear Mack's pants away, but he stopped himself.

Never so soon.

He kissed a trail across Mack's cheek and then buried his face in his neck. Mack's head thrust back. Ben strolled behind Mack, kissing the other side of his neck and cupping his ass. Patrick's tongue snaked into Mack's mouth and he squeezed his cock, stroking and kneading.

Mack breathed the heaviest of the three, moaning and gasping, plastering his hand to the back of Patrick's head.

Hunger pangs struck Patrick, and he swatted them away like flies, but they always returned. Problems always began this way, he realized. Sometimes the hunger crept in after sex began, but they never completed the act before his appetite swelled.

As Patrick lifted Mack's shirt over his head, he recalled how the thrilled expressions of previous lovers turned to terror as their hunger swelled unabated. He beheld the ovals of Mack's chest and then leaned in to kiss them. It was all he could do to nibble his nipples gently and not bite them.

Patrick unbuckled Mack's belt and pushed his jeans to the floor. Mack tented his boxer briefs, which Patrick and Ben peeled back to free his cock. Crouched before him, the duo took turns tasting the young man's meat.

Mouths opened wide, Patrick welcomed Mack's cock deep into his throat. Again, the young man groaned, combing his fingers through Patrick's hair as Patrick worked his hand into action.

Ben stooped behind him, spreading Mack's ass open. When Patrick heard Mack gasp with great urgency, he knew Ben had probed his tongue into the perfect spot.

Before, Mack had shied away from deep conversations about his likes and dislikes. They knew he'd only share himself when he felt ready. Patrick saw the upside but appreciated the downside enough to take caution.

When Patrick stood up, he kissed Mack deeply again and reveled in his flavor. That stoked the fire that threatened to consume him, but he couldn't turn back now.

Mack helped them out of their clothes and they climbed into bed together.

Patrick slapped his leg to summon Mack aboard. Mack had described himself as a versatile bottom. When he threw a leg over Patrick's hip and crouched, Patrick slid into him steadily. Bashful, yes, but Mack seemed like a willing sport.

Mack grinded on Patrick's hips, working his ass into motion as Patrick maneuvered his hips. When Patrick took Mack's hand, he drew the fingers into his mouth, biting down hard. Before, he'd nibbled on his flesh, but now he worried he'd tear skin and snap bones. He wanted to stop, but his hunger arrested him.

Mack snapped his hand back, but asked no questions. Patrick might've called it their version of kink, one of those things he wouldn't push him into. Later, he would apologize profusely and promise to stay at Mack's pace.

At Ben's command, Mack's dismounted, turned in the opposite direction and squatted onto Patrick's cock. This time, Ben stood over them, sliding onto Mack's waiting meat.

Sandwiched between them, Mack's head rolled onto Patrick's shoulder. He nibbled on Mack again, certain he'd leave marks this time. Ditto for Ben. As climax approached, he worried he'd tear a chunk out of Mack's shoulder, arm, or closest delectable spot. With flesh and blood in his mouth, he would continue until sated.

If either gave in, they would ruin what they had, which would send them on the run again. Worse, Patrick would remain more animal than human, more devil than angel, an idea he loathed.

All having climaxed, they lay in bed together. Mack's taste remained on Patrick's lips, and he worried he couldn't hang on forever. He likened it to the final thread on a rope, ready to snap.

Each encounter would draw him closer to breaking.

* * *

"You nearly did it this time," Patrick said. "If we didn't slow down, Mack would've caught on to us. Maybe worse."

"*Me*?" Ben said. "Don't you mean *we*? You eyed him like filet mignon. Why are you pointing fingers here?"

"Okay, we. Point is, we pierced the skin this time. We made him bleed. Sooner or later he's going to put one and two together."

"A little bit of kink. It's just our way."

Patrick wanted Ben to can the used car salesman

talk since no one should fall for his act. He couldn't play innocent, though. His hunger had swelled at Ben's rapid pace until his teeth sank into Mack's flesh. He'd tasted the young man's meat, but he wanted to tear it off and chew it. Taste alone wouldn't suffice.

That was why he must stop before things worsened.

He would remind Ben of his promise.

"You remember the last one?" Patrick asked.

"Blond, blue eyes, lean. How could I forget . . . what was his name again?"

"That's not funny, Ben."

Patrick expected him to add how wonderful he'd tasted. Patrick's mouth would water from remembrance, and he'd lose his quest for morality.

"You remember how much we had to hide," Patrick said.

"Of course I do."

"And you remember how we were almost caught."

"But got away with it."

"And you remember when his family started calling, sounding frantic, worried about where he was."

"We said we didn't know. We said he had itchy feet and took off."

"Yes, that's what we *said*, but that wasn't the truth."

"Of course not. What were we supposed to tell them?"

"Obviously we weren't going to tell them what we did, what we really are or that we've used fake names in every town we've lived."

"Exactly. And we cleaned up the mess before anyone got wise. What's the problem?"

Ben turned his back to him like when he lost any argument. Losing a fight meant nothing, not in these matters. For all Patrick knew, Ben could take matters into his own hands, leaving them with a new mess to cover up.

"It's not just being on the run," Patrick said. "It's about right and wrong."

"I know." Ben acted like he'd heard it 1000 times. "I don't like it any more than you do."

"But you're willing to give in."

"Look, it's going to happen sooner or later. I don't know why you're putting on this act like we're a couple of angels."

"I never said we're angels."

"Good, because we're not. We're—"

Ben lost himself in assigning a label, which suited Patrick fine.

"Ben, I don't care. Whatever we are, I don't want to be it anymore."

"Too late for that, Patrick. You were a lost cause the first time you tasted human meat."

Patrick closed his eyes and ignored the sinking feeling in his gut. Ben leveraged the argument to remind him of how much he'd enjoyed men both raw and cooked, and how he'd relished them like a delicacy.

No better than Ben at all.

He wanted to believe they were good-natured, that something had come over them. And something had. Together, they created a lust so great that they couldn't sate their appetite. Those appetites had twisted into something alien, something monstrous.

Never too late to stop, he told himself. *Never too late to reinvent ourselves as decent human beings.*

And yet Ben seemed uninterested in decency. Their crimes made him feel bound to his partner, but he wondered if he had to be.

"You made a promise," Patrick said. "A promise that we'd control ourselves no matter what. A promise that we'd never hurt anyone again."

"Promises are meant to be broken."

"Ben, how can you be so callous?"

"Back to *m*e again, huh? Remember, everything about this is *we*, not *me*. We committed those crimes. We devastated those families. Not just me."

Patrick bit his lower lip, unable to refute his partner. Until he stopped this, he would remain as dreadful as Ben.

"We'll take him tonight," Ben said. "Before anyone knows Mack has anything to do with us. Fewer arrows pointing to us."

Patrick balled his hands into fists desperate to defy Ben, but he was lost for an argument.

"I know that look," Ben said. "If you refuse, there'll be nothing left for you. I'll take it all for myself."

* * *

"We've really got to talk," Patrick said. "Privately. You can't ever tell Ben about this conversation, understand?"

"I guess so," Mack said. "What's up?"

"Come this way." He waved Mack aside. "I want to make totally sure no one hears us."

Mack turned stony.

"We need to get away," Patrick said. "Tonight, if we can. I don't know where we'll go, but we've got to get as far away from Ben as possible."

"Why? What's going on here, Patrick?"

"I can't explain it all to you. There's too much."

"Can you try?"

Of course you can, an inner voice said. *You just don't want to. The thought sickens you, Saint that you are, but you'll blow everything if you blab.*

"You're in danger," Patrick said. "Yes, you specifically. We can run away and have a relationship of our own, free of Ben. It's for the best. I mean that."

"But what about all that business about how we can make this arrangement work? Didn't you promise there wouldn't be an odd man out?"

"I'm not talking about an odd man out." He combed his fingers through his hair. "I'm saying it'd be deadly for you to stay. Neither of us is good for you, but together we're..."

"I still don't understand."

"How much attention do you pay to the news?"

"Enough."

"Then you've heard about the murders in Tucson, Evansville and Albany? And other places like Altoona and Towson?"

"Don't murders happen everywhere?"

"Not ones where the murderers only left bones when they were through."

Mack turned, ready to run, but Patrick grabbed his wrist and dragged him back in.

"I'm not going to hurt you, Mack. I promise. In fact, I want to save you, but you'll have to listen and—"

"Is this what you two do? You find some dopey third person and then you—"

"It's not like that. At least it didn't start that way. The first time we invited a third to join us, we had good intentions, but we grew hungry like never before. So much that we couldn't stop ourselves. We thought it would be a one-off and we cleaned up the mess, but it happened again and again. It's been a nightmare staying one step ahead of the law, let me tell you, but it's become part of who we are."

"You two are..."

"Don't use the word, Mack. Please.

"Why shouldn't I?" Mack asked. "And why should I believe you?"

"Are you kidding? Why would I make up a story like that?"

"No Patrick, I mean why should I believe you're on my side? Why would you want to help me?"

"Because I'm good, Mack. I've done evil things, but I'm not... you know, *evil*. Ben, on the other hand..."

"So, he's evil and you're not? Right."

Patrick paused, feeling backed into a corner.

"Okay," Patrick said. "I know how it sounds. But we made a pact to stop and Ben spit on that promise. And he wants to hurt you. He even said so. I decided right then that I was done, but I at least had to warn you. Besides, we made a commitment to you, and I don't want to leave you hanging."

So honorable of you, his inner voice returned. *Why don't you tell him how close you came to devouring him yourself?*

"I know it'll be hard to trust me," Patrick said. "But you'll have to. Your life depends on it."

Mack looked ill. He understood why. Wouldn't he feel sickened to learn he'd nearly been served for dinner?

"Where would we go?"

Patrick considered it. He'd hung on until now, but couldn't promise his desire wouldn't overcome his intentions. He needed some way to stop himself from acting on his impulses.

"Tie me up," Patrick said.

"What?"

"Tonight, when we make love. Tie me up. That's the only way you'll stay safe from me. Tell Ben you want to explore some kink and you want to tie me up. That way I'll be incapacitated."

"Think he'll buy it?"

He shrugged. "Hard to tell, but we're short on options. I hope he'll think you're finally coming around."

"I can do that. It'll be a little weird, but…"

"Don't flake out on me. Remember, the ropes are in my bottom dresser drawer. And we can't take any risks, so tie me up tight and don't let me loose."

* * *

"Aren't we getting adventurous?" Ben watched Mack produce ropes from the drawer.

"It was Patrick's idea," Mack said.

"Yes," Patrick answered, "but I knew you were ready for it. You seemed so… hungry."

Mack threw the ropes onto the bed, his first show of confidence and control.

Normally, he would've taken Mack into his arms

and kissed him, but instead he let Mack take the reins. Mack ran his hands up and down Patrick's back, showing his strength. He cupped Patrick's ass and then squeezed him tight.

"Get in bed." Mack didn't sound dominant, but definitely more authoritative than his usual mild self.

Foreplay normally consumed the first act of sex, but Mack seemed eager to reach the bed. Dreams of bondage might've arrested him and pushed him to consume the main course early.

Patrick followed orders by climbing into bed and submitting to Mack. Mack bound his hands and feet to the bedposts. Like he'd asked, Mack tied the ropes tight. Then he kissed him again, slithered down his body and took his cock into his mouth.

Foreplay not forgotten, Patrick's eyes rolled back in his head. Mack worked his cock hard and fast, bringing him to the edge of climax and then withdrawing. Just as well, Patrick thought. No need to get off early and ruin the whole thing.

He brought Patrick to the brink of climax multiple times, always easing up the split second before Patrick exploded. Since that made the eventual payoff more satisfying, Patrick didn't mind, but something felt different now.

Something seemed off.

Mack could be a great actor, but he seemed more natural with rough sex and bondage than he would've believed.

Aside from sliding his dick into Patrick's mouth, Ben sat out. Normally Ben stayed in the thick of things, even when Patrick took most of the control, but he seemed content to watch.

Mack had convinced him that he'd enjoyed some kink. After all, he hadn't missed a beat when tying him up, almost like he'd done it before. But soon enough, Mack would let him climax, they would satisfy Ben and escape in the morning.

When he looked up, something else had changed. Patrick couldn't see much, what with the bed rocking ferociously, but Mack looked more intense than usual. Innocence lost, maybe. Up until then, Mack had been innocent by most people's standards, especially his and Ben's. But something else had changed and Patrick couldn't nail it down.

Finally, Mack granted Patrick his orgasm and then dismounted him with a kiss. Patrick expected Mack to free him, but he stood back with Ben and watched him. A devilish grin appeared on his face.

Patrick tugged on the ropes.

They wouldn't budge.

And Mack didn't move to loosen them.

"Okay," Patrick said. "First rule of bondage is to free your partner once you're finished making love…or any other time they tell you to."

Mack opened the dresser drawer and dug out a ball gag.

Mack strapped the gag over Patrick's head and stuffed the ball into his mouth. Patrick tried to scream, but couldn't.

Mack and Ben stood over him.

"Sorry to betray your trust," Mack said. "But you weren't exactly honest and straight-forward with me, were you?"

Patrick struggled against the bonds until his arms turned rubbery.

Mack said, "Forget how you lied about only doing this once before. You fessed up to that, for what it's worth. You told me there wouldn't be an odd man out and you were wrong...partly. The man you thought would be the odd man out isn't...and he'll still be alive come morning."

Mack took a pair of knives from the drawer, the ones Patrick and Ben had used to carve so much meat. Mack ran his finger along the blade.

Patrick's eyes opened wide. He fought until his body quit.

Ben said, "You took so much credit for finding Mack, but *I'm* the one who found him before you did. Mack ran errands at my work before moving on to his next job. Such a sexy guy I had to know him better. Sparks flew and plans were made. In fact, we've had this whole plan in place since you and I moved here."

Patrick used the last of his strength for one final struggle.

"What was I supposed to do?" Ben said. "You started throwing pacts and morality at me, like we're supposed to deny what we are. When I met Mack, I finally met someone as sick as us. We can accept that. That's the difference between us and you."

Mack and Ben drew closer with their knives. They licked their lips.

"Maybe you think I betrayed you," Mack said, "and this whole tying-you-up business is part of it." He brought the knife to Patrick's skin. "But no guilt here," he said. "After all, this was your idea."

Affliction

Spinster Eskie

What would you like to know? Did I do it? Of course I did. I'm not going to waste your time trying to convince you otherwise. The lie would be useless to us both. No, he didn't attack me. No, it wasn't self-defense. I killed him because I could and I wanted to. This really destroys your whole plan to position me as the victim, doesn't it? But that story is too easy, and let's be real, it's a bit of a cliché, don't you think?

I know people want to believe the Hollywood tales, but I didn't get into my line of work because I was a victim. My father never hurt me. He was a good man. One of the best. I didn't become a whore to pay the bills or provide for any children. I can't claim a reason worth pitying. My IQ is high enough that I could have pursued any number of lucrative careers. At one point, I thought to become a doctor or even a lawyer like yourself. But I didn't have the patience for all that schooling, and I wanted to be entirely in charge of my business and my fortune. I wanted to answer to no one.

You may have discovered that I do not work for a manager, as I manage myself. I promote myself. I take everything I earn and I put it toward *me*. And I have earned *a lot*. That is why I'm able to afford your services. I know you come at a steep price and I'm willing and able to pay. I have the means. As you may know, I don't come cheap either. Peloni, and some other powerful men I cannot mention by name, men of wealth, would pay me ten grand a night, minimum. Peloni was my most loyal client and he often paid in cash.

I know what you're thinking. She doesn't look like she's worth a grand and you'd be right. There's more attractive competition. I wasn't blessed with a full rack. There are women of higher quality and even greater skill, comparatively, but it isn't just the sex that men sought from me. Sometimes it was, but they were extremely specific in their requests. You see, there's one talent I became in high demand for. I feel nothing. Before you jump to conclusions, let me remind you that I am not talking about some kind of sexual trauma. While emotional nothingness is certainly part of this condition, most doctors are amazed to note my basic lack of nerve endings.

Do you see these scars all over my arms and legs? Some of them I did to myself. Most of them are from clients who fantasize about slicing someone up. My niche is that I am able to withstand the most heinous afflictions and the most brutal beatings. My body does not register agony. I feel nothing. If you place a flame beneath my palm, I won't even notice the heat until the skin starts to bubble. If you throw me down a flight of stairs, my broken bones are a mere inconvenience. I am not just a whore. I am a catalyst for man's most twisted and ruthless desires. Fantasies that most men would be imprisoned for acting upon.

You now believe you have your defense, don't you? You're thinking at some point I must have had enough, and I cracked and that is why I murdered Peloni. You would be wrong and I refuse to give the media the satisfaction of adhering to a false and deceptive story. Sure, it makes sense, but it's too simple. I planned Peloni's death weeks in advance, and not because I grew tired of him. The conditions I had with Peloni were completely adequate. He was rich and reliable and had a personal doctor that would fix me up when things got too rough. Broken bones immobilized me, so I insisted upon some guidelines that Peloni was willing to follow. My nerves are inactive, but as far as I know, I am not immortal. At least I don't assume I am. So whatever Peloni thought to do to me, he had to be certain I didn't lose too much blood. That was really the only regulation. Everything else was free game and believe me, men will pay good money for a woman who won't say no too much.

Like I mentioned, Peloni was a regular. And he was the most sadistic of them all. He would inflict upon me every possible means of harm; kicks, punches, hair yanks, lashes, choking, biting, cutting, even smashing my face into hard surfaces, causing my nose to become bent out of shape. I know. What kind of self-respecting person allows someone to treat them this way? Well, what kind of self-respect exists if you're numb? I have no more self-respect than I do self-loathing. Really, any type of self-worth requires some kind of emotional competency, of which I have none and I do not apologize for that.

It's the nothingness that I need you to understand. The numbness. No fear, no pain, no joy, no pleasure. I am as artificial as any person of flesh and blood can be, but I doubt that makes me evil either. How can one be evil if one lacks the ability to sufficiently hate? I did not hate Peloni. I did not love him. Even apathy is too strong a word. Somehow it suggests meaning. If people could understand what it is to not feel, what it is to just exist without any spectrum of passion, they might sympathize with my motive. I sought to counter this numbness by killing a man.

Perhaps I should take you back to the time when this discovery came to be. And that my heart, at least the metaphorical one, had died. No doubt, you know of the tragedy that occurred when I was a child. I do recall having some amount of feeling before the accident. I recall screaming from a bee sting and laughing as my father kissed the sore bump it left on my fingertip. I recall the cooling ointment that he used to calm the sting and the affection I had for him within his solid, hairy arms.

In summer, my parents opened the pool in the backyard and those are my favorite memories. The absolute delight in splashing and twirling about in a giant liquid playground, while Mother sipped her martini by the poolside, soaking in the sun and looking like a tan bikini goddess. I admired her beauty and felt blessed that she was mine and I was hers.

All these things came to an end when my father's plane came crashing into the Sierra desert. We were on our way to visit family in the North West, but little did we know, our pilot was on a suicidal mission. He had been drinking and he didn't plan for any of us to make it out alive. I woke up among blazes, strapped to my seat, my mother on top of me. Perhaps she had been protecting me or perhaps she just ended up that way. I will never know. She was limp and heavy, and I had to push her off in order to assess my unfamiliar surroundings through the smoke. The body of the plane was engulfed in raging flames and a mangled hand that came through the glass may have very well belonged to my father, but I couldn't quite tell with all the fire and smoke spreading with fury. I could have maybe dragged him out of there, but I was seven years old and he would have been a lot to manage for my tiny size, so I watched him burn.

Bone protruded from my ankle and I could barely breathe. As the sunset, I somehow was able to pull myself away from the fire and into the crevice of some nearby heap of land. I had with me my backpack that Mother had packed cookies and a couple of juice boxes in. Something told me not to eat it all at once, but I wasn't exactly hungry to begin with. The pain in my wrists and ankle was searing, but I could hardly weep with the sharp cracks in my ribs. Eventually Mother and Father would find me and bring me home. This I believed, even though I saw with my own eyes that they were done for. Still, my whole body shook in the icy air and my heart raced with dread. Experience had taught me that Mother and Father would be there any time I was frightened. Two and a half days passed, and I continued to wait for my parents to rescue me.

A lizard crawled onto my shoulder and I threw it into the dust and stomped on it, believing it would eat me up like a vicious dragon. Perhaps I did know something about death at the time. When the helicopters appeared in the sky I believed they were angels, coming to take me to Heaven. I wish they had.

71

Instead they carried me to the nearest children's hospital where I was operated on and bandaged up and kept isolated from the television people. I asked the doctors when my parents were coming to get me, but nobody would tell me they were dead. Even when my Aunt Louise came to take me to her house, I still waited for my father's sleek and shiny black Mercedes to pull into the driveway. I loved that car because he loved it and it was handsome like him. Every day I waited and every day, he never showed. Even at my parents' funeral, I waited for my father to lift me up with a sturdy embrace and carry me back to our big, luxurious palace. But he never did, and Mother never showed either, and after a while the anticipation became suspension and then void; like I was put on hold, every part of me.

So there's your defense. Post-traumatic stress? Maybe. But you know the prosecution will undoubtedly frame me as an angry prostitute with a vengeance. I need you to somehow prove that I don't get angry. I don't get vengeful and I don't get sad. The truth is, I'm not even worried about going to prison for the rest of my life. What can prison do that hasn't already been done to me? I don't respond to food with any supreme enjoyment or disgust. It's just nourishment. I won't miss any kind of cooking on the outside. More than likely, I'll just get some reading done in lock up.

That would be nice. I guess. To read some books. Reading was a favorite pastime before the accident. I still read quite a bit, but it's more of an intellectual pursuit than an emotional fulfillment. I'm always learning, always taking things in, but rarely do I have an opinion about a subject matter. My values are strictly based on survival instincts. Make money, eat when hungry, sleep when tired. I have trouble developing values that require empathy or compassion. I know that murder is not right, but that's because I know what the written law is. I also know that freedom is frequently preferred over imprisonment. Intellectually, I know that my life is better outside of a jail cell.

So ask me. I know you're wondering. If sex is how I make my money, am I able to reach orgasm? It's a redundant question. No. But when has that ever been part of the job requirement for sex workers? My inability to feel sexual pleasure makes prostitution the perfect gig. I'm sure I'm not the only sex worker you've ever met to describe fucking as "just a job." That's what it is. There's not much else to say about it, except maybe that Leah complicated things. Of course, I didn't fall in love with her. That would not be a possibility. But she was in love with me and she made it very much known that my existence, and the way that I am, hurt her at all times.

I told her not to expect anything from me. I said I was a shell. She just kept pushing, trying to get close, trying to wake me up inside. We fucked a handful of times and she said she could see it in my eyes, a desire for intimacy growing each time we were together. It was her imagination. She projected upon me what she wanted to see. I knew how to feign closeness and attachment. I did that for a living. But it was difficult to get Leah to realize what emotional vacancy actually is. It's not some self-absorbed Emo bullshit that is used for attention. I was never trying to get attention.

The best I could explain to her was that I felt about her as a reptile feels about its hatching eggs. She was in my vicinity and I thought it made sense to guide her. But that guidance was not the loving, sensitive nurture that a human mother might give her young. She cried when I said this and she wanted me to feel bad, but I couldn't give her what she wanted, so she punched me in the face and left. That was the last time I saw her. She knew she could get away with punching me. I think the attack was more for her release than to get a reaction from me. What I know about Leah is that she is defined as a good person and I expect moving on will be nothing less than rewarding once she is able to do it.

So, indeed, I may have become relatively curious about reclaiming my emotions due to Leah's excessive preaching about all the "wonderful" spectrum of positives and negative feelings. She was an artist, after all and attempted to teach me the idea of emotions through her creative compositions. The colors in her paintings helped me make connections, like a blind person learning to see through another sense. However, it's not that I didn't have any personal experience. In my memory, I could recall laughter and tears. I could recall being whole at one point, and I figured since I lost my ability to feel when I lost my parents, something major needed to occur in order for me to regain sensation in my entire being. It could be argued that I took on a career in violence, hoping that one day I might flinch at a sharp object near my vein. That hadn't happened, and so I decided to kill Peloni. I figured no one would miss him.

If Leah was a good person by definition, with her

unyielding volunteer efforts for dozens of charitable organizations, then by definition, Peloni was a bad person. When he wasn't beating me, he was beating his wife and kids. He only ever spoke with disdain for the poor and he relished only in what he could buy, and he could buy anything.

I didn't kill him instantly. I opened up his stomach in order to watch his organs spill out. He took a few clumsy swipes at me, called me a "fucking bitch," stumbled, and collapsed to the floor. His heavy weight caused the wood to rattle. I then sat on his legs and grabbed his face to stare into him, and I observed his confusion and fear as I watched the life go out of him. My theory was baseless, but I thought that maybe his fear would bounce off him and onto me. Maybe I could absorb his terror and make it my own, but when the police came I was not afraid, and I fully cooperated, knowing that any resistance would be pointless. That's when I asked for you, Counselor.

I had already done my homework and I wanted an attorney that was known for defending the very worst in humanity. You were that guy. I read all about you online. You've made a name for yourself keeping serial killers out of jail. You make sure rapists and terrorists go free. Many call you a monster, and yet you don't seem to care. You do your job without guilt or remorse. You are meticulous and without judgment, because for you, justice is not about right and wrong. It's about strategy.

I wonder Counselor, when your wife killed herself last year, did you mourn her? If I could squeeze my chains around your neck, would you scream? If I cut you like I cut Peloni, would the gash in your flesh burn and throb as his did? You see, Counselor, I theorize that you have been dealt the same affliction, which is why you are so good at what you do.

Most lawyers try to pray their sins away, but unwanted intrusions do not seem to interfere with your particularly gruesome daily business. You do not weep for these criminals, nor do you weep for their victims. You know only what you must do and you are not bothered by morality. That is why I chose you to represent me. I instinctively knew that you'd relate best to my story and that only you can educate a jury about why I did what I did. And by the look on your face, I'm guessing my assumption is not so far off.

So now tell me, do you consider our desolation freeing? Or do you consider it a curse?

Sometimes Peloni would beat me with a metal bat, causing welts and fractures that I'd regard as having tattered my outerwear. And I'd want to die. Not because of any unbearable wound, but because dying was something and something seemed like it might be better than nothing. Anything seems like it might be better than nothing. So what do you say, Counselor? Will you be taking my case?

His Type
Sèphera Girón

"What's your type?" Jamie leaned over the table towards his friends, his lips turned up in a playful grin, dark eyes twinkling. Around them glasses clanked, voices burbled, and music pulsed. Streaks of the setting sun sliced across the metal tables casting reflections across the walls and ceilings, bouncing from the hanging glasses at the bar like strobe lights.

"Big brawny bear, lots of fur, and dark eyes," John said without even thinking. He looked around the table and raised his pint of lager to his lips.

"Well, you sure didn't have to think twice about that one, now did you?" Jamie teased.

"Mmm yes, bears are good, but I also enjoy the sight of a glistening hairless muscleman donning merely a studded leather harness slowly licking the filth from my boots," Francis offered. The men nodded as they thought about it.

"Of course, a sharp-dressed man in a business suit is never wrong," John said.

"Everyone loves a sharp dressed man," Francis sang.

"Or..." Jamie said, "how about that guy over there?" Jamie nodded his head as he stage-whispered. "Check out that ass."

The four friends turned to leer at a 20-something man who had just walked through the door and towards the bar. He wore a tight purple T-shirt that enhanced every ripple from his biceps to his six-pack. Tiny jean shorts barely covered his ass as he shifted his weight from one leg to another while waiting for a drink at the bar.

Jamie, John, Francis and Tommy were buddies who'd been meeting at the same bar on Church Street in Toronto since their high school days; nearly 15 years. They'd been through school, through a myriad of relationships, and several career changes. Through it all, they liked to grab a few drinks and catch up with each other while looking for new loves and new lives.

"Young...so young, I can barely remember being so young," Tommy said.

"And lord knows, you've never been as pretty," Francis chuckled. The men watched the young man pay for his drink and then move down the bar a bit. He stood, taking little sips of his mixed drink, likely a gin and tonic, Tommy thought, and nervously stared around the bar.

"Aw, look at that. A newborn hatchling," Francis said.

"He looks so lost, poor thing," John said.

"Oh hey, and he's totally my type. See ya later!" Jamie waved with a kiss to his friends.

Tommy and John sipped their drinks as they watched Jamie work his magic on the beautiful stranger, a new kid in town. Jamie and The New Kid were laughing within minutes, their glasses clinking, their hands on each other's shoulders.

"Well, shit, that was fast. No wonder we never see him anymore," John said.

"He always was good with the gift of gab and of plucking out the hotties before the rest of us can even think to stand up," Tommy said sardonically.

"Well, he's welcome to the hatchling," John said.

"I guess it's easy when you don't have a day job and a million responsibilities," Tommy said. "Easy on the brain."

"Gotta love the trust fund babies," Francis nodded. "Every day's a party."

"Party… always gotta party," Tommy said.

"Oh, and what responsibilities weigh you down too much for some weekend fun?"

"Just my brain, I guess," Tommy sighed. "Don't really have much time to unwind with the latest round of research work."

"Research work, my ass. Don't tell me you're still hung up on Martin?"

"Martin?"

"Yeah, you remember—the asshole who cheated on you and left you nearly homeless, who stole your…"

"Yeah, yeah…No. Of course not, how could I be?"

"But you still…oh wait, maybe it was Stanley, the one who borrowed 20 grand and never paid it back? The Blue-Eyed Bandit. That guy?"

"Please…" Tommy shook his head.

"You know then there was Bernie. Sweet Bernie, you wanted to take care of him, his pretty blue eyes, and his thick long cock but meanwhile he was an escort and others were taking—ahem—care of him, too."

"And your point?" Tommy said.

"You don't want to date, Tommy. You're too bitter."

"It's not that at all," Tommy said. "I'm just not good at choosing people…"

"Who is? Maybe there is no perfect choice," Francis shrugged.

"And maybe there are just bad people who want to ruin it for everyone else," John said.

"If there were no assholes, how would you ever tell the good guys?" Francis asked, finishing his beer.

"True," Tommy nodded.

"And not everyone's an asshole. There're a lot of great people out there, people who just want to have fun with no fucking drama."

"I know, I see it. I've had it…them…fun that is…more often than not. It's just hard to forget the shitty ones," Tommy said.

"That's because they take so much…your money, your heart your soul…real live vampires," Francis said.

"Or maybe demons…" John said. The men nodded solemnly. The door opened again, and a burst of orange sunset flooded into the room and then was gone.

"Oh look, my date has arrived," Francis said as he looked towards the entrance. A tall, muscular man in a burgundy tank top and shorts stood waiting. "Check you later, honeys." Francis waved as he stood. "You going over to the *Hang Dog* later on?"

"You bet. Just have to go run some errands first," Tommy said. John nodded.

No sooner had Francis and his date slid over to the bar, then John was waving good-bye to Tommy as his own date arrived.

"Later, 'gator," he said as he left the table and hurried towards a curly-haired man carrying a book bag.

Tommy finished his beer as he watched his buddies gossiping with their dates. It'd been a while since he'd had a date of his own, but he only had himself to blame.

He had a type.

* * *

Later that night, Tommy stood outside the *Hang Dog*. He stared up at the moon that was visible just over the club's roof. It glowed.

"Full moon tomorrow night," someone said to him as they passed him, nearly bumping into him while he stared up at the nearly perfect orb glowing in the sky. Tommy fingered the vial in his pocket. It just fit into his hand as he palmed it. He popped the cork with his thumb and sprinkled small drops of the liquid content along the walkway and into the lobby of the *Hang Dog*.

* * *

Later, Tommy was dancing by himself at the *Hang Dog*. The place was packed with dozens of half-naked sweaty bodies that gyrated and throbbed in the strobe lights. His buddies were also haunting the dance floor with their dates. The booze was flowing, the vibe of the place was electric. Men were kissing in every corner, on the dance floor, and at the bar. Slick, firm, flesh was everywhere. Curved thighs, toned calves. And faces, so many glorious faces. Sharp cheeks, firm chins, round cherub faces, full lips, small lips, smooth clean faces, beards and moustaches…As if heaven had spared only the most beautiful angels to grace the club that night. Tommy went through the motions, his gaze hovering over the stunning go-go dancers on the speakers to the well-muscled bikini-clad man clutching the bars in a cage by the DJ booth. It was Saturday night, and everyone seemed to be living in the moment, for the moment, the future a vision that existed only in the outside world, beyond the vibrating walls of the club.

Tommy took a break and hit the bar for another rye and coke. He looked around through the flashes and thought he saw one. His type. That elfish face with bright eyes and dark hair. Tommy looked again but the man was gone. In his space stood Martin. Was it Martin? Martin's blue eyes glared at him, his firm cruel mouth a sharp line in his face. Tommy blinked, and Martin was gone. Fuck Martin. Why was that asshole haunting him?

Tommy returned to the dance floor, looking for His Type, but hoping to avoid Martin, if Martin had been there at all. The place was packed, and bodies danced together as one writhing being, amped up with adrenaline and booze, uppers and weed, you name it, someone was likely on it that night.

Tommy walked through the dance floor and out to the back patio where people were still allowed to smoke in a very small area. Tommy wasn't sure if these days they were *actually allowed* to smoke in that spot anymore, but he'd been smoking here for 15 years and didn't see the point of stopping now. Others seemed to share his opinion as someone offered him a light while he patted his pockets. Tommy stared up at the moon, now higher in the sky, smoking his cigarette. Someone else offered him a joint and he took a hit, passing it along to another stranger. Soon Tommy was laughing over trash pandas with several others, the joint growing smaller until it was finished. That much hadn't changed in 15 years either. Racoons in the bushes. Smoking joints on the patio. And though weed was now legal, it was still illegal. Nothing made sense anymore if it ever had.

As he made his way back to the dance floor, he saw His Type, down at the end of the hallway. That confident swagger, the dark tousled mane of hair, the slender frame. Tommy walked faster, hoping to catch up with the stranger but he disappeared into the throng of dancers. Tommy began to follow but then succumbed to dancing, the darkness and the strobes with the green glowing lights made it far too difficult to find anyone.

Yet, for a moment, he saw, he could swear, he locked eyes with Stanley. That friggin' Blue-Eyed Bandit asshole. Tommy's heart skipped a beat and his body grew stone cold. Why would Stanley come here, to his dance cave? They had agreed that Tommy got *Hang Dog* and Stanley got *Suspenders*. Maybe if he was here, he was with someone else...but of course he'd be here with someone else, he was always with someone else...he's the fucking Blue-Eyed Bandit. Tommy blinked, and the Blue-Eyed Bandit was gone. He looked around but never saw him again. Tommy caught another glimpse of His Type, over here then over there. Dancing so light and spry. Graceful yet forceful. An undulating package of flesh and charisma.

Funny how he could spot him now, so rare and yet there he was.

* * *

Tommy left long after his friends, and in fact, danced until the lights went on.

He finished out the night, going home alone once more.

* * *

Tommy liked nothing more to do on a Sunday morning than to go to the neighborhood coffee shop and sip on a double cappuccino with a sprinkling of cinnamon while reading either his Facebook wall on his tablet or an actual real paper book that wasn't over 100 years old.

It was a hot day, another August day in the humid city, and the fumes from the sidewalks were already wafting up. Yet coffee beckoned.

"Double cappuccino…a dash of cinnamon, please." Tommy heard a soft sultry voice place the order. He turned around to see the elvish dancer from the previous night. His heart skipped a beat.

"Hello!" the man said.

"Hello to you too. Do I know you?"

"I've seen you around but no we've never met. Chip," Chip held out his hand.

Tommy took the young man's hand and wrapped his fingers around it. Long slender pale fingers, his touch was slightly cold despite the heat of the day; probably the air-conditioning.

As Tommy shook Chip's hand, a chill rushed up his spine. Chip looked at Tommy with big blue eyes. Tommy didn't think he'd ever seen eyes so blue, so big, so beautiful, and so clear looking at him with such intensity. It was a struggle to form words as Chip waited for him to speak.

"Chip. Certainly don't hear that name around much anymore," Tommy said.

"No, it's old-fashioned. Gotta love the parents who fall in love with nostalgia."

"Oh, does Chip stand for anything...or rather, anyone?" Tommy asked.

"No, not unless you considering 'chip off the old block' an endearing moniker. I'd rather just be thought of as a Tollhouse cookie, really. At least people know what they are."

"Your parents...you don't get along with them?" Tommy asked.

"Oh, well, you know. They like to show their affection with their wallet. I'm certainly a chip from an era gone by indeed. But let's not talk about such boring stuff on a such a beautiful Sunday morning," Chip said.

"What brings you here today?" Tommy asked as he took his cappuccino from the barista. "Besides the coffee you mean?" Chip asked playfully. "Just lounging around on a nice Sunday morning, probably like you are."

"I don't think I've ever seen you here before," Tommy said.

"I get around," Chip said. "But I will admit, that I stopped in because something, or rather, someone, caught my eye."

The barista turned on the espresso machine again and as milk foam frothed, Tommy studied Chip with a newfound interest.

"Love that shirt," Chip said.

"This?... oh..." Tommy stopped speaking and then flashed a smile.

"And your shoes..." Chip said. "Tell me, where did you ever find them in that color?"

"There's a boutique over on Church, a bit north of..."

"Right, right, I know the one. I frequent it often. So lovely... you're... so lovely..."

"Nonsense," Tommy squeezed his cup slightly tighter as he moved through the cafe towards the exit.

"What are you doing, later...now...oh I'm sorry, I'm much too forward..."

Tommy grinned and studied the man; earnest blue eyes, thick pink lips, tightly packaged shorts....

"Forward is appreciated in these days of smoke and mirrors," Tommy said as he found a bench and sat. Chip sat as well.

"What kind of work do you do, Tommy? I personally am a stock broker, well, I'm on Bay Street you know, an office there with a rather large firm, perhaps you've heard of them...?"

"I-I don't follow stocks. I wouldn't know them if you named them. I'm a historian. I work over at the Museum. Mostly behind the scenes."

"Oh, an intellectual. I bet you make good money over there."

"I do okay...between that and government grants." Tommy smiled.

"Government grants? For what?" Chip sipped his coffee, looking up at Tommy with earnest, his blue eyes wide and endearing. Tommy could have stepped right into them but instead he cleared his throat and explained the grant process.

"My research itself is likely quite boring to you, just a professor rolling through old texts searching for eternal youth, eternal power, a money tree, you know, any type of lore pertaining to obtaining our wildest desires."

"You get paid for reading old fairy tales?" Chip asked with awe. He raised his cup. "Well, good on you. Best scam I've heard yet."

Tommy smiled and clicked his cup to Chip's.

"Oh, it's no scam. There are secrets to be unearthed that would be detrimental in the wrong hands. Spells, conjurings, prayers…"

Chip laughed.

"Again, fairy tales. I live in the real world. Money talks, and I admire the fact you're making it."

"Money isn't everything," Tommy said, wiping his mouth with his napkin. "Peace of mind is good too."

"Now I know you're crazy. You have money, you have it all. Power, love, house, car…it's all there."

"Well, I'm a historian not a jet setter. My income is modest, possessions, well…" Tommy winced thinking about his tiny room in a boarding house thanks to his poor choices in mates. "…but I do love my work."

Chip nodded.

"You certainly make enough to be a sharp dressed man on a Sunday morning, now don't you?" Chip said as he put his hand over Tommy's. Tommy looked down at their hands and then slowly put his hand over Chip's and squeezed.

"Tommy, would you like to go, somewhere?"

Tommy shrugged. "Why not? Would you like to see my office at the museum?"

"You know I'd love to," Chip said.

* * *

An hour later, Tommy was tying the last knot of a long purple scarf around the wrist of Chip, who let him. In fact, Chip wasn't even paying attention to Tommy, he was looking around the room. Tommy stood back and surveyed his work. The man was face down, spread naked across a two-level metal bondage bench that allowed him to move his head around but forced him into a kneeling pose. The men were in a small room behind a wooden wall panel in Tommy's office. There were tall objects around the room that were draped in red sheets. The garish color brightened up the room and highlighted the red padding and black metal framework of the bench. Chip's ankles were individually fastened to posts with purple scarves as if he were kneeling, his wrists affixed to posts by his head. Chip's face was turned to the wall where there was a large mirror. Chip stared into it, his pink thick lips barely brushing together.

"Your ties are perfectly knotted...master," Chip whispered with admiration. Tommy's lip twitched but he said nothing. He stared at the young man on his bench.

Perfect round buttocks, just as he had hoped. So many men wore those shape-shifting under gear and reality often disappointed, but not in this case. Chip had the goods that had been advertised.

Tommy ran his hand along one of Chip's smooth firm cheeks, wondering how it felt to be so young and daring, how must it feel to have life laying before you like a red carpet, knowing the power of being alive and using it.

His fingers glided up Chip's back and along his muscled shoulders. The inviting curve of neck, the shaggy tips of black hair gracing broad shoulders. Tommy nuzzled his face into the soft scented hair of Chip. He sniffed deeply, sucking in the youthful exuberance. Tommy's tongue danced along Chip's cheek and then lips met lips. Tommy kissed with hunger that threatened to consume him. Chip kissed him back just as passionately. Tommy's urgency swelled but he pulled back, breaking the kiss. His forehead glistened with sweat as Chip watched him with soft, blue eyes, his lips moving seductively. There was no denying the tension that bound them and Tommy ached to return to Chip's soft firm lips.

Instead, he stood up and paced around the tiny room, catching his breath. He wiped his lips.

Slow down. Take it easy.

Tommy looked at Chip's reflection and Chip turned his head towards the mirror, their eyes meeting in the shadows created from electric candles and the mirror.

"You like to watch, don't you?" Tommy asked. Chip smiled.

"Doesn't everyone?" Chip asked.

Tommy laughed.

"Some do, some don't." Tommy walked around the room and stood before one of the tall objects. He pulled the sheet to unveil a standing mirror and draped the material underneath on the floor. Chip found his reflection in it by lifting his head. He smiled as he studied himself.

Tommy walked around to the other side of the equipment and revealed another mirror. And then another until five mirrors glinted with shadows and secrets in the room.

Chip laughed.

"A mirror for every angle. I bet there's one on the ceiling as well!" Chip struggled to turn his head to look up, but he was restrained by the scarves.

Tommy studied the lithe figure on his bondage bench who was enjoying his own reflection in the reflections. Chip looked upon his own body, studying the curve of his own thigh, the swell of his ass jutting out on the bench. Tommy wondered how sticky Chip's knees and chest were getting from the plastic coverings he had put over the cushioned leather. Plastic coverings that still had a misty sheen on them from where he had lightly sprayed the elixir.

Beside the bench was a cabinet with a whip, cat o' nine tales, handcuffs, and other tools created from leather and metal hanging from hooks in the opened doors. There were belts and feathers and beside the hanging ornaments, there were more tools on a side table. Several knives, a sword, a couple of antique handguns, and a pick. The metal bits gleamed in the many mirrors, creating rainbows and halos that combined with the curtain shadows like a canopy.

Tommy wiped his mouth with the back of his hand and turned away from Chip.

"You like to watch as well," Chip said.

"Definitely," Tommy's voice was low as he turned back, holding a riding crop in one of his hands. He raised it and then struck one of Chip's fleshy ass cheeks. Chip moaned low in his throat. A shiver of lust ran up Tommy's spine as he watched the red mark of the crop welt up and then slowly fade but not quite away. He brought down the crop again, watching the red line streak across the white. Chip grunted. Tommy put the crop away and then reached for a flogger that had many strips of soft black leather. He teased Chip, running the flogger up and down Chips legs, ass, and back, the soft material likely soothing after the sharp bite of the crop.

He ran the flogger more firmly across Chip's body and then lifted it. The flogger fell against Chip's body with a crack, creating several lines. Chip grunted, still staring at himself. Tommy raised and lowered the flogger repeatedly.

* * *

Tommy caught a glimpse of himself in the mirror, his face flushed and intense as he fucked Chip. In the mirror, his face reflected lust, and a hardness he'd never noticed before. His own eyes were dark pools that told everything and yet nothing at all set in the shadows of sleepless nights pouring over old books. Tommy's body quivered with the lust the young man had inspired in him. He nearly cried, reminding himself of when he was a teenager fucking the very first beautiful man he'd ever had. A true beauty, he'd been. Much like the beauty he was fucking right now. He ran his hand down Chip's back as his cock plunged in deeply. He pulled Chip's hips towards him, letting his cock impale him, feeling Chip tighten and loosen, twitching his warm flesh around Tommy. Dark hair flipped over Chip's dark eyebrows, his mouth an 'O' of ecstasy. The pretty face, youth and freshness caused a hollow ache in Tommy's stomach, an ache that continued to grow. Chip's beauty overwhelmed Tommy as he pulled back then plunged in again, deeper, harder. He quickly checked Chip's face in the mirror between thrusts.

Still exquisite from every angle; full pink lips, vivid blue eyes now half-closed as he received Tommy.

Tommy leaned over, still inside Chip, laying across his back, biting his shoulder, nipping at his triceps.

"You're so beautiful," Tommy whispered. "What do I do to deserve this?"

"You are the beauty," Chip gasped.

"Not likely."

Tommy fucked Chip some more, letting himself fall into a pleasurable rhythm. He almost lost himself but then he remembered the work he had to do.

He pulled back and pushed into Chip as far as he could, holding back his come, trembling while watching Chip's face in the mirror.

Chip's face had morphed, rippling into Martin's, that damn Martin who had taken so much from him. Tommy gasped as Martin's leering blue eyes stared at him in the mirror. They blinked, long thick eyelashes flashing across those bright blue eyes and then disappearing again. Chip's face returned. Tommy clenched Chip's hips, his nails digging in hard as he kept watching Chip in the mirror.

"Fuck me harder," Chip whispered.

Tommy obliged, still watching Chip's face. Sweat rolled down Tommy's face, stinging his eyes. He wiped it away, still watching Chip staring at himself getting fucked in the mirror. Chip's face rippled again, this time revealing Stanley. That fucking bastard Stanley. Beautiful Stanley. Blue-Eyed Bandit Stanley who was such a lying bastard. Tommy wanted to rip Chip's body in half but instead, he waited until Stanley's face sank back into Chip's.

As he looked at Chip in the flesh, in front of him, impaled on him, he couldn't see any of the faces. It was just Chip. Shaggy hair, broad shoulders, muscular back. Chip's round red-streaked ass slapped against his thighs as he pushed and pulled him. The bindings on Chip's wrists and ankles kept him at Tommy's mercy. Tommy reached over and grabbed a fistful of Chip's thick, black hair. He pulled his head up and held it. They both looked in the mirror.

A flash of Bernie flickered across Chip's face and was gone. Chip's flesh rippled, his back undulating as if a million beetles were scurrying just beneath his flesh. Then more ripples, as if a wind was blowing across a river.

Tommy reached around with both hands towards Chip's face and hooked his fingers into either side of Chip's mouth. Tommy tugged at the skin, the flesh split roughly, a squelching tear, as he peeled it back from Chip's head. The skin sloughed off in his hands, steaming with meat, stinking of rot. Tommy flapped his hands, blood splattering the plastic wrapped bondage bench and the mirrors.

Fleshless, Chip laughed as he slipped away from the rest of his skin. Tommy's cock was still in Chip, yet Chip stood before him, a glistening fleshless human that was not human at all. The husk of the flesh that had been Chip lay across the bondage bench. Tommy shuddered and stifled the urge to puke as he wrangled his now limp dick from the sloughed off skin.

"You can try but you'll never stop us, never," the demon taunted, dancing with glee. "We're greater than you, we're always one step ahead," the demon said, his voice deep and menacing. He dripped blood as his veins pulsed, lunging from side to side as his legs grew longer, his arms spindly like a spider, his teeth long and rotten. He transformed and twisted, lumps of meat falling from him. He looked down at the ground and picked up pieces of himself. He pressed the pieces back into his abdomen, staring at Tommy. His eyes still were the eyes of Chip, of Martin, of Stanley, of so many others. Those eyes that were always an echo of someone familiar, from once upon a dream yet the future only held the promise of nightmare. Demon-Chip stopped and stood still. Slowly, new flesh grew over his form and knitted itself together, and soon, he stood tall and slender, perfumed, naked and aroused. He was Chip from the coffee shop once more.

"Hey, Tommy, what's up. You look like you've seen a ghost. You feeling okay, man?"

Chip walked towards Tommy, his huge erection nearly touching Tommy before the rest of him did. Tommy stared at Chip's cock for a moment. He licked his lips. Chip ran his hands along Tommy's arms.

"Come on, Tommy, let's finished what we started, okay? I don't know what happened but it's cool, man. It's cool."

Chip reached up with long pretty fingers to touch Tommy's face. Tommy leaned back, licking his lips as he stared into the crystal blue eyes. He moaned as Chip's fingers firmly wrapped around his cock, tugging on him exactly how he liked it, renewed pleasure surging through him.

"No…" Tommy moaned. "No, stop…"

He leaned into the pleasure for a moment, wanting it to continue, the firm practiced fingers dancing along him as if they'd known him forever, that handsome face…

The mask was slipping…droplets of blood seeped through a slit on the side of Chip's face. Tommy pushed him away, unlocking Chip's fingers from his cock.

Tommy turned away and reached over to the cabinet, to the table beside it. He scooped up one of the guns, aimed it at Chip, pulling the trigger repeatedly.

Water sprayed out, drenching the demon. Sparks and then smoke exploded out wherever the water hit Chip's flesh. The demon shrieked and wailed, dissolving into nothingness before Tommy's eyes.

Tommy grinned. He twirled the gun around on his finger a few times before putting it on the table. He reached into the cabinet and brought out a wooden box with letters and numbers carved across it. He untied the scarves from the bondage posts, shaking them out. He folded each one and put it into the box.

He carefully peeled the shucked skin from the bondage bench, his eyes welling up as he rolled up what had been a beautiful face, a perfect body. He put it into another much larger box. He folded it in, the texture melting as he touched it. He stood above the box, remembering. His hand fondled himself, touching his own chest, his arms, his eyes. He watched himself in the mirrors, fingers tracing along his erection then firmly gripping it. He closed his eyes, remembering bright blue eyes, the soft smell of youth, the eager grin of victory. His hand pumped faster as he thought about how tightly Chip's flesh had wrapped around him, pulsing and quivering as he fucked him. And the lips. Soft and full, like velvet, soft and sweet. Tommy came with a groan, letting his come pulse into the box and along the discarded flesh. There were small wafts of smoke and a sizzle, as if he were putting out a fire, and perhaps, in some small way, he had. The come mingled with the skin and seeped into the box, steaming and sticky; Tommy closed the lid on the rotten smell.

He put the gun into the box that held the scarves. He also took a small bottle of water along with the vial he had taken to the club and lifted them into the air.

"Who knew how handy this stuff could be?"

He stared at the murky water and then put the bottles gently in with the scarves and the gun. He closed the lid and put the box back over by his tools.

He picked up the larger box, the one with Chip's skin, and made sure the lid was tightly shut. He took a knife from among the bondage tools and carved 'Chip' on the box. Then he pressed a panel on the wall. A secret door popped open, revealing several shelves. There were a few boxes on the shelves. Some had no labels. He slid 'Chip' in. For a moment, he looked at the boxes with the labels, 'Martin,' 'Stanley,' and 'Bernie.' He nodded his head, sighed, and then shut the door

The Life Model
Jim Towns

1.

Tara had started doing life modeling at the college for the extra money. But it had become something more than that.

It was a strange thing, to walk into a room full of strangers—guys and girls—and take off every stitch of clothing to sit or lie, fully exposed, as they drew her. Sometimes the poses went on for an hour, and she would find herself slipping into an almost meditative state. And sometimes, especially during a Saturday morning class, she would straight up fall asleep lying there naked in front of everyone.

It was a kind of sacred space, the life drawing classroom. For the most part the students took what they were doing very seriously. After all, they were paying to be here... or at least their families were. During breaks and after class, Tara—wrapped in her thin kimono robe—would walk around the room and look at all the drawings. Some of them were remarkably lifelike—she felt that she could almost reach out and touch her own self on the heavy paper. Others—well, it was fascinating to see how some people saw her, and how what they saw translated into their work.

Tara had always been shy in high school. A classic wallflower, she'd had a lot of anxiety issues. Taking tests had been an ever-present problem for her. Tara would begin thinking about the ramifications should she fail. That would lead her to horrible visions of her compromised future Suddenly she'd be all light-headed and next thing she knew she'd be throwing up in the girl's toilet. So after her freshman year of college, she'd decided to take a few credits at the local community college for a year before coming back. In her first week at the community college she'd seen a posting on a bulletin board that the art department needed life models.

She was amazed at the way the possibility of doing it made her feel; the tingle that shot through her pelvis at the idea of actually stripping everything off in a room full of total strangers. Before she could stop herself she'd called and then come in for an interview and was scheduled to pose the very next Tuesday afternoon. Tara had never even been fully naked in front of a boy.

That first time she'd almost not shown up. She stood naked in front of her mirror at home the morning of, looking at herself from every angle, imagining how 20 people would view her when the moment came for her to drop her robe. Would they think she was attractive? Ugly? She was on the short side, slender of build with short-cut red hair. A million tiny freckles dotted her face and shoulders and ran down towards her breasts. Her breasts were sizable for her tiny frame, she thought. The nipples were very pale, almost the same color as the flesh surrounding them. Did people find that weird? Was it harder to draw, she wondered?

Her hips flared out a good deal as well, giving her rear a funny inverted pyramid shape she'd always felt awkward about. Her legs were on the short side, the thighs a bit stockier than she would have preferred, tapering down to narrow calves and relatively small feet. She'd spent some time staring at her privates. She never trimmed her pubic hair like other girls she knew. It grew in a very faint patch of almost colorless fuzz, so she'd never seen the point. But now she looked and could see every detail of her labia, and realized everyone else would be able to, as well. Would they draw it? The idea terrified and tantalized her at the same time. She'd actually touched herself in that moment, something she'd rarely done, and found herself climaxing in mere seconds as she imagined what it was going to be like.

2.

When she entered the room that afternoon she'd been hesitant to meet anyone's eyes. The instructor, a younger woman named Mrs. Stevens, had shown her to the center of the room. She'd obviously been told Tara was new. It would be several poses, she told her: short standing ones at first, then longer seated or reclining ones. Tara glanced about her at the surrounding people. The time had come, and she stepped to the side to put down her bag and take off her robe.

She felt every minute sensation as the silky belt came loose from around her waist and the robe opened in the front. This was it, she told herself. There was no going back. She let the robe fall off her shoulders, set it down, then turned and stepped into the center, where there was a raised 5x5 wooden platform with several cushions and a cloth-draped stool.

Tara felt the light on her bare body immediately. She opened her eyes and raised her hands above her head, stretching her back out. Suddenly, she wasn't afraid anymore. She pushed her bare breasts out, feeling the nipples harden with excitement. She took several poses for 30 seconds, a full minute, then three as the students furiously sketched her rough form. There was a minute-long break during which she sat on the edge of the platform, a little unsure of what to do. She wished she'd brought a bottle of water and made a mental note for the future.

After the break was a 15-minute pose. This is what Tara had been dreading—the long protracted stillness of others studying her as she sat exposed before them—but surprisingly it was at this moment she finally felt freed from her worries. Thus far she'd been crossing her legs, self-consciously hiding her more intimate areas from the students, but now, on the next pose, she finally spread her legs apart on the stool—one foot up and one down on the platform— and felt the damp hair of her genitals open up... the people were looking at her and she liked it. For the next poses she actually leaned over, giving everyone behind her a full view of her labia, and even between her cheeks. If they wanted to draw it, let them. Before she knew it the time was up, and it was over—but really it had just begun.

That night at home, Tara took off all her clothes again, standing once more in front of the mirror and staring at herself; turning, bending over, and spreading herself open to look... it was really quite amazing there, the way the light colored flesh of her labia parted and came back together, the soft centimeter of skin below it that then fell away into the darker colored tiny puckered crevice. Her fingers again found their way in between her legs and she came like she'd never come before.

3.

Tara had been modeling for a few months when she noticed Robyn staring at her. Spring Quarter had started. The college had received an endowment that enabled them to build more computer labs, so the foundation drawing classes were moved into Chancellor's Hall, the oldest building on campus. It was a two-story brick structure that had originally been an elementary school before the new college had annexed it back in 1911. Instructors and students grumbled, but Tara liked the old rooms. She liked walking around on the old soft wood floors between poses.

So far her life modeling experience had been overwhelmingly positive. In fact, it had been a bit of a life-changing thing for her, challenging her and opening up her horizons in many ways. Her confidence was up, and she was looking forward to starting classes again in the fall.

It happened during an evening class in the old building. Tara was holding a long pose, curled into an almost fetal position with her one arm wrapped around her knees, the other stretched outward, a strong lamp on a stand shining warmly on her. Her mind had gone away to that place where there was no time and no fatigue and no cramping muscles, but something had pulled her back to reality—that ancient mammalian sixth sense that warns someone when a pair of eyes is locked upon them. Her eyes had been shut, but now they opened and she searched around the room as much as she was able to without moving her head.

Of course they were all staring at her. That was what this job was about—she wasn't a person, she was a figure. A human-shaped subject for light to play off of, casting shadows across her form and molding her shape, so that the students could study, draw, and learn about anatomy and rendering the human body. But she was now acutely aware that there was someone in the room who wasn't looking at her that way. Someone here was staring not at an object, but at Tara. At *her*.

She felt the eyes on her. Not in any threatening or challenging way, but with a definite raw intensity. As she carefully cast her gaze down past her knees she found the source of the feeling: a smallish girl towards the back with dyed black hair, black sweater and skintight black jeans. Her eyes were locked onto Tara, her charcoal barely moving across the surface of her paper. She could see Tara looking at her, and there was a silent frozen moment as the two women stared at each other before Tara slowly closed her eyes again.

She was a bit unnerved by the intensity of the girl's gaze, and it brought her back to her first afternoon posing nude for the class—the insecurity swelling up all over again. Better to go back to her away place for the rest of the pose. It took some effort, but Tara managed to forget the arresting green eyes watching her, and the next thing she was aware of was the timer ringing. The class was over.

4.

It was Tara's normal custom to wait until most the students had packed up their materials and left before going to gather her things and go to the women's room to change into her street clothes. It wasn't really out of modesty—she was past that—it was simply less awkward than having to make conversation with the girls from the class while meantime trying to pull on her panties and jeans. She also used this time to stretch out any of the kinks she'd acquired by holding the longer poses during the session, so she was still sitting on the platform pulling on her robe when she realized the only other person left in the room was the black-haired girl.

The self-conscious feeling returned again. Tara got up and went to her pile of stuff. The girl's easel was right next to it, and she was collecting her pencils and charcoal, but Tara sensed that she was acutely aware of her proximity, and caught a furtive glance from the girls' green eyes at her nude body as she bent to pick up her robe. From this angle Tara could see the girl's drawing.

"Wow, that's good," she heard herself say. And it was: shockingly so. From her angle the girl had had a clear view of Tara's curled legs, and while much of the drawing had been only loosely blocked out, certain areas—the soles of her feet, the space in-between her thighs—had been drawn in incredible detail. Without thinking, Tara leaned in for a closer look. Every fold of flesh, every crinkle was rendered with utmost skill and more than that: with care. Tara felt the familiar tingle just looking at it. It was then she realized she

103

was still holding her robe and hadn't put it on yet. She was standing inches from the girl and still completely naked.

The girl's fingers reached out gently and brushed some stray erasings from the artwork, and while doing so caressed over Tara's privates in the drawing. "Thanks, you can tell I got a little—caught up in some of it... I wish we'd had more time with the pose." Her voice was soft and low.

"I had plenty—my hip is killing me." Tara had still not pulled on the robe. Now it was a bit hard to figure out how to do so while standing so close.

"Oh, I'm sorry," the girl's hand then impulsively caressed Tara's hip and the touch was alarming and comforting in perfectly equal measures.

"It's fine. I'm used to it. I'm Tara, by the way."

"I'm Robyn," the girl replied. Her eyes were locked on Tara's. Tara was barefoot and Robyn was still a little shorter than her. "You're a really great model. I like drawing you."

"Thanks, I'm still pretty new, but I like it."

"What is it you like most?"

Tara had to think for just a moment: "It's—open. Honest, I guess? Maybe that sounds dumb."

Robyn's hand moved to trace over the skin of Tara's upper arm now. "No, that's it exactly. That's why I love figure drawing." Her hand slid down Tara's freckled arm and Tara could feel the hairs standing up on it. "Everyone's body is so different, different shapes and colors, with different parts... but they're all sort of one shape, you know? All of them beautiful." Her hand had come to rest holding Tara's own hand. Her bare body was very close to Robyn's now. She could feel an acute ache in her nipples she'd not experienced before. "It's wonderful, really."

Tara stared at the girl. Alone in this room together, they were sharing a degree of intimacy that Tara almost never felt comfortable with around anyone, even her friends. The thought of how beautiful Robyn's body must be under her clothes raced through her mind and was gone so quickly it was almost like she hadn't thought it. She spoke before she had even thought:

"Would you like to draw me some more, Robyn? Right now?"

"Yes, I really would."

"The same pose, or—?"

"No, something different. Something you wouldn't do for the class."

Tara liked that.

5.

"You don't need a break?" Robyn asked.

"Nah. I want to see what you draw." She stepped up onto the platform.

Robyn moved her pad and materials to an easel closer to the front, as Robyn sat down on the cushions, grabbing her bottle of water and taking a drink.

Robyn asked, "I like to get a little more comfortable when I draw, is that okay?" Tara told her of course, and watched out of the corner of her eye as Robyn slipped out of her shoes, then pulled off her sweater. Underneath she was wearing only an old thin tanktop. She was very skinny and pale, with several tattoos running up her left arm.

"I like your work," Tara nodded to her ink. Robyn smiled.

"Thanks. I wish my parents did. You good?"

Tara nodded again. Robyn switched the spotlight back on, and Tara eased herself back down onto the cushions.

"How do you want me?" the question was out of her mouth before she realized it. But Robyn just smiled.

"Would you mind if I pose you?"

The idea sent a tiny thrill through Tara's lower regions. She was becoming very aware that they both knew where this was going, yet they were both enjoying the slow pace it was taking. "No, of course," She said. "Please."

Robyn moved forward a bit timidly, and then seemed to summon the courage to step up onto the platform. Her feet were slender; her toenails were black like her hair. She leaned forward and Tara felt gentle hands take hold of her shoulders and ease them back. She let Robyn shift her hips to one side, intently aware of the feel of the fingertips touching the flesh of her rear. Robyn gently lifted her right thigh up, taking her foot by the instep and turning it to face her opposite thigh, opening up her crotch wide. Those fingers inches from her sex. Tara found it almost hard to speak:

"What about my arms?"

In response Robyn leaned over her, positioning Tara's arms above her head. In the heat of the room, Robyn's shirt clung to her chest, and her nipples protruded clearly through the material, inches from Tara's mouth. They were dark, she could tell, and large for so small a girl. Tara had a sudden compulsion to reach up and lick them, which surprised her. She'd never had such an intense urge before, especially not for another woman. She resisted, but the idea of what it would be like stayed with her even after Robyn had retreated back to her easel.

"Are you comfortable?" Robyn checked.

"That's one word for it." Tara chuckled despite herself, but Robyn chuckled as well, and began drawing.

During the drawing part, Tara was usually accustomed to slipping away into a kind of meditation, distancing herself from what was going on in the room, the little noises and occasional voices; and instead focusing on the tactile feel of the cushions against her back, the wood beneath her feet, the warmth of the light on her skin. But tonight was different. She listened intently to every scratch of Robyn's charcoal on her paper, every shift of her naked feet on the wood floor. She was hot under the light, and could feel her body covered in the thinnest film of sweat.

Robyn's voice came to her: "It's hot."

"Seriously."

"So would you mind?" Tara looked up to see Robyn was unbuttoning her jeans.

"No, sure, go for it. I mean—it's nice like this."

She closed her eyes again, but not all the way— under her lids she saw Robyn peel off the tight black jeans and toss them onto a stool. Her underwear was black and hung very low, well below where her hip bones protruded. Robyn's shirt ended above her navel, showing several inches of a small belly that curved down to where the black lace barely covered where her privates began, and Tara could tell that Robyn shaved bare.

"What if like the janitor comes in?"

"Well he'll have a good story, won't he?"

6.

Robyn had been drawing for a while now, and Tara's mind had just started to drift away. Fantasies were dancing around in it—possibilities of what would happen when she walked over to look at Robyn's drawing. Robyn's soft voice brought her back.

"Do you want to take a break?"

"I'm okay. Are you close to being done?"

"More-or-less." She drew for another moment. "Can I say something without it being weird?"

"Yes, of course."

"Are you sure? It might be a little—"

"No, I want to hear..."

"You really have a beautiful pussy."

Tara's heartbeat nearly palpitated. "I—thanks... I've never had anyone... thank you." She paused—it was on her to take the next step, she'd decided.

"Do you see a lot of pussies, Robyn?" The question was loaded, she realized—filled with anticipation of what she was quickly beginning to desperately want to have happen.

"I've seen a few pretty close up, yeah. You?"

"Not so many, no... But..."

"But..?"

"But I think I'd like to see yours... close up."

The comment hung there for a minute and Tara

worried she'd moved too fast, or somehow misread the signals. But the next thing she was aware of was feeling a slight weight land on the platform next to her outstretched leg. Gentle fingertips grazed along the top of her foot and up her shin to her knee, then to her hip. Tara opened her eyes a bit and saw Robyn kneeling above her, staring down at her.

"So the drawing portion of the evening is over?" she asked.

Robyn grinned: "Definitely."

Her hand brushed through Tara's short-cropped hair, running down her cheek and over her collar to caress the soft skin of her breast.

"I haven't before—with a girl."

"That's not a problem... as long as—"

"I do. Let the janitor come in, I don't care."

And they kissed. Robyn's tongue was instantly exploring every corner of Tara's mouth, then working down her neck. Tara could feel Robyn's hands running down her sides, wrapping around under her buttocks and squeezing. Tara found her own hands instinctively reaching out, her fingers dipping underneath Robyn's underwear and moving over her smooth rear.

Robyn's mouth finally found Tara's nipples and her breath caught in her throat. She'd never had someone so skilled work magic on that tender skin before. Robyn's tongue danced from one to the other, she alternately suckled and bit them gently with her teeth. Tara's back arched upwards with pleasure, meeting Robyn's chest. Her hands fumbled with the damp tanktop.

"Take this off. I want to feel your body against me."

Robyn rose up and peeled off her top. Tara's hands moved up the smooth skin of her stomach and over the small mounds of her breasts. They were wonderfully soft, softer than anything she'd ever felt, Tara thought. Then Robyn was on top of her again and her nipple was in Tara's mouth. It felt like the most instinctive thing, to lick and suck on it. It tasted fleshy and deliciously salty from her sweat.

Robyn's hands were sliding downward along Tara's sides. With what could only have been experience, she effortlessly lifted Tara's leg, kissing the tender back of her knee. Tara found it ticklish and delightful. Robyn lowered her leg back down on the outside now, placing herself in-between Tara's thighs. She spread Tara's legs wide apart. Tara knew what was coming and her body burned in anticipation for it.

Robyn's tongue explored all around first: moving along the inside indentation where her legs met her pelvis, running up to Tara's navel before sliding downward. The first contact of the tip of her tongue with Tara's clitoris was an electric jolt, sending her into a convulsion. But more gentle wet caresses came, and faster—a sensate drumbeat that quickened and grew more frantic in tempo to Tara's rapid breathing. Robyn's hands spread her wide open, and then she felt her fingers exploring inside her, swirling around her rapidly moistening sex, before what must have been her thumb finally penetrated deep up into her. Tara gasped as all the while Robyn's tongue danced over her ultra-sensitive locus.

When it came it crashed across her like a blow, taking the wind out of her lungs and leaving her almost insensate for a moment. Tara turned and twitched, holding Robyn's head tight between her legs. She didn't want it to end, but Robyn had no intention of stopping—she kept licking for a protracted moment, and a half-dozen smaller shockwaves ran up Tara's body, finally dwindling down to the gentlest buzzing.

7.

"Oh god... oh god I didn't... I've never..." she could barely speak. Coming back to awareness, she looked down at Robyn's beautiful green eyes gazing up at her from between her legs. "Shit, was I loud? I didn't—"

"Shhh..." Robyn crawled up, taking Tara's body in her arms. "You were fine. More than fine."

Tara leaned up to kiss her, and tasted herself on Robyn's lips—it was salty like her nipple, but something else to—a little like a sour fruit. She ran her tongue over her own lips.

Robyn grinned down at her: "You've never tasted a girl."

"No."

"But you like it?"

"I do. It's like a grapefruit." Her hands moved under the waistband of Robyn's underwear. "I want to see what you taste like."

She felt clumsy at what she was attempting, but Robyn's low groans reassured her she was doing all right. She had been right before—there was no hair down there to get caught up in, just a smoothly-shaven slide down into the soft folds of Robyn's intimate parts. Tara tried to be gentle, caressing the tender flesh, feeling its wetness, searching for the right spot.

111

It took a moment, but then under her middle finger Tara felt the tiny solid spot and Robyn gasped and kissed her forcefully. Tara swirled her finger around and around, and Robyn moaned harder and harder.

"You don't have to if you don't want. Sometimes when you're new to it, it's strange."

In answer Tara brought her fingers back and put them in her mouth, sucking the juices from them, then kissed Robyn, letting her tongue dance inside the other girl's mouth before licking all the way up her cheek, to whisper in her ear. "I want your pussy on my face, woman."

Without another word Tara rose up, yanking down her panties and stepping out of them, tossing them to the far corner of the room. Tara could see the darker skin of the girl's pussy above her, the lips already spread wide in pleasure from Tara's fingers. Then Robyn knelt down and her sex came down on her in a sweet rush and Tara grasped two full hands of Robyn's ass and licked her all the way from back to front, making the other girl hiss with ecstasy.

Tara began licking furiously—she had discovered an amazing secret world that had been hidden from her for her entire sexual life. Robyn tasted glorious, like honey and milk mixed together. She was dripping wet, and it ran down Robyn's cheeks as she dappled her tongue over Robyn's clit. It didn't take Robyn long at all before her body clenched and she let out a harsh gasp that transformed into a moan. Her face so deep inside, Tara could feel the muscles in Robyn's vagina clench through her cheeks.

"Fuck... fuck... oh fuck, honey..."

But Tara didn't want to stop. She wanted to stay

where she was. She kept licking and within seconds Robyn had climaxed again. And again.

"Oh God, please... no wait—Oh my God..."

The girl lurched back, planting her lips on Tara's and kissing her with ferocious intensity.

"You... I can't even—"

"Shh..." Tara soothed her, wrapping her arms around her, even as one of her hands moved between Robyn's thighs again. Robyn clutched her wrist and gasped.

"Do you want to stop?"

"Are you fucking crazy?"

8.

They spent another hour locked in their ecstasy together, before Tara finally had to get up and use the bathroom. Her legs were weak and shaky as she wrapped her robe around herself and went down the hall. As she urinated, it began to sink in that her life had changed tonight—it wasn't an orientation thing, it was more an awakening into a larger way of seeing the world, and people as well.

When she'd left, Robyn had been stretched out naked on the platform—leaning on one arm and watching her with a smile. She'd been gone perhaps five minutes, and she'd expected to return to more-or-less the same situation.

She was disappointed.

As soon as she stepped in the room she knew something was different.

"Robyn?"

The spotlight was off, and Tara searched around

for the master light switch a moment before finding it and illuminating the room. Her eyes scanned the entire space, every corner: Robyn was nowhere to be seen. Maybe she just went to the bathroom too, and they'd missed each other? The thought lanced through Tara's mind. But now she saw all of Robyn's things were gone. Her art materials. The jeans she'd tossed onto the stool. Even the underwear she'd tossed into the corner. Tara was dumbfounded. Why would she leave like that? Had she done something wrong? Was this some bizarrely cruel prank?

As cold panic coursed through her, Tara turned and saw something she hadn't noticed at first. On the platform, placed gently upon the cushions, was Robyn's drawing. Tara reached down and picked it up. It was smaller rendering—similar to the other with some of her shape loosely sketched, while other parts like her face and her sex were incredibly detailed. Tara stared at it a long moment and felt hot tears coming up into her eyes. Then she quietly got dressed and left, taking the drawing and turning off the light.

9.

The next class was two days later. Tara had spent the last 48 hours quietly at home, going over and over what had happened that night after class. None of it made sense. She could still smell Robyn's sweet scent on herself. She stared at the drawing with its careful lines shaping her contours, trying to see herself the way its artist saw her.

Thursday came and she got there far too early, hoping to get a chance to figure things out with Robyn.

114

But as the students filed in and class began, she realized she was again going to be disappointed. Robyn was nowhere to be seen.

Tara debated with herself the entire class, as she lay naked on the cushions with everyone drawing. Finally after class she approached Mrs. Stevens and invented a reason to ask if he knew Robyn's last name. The teacher's expression was puzzled. There was no one named Robyn in the class, he told her. Tara described Robyn's hair and dress to him—even the style she drew in, and the man's expression grew even more strained. He'd had a student with that name on campus his first year teaching in the 90s, he told Tara. She'd been a quiet girl but a gifted artist, and had taken classes in this building. She'd been walking home from a late class and had been waiting for the light at an intersection when a car full of teens cut the curb. Robyn had gone under the wheels. She had died on the spot.

10.

Tara continued modeling through the summer quarter, when the outside air would drift in through the open windows of the old building and float sensuously across her bare skin like a feather. Like Robyn's delicate fingers. She volunteered for every evening class available, but Robyn didn't show up again.

That fall she went back to college.

The God Modulation
Kimberly Gondrella

"Cass! You gotta see this shit!"

Cassidy had barely pushed open the industrial door into Maverick's 'Inner Sanctum' and already the reverberations hit her like a wall. That Lucien had to scream be heard over the din didn't help matters. It was at times like these that she was grateful there was no one else in the building who might be inclined to call the cops (in all reality, it was highly unlikely the cops would be bothered to come out to this part of town even if someone did).

She dropped her messenger bag next to the door and was about to do a little screaming of her own, the exact words being, *'Turn that shit the fuck down,'* when her agitated brain abruptly registered what the two morons were staring at. In the center of the room sat a table that Maverick had no doubt scavenged from a dumpster somewhere. It'd obviously been recently installed. The metal walled room was usually sparse. Other than his equipment, the only furniture she'd ever seen in Maverick's music studio cum squat, which also functioned as a Faraday cage, had been a sad little futon in the corner.

On the center of the table was a cage of a different

117

kind, a smaller one, whose occupants were smaller still; two white rats. As Cassidy neared the table she noticed something was wrong. The rats weren't eating, sleeping, or nosing about—in fact, they weren't being very ratty at all. They were, however, pressed hard against the bars on opposite ends of the cage, in what appeared to be a state of great distress. Their eyes seemed frozen and they twitched in a spasmodic and pathetic way. The whole scene turned her stomach. She wasn't sure what she was supposed to be looking at, but she certainly didn't like it.

"The fuck, Lu?!" She hollered and shoved her boyfriend back a pace.

The cacophony ended abruptly, and the absence of sound seemed to ripple through the space. Maverick leaped to her side, peering over the top of the cage with a gleeful expression, like a little boy with a killing jar full of fireflies. The rodents slumped to their sides as if released from an invisible grasp and then stood on all fours and began wandering around the cage, as alert and purposeful as rats could be. Lucien was shaking his head, a conspiratorial smile on his face, he should've known Cass would over react. She was a vegan and probably rescued ladybugs out of the pool while growing up in the 'burbs back East.

"That's some weird shit man!" Lucien chuckled, avoiding his better half's disapproving stare. "How'd you know they'd do that?"

Maverick had already abandoned the rodents and was back behind his wall of equipment. Monitors and speakers towered above him and a hive-like tangle of wires, synths and computer components separated him from the table and his two friends—that and a sliding metal grating that passed for a door between the

118

rehearsal space and the 'sound room.' He fiddled with a small video camera mounted on a tripod and pushed stop on an old, beat up tape deck he'd set to record.

Cassidy rolled her eyes, Maverick had a fetish for dead tech.

"I didn't... at first anyway. I just noticed the effects of the modulation this morning." He cast his eyes over his hardware lovingly. "And before you get your panties in a bunch, Cass, that was not the reaction I was going for, but shit, any reaction to the experiment is a success in my opinion." He spread his hands out over his laptop keyboard and stared at them as if pondering the juxtaposition of living flesh over impassive circuitry.

"What experiment? It looks like all you managed to prove is that even mammals with limited cognitive capacities think your music sucks. Good work, but I could have told you that."

Sometimes Cassidy felt like she merely tolerated Maverick. He was her boyfriend's best friend and somehow, he'd gotten her to agree to front their band, but if she were to be honest, there had always been something rather *off* about him. She couldn't put her finger on it, but at times like these, she had a niggling suspicion that her band mate was quite possibly a sociopath. Cassidy sighed and swallowed her distaste. She would ask Lucien about it later. They had practice and she wanted to get it over with. She disliked the abandoned warehouse and its weird metal room. It bothered her that there was no cellphone reception inside and that any tweaked-out derelict might come stumbling in. Her parents back home in Massachusetts would drop dead to see her in a place like this, and they certainly wouldn't be too thrilled to learn how she'd been utilizing her Vassar education.

"Touché, Cass but I guess small minds think alike." Maverick seemed nonplussed, his face was usually an emotionless mask, except of course when he was torturing small animals. He wore that mask now as he gingerly unplugged his modulator and set it to the side.

"The effects of sound waves on biological functions have been studied by many. There have even been inroads into military applications." Cassidy thought she saw a glimmer in Maverick's eyes as he spoke. "We know that music can have profound emotional and psychological effects on humans. It can stimulate and activate the parts of the brain that access long-term memories. But what if you could create music that would impact your audience on a physical level, yet do so almost subconsciously? What if you could cause involuntary physiological reactions to the sounds themselves?" Definitely a glimmer now.

"You're talking about the Brown Note I assume." Cassidy rolled her eyes haughtily. Maverick thought she was a square. In his world that was worse than being a Yankee. She wasn't about to let him mansplain the experimental electronic scene to her. "Yeah Mav, I've heard of Throbbing Gristle. And Coil. And Psychic TV and, you know what? I've always wondered why anyone would try to find a note that would make a person spontaneously loose their bowels, but now, after spending so much time with you boys, I'm beginning to understand."

"You might find it juvenile, but it was an interesting line of study. As a concrete, undeniable, yet ultimately, harmless reaction, it was an obvious choice for sound pioneers. Other, involuntary, biological reactions would be hard to quantify. Remember, Clive Barker once said that Coil's *Hellraiser Themes* made his bowels churn, but how can you prove this without a more explosive reaction? In this case, I was going for something a little less messy." He smiled slightly at this and then his face went dead once more.

"The *Hellraiser Themes* are beautiful and that quote is great marketing." She yanked her ponytail forward and pulled out the hair tie, letting her heavy, dark tresses spill over her shoulders. She tossed her head and rubbed the back of her neck. Upon seeing this, Lucien moved toward her and brushed the wave of hair aside. He placed his hands on her shoulders and went to work, kneading her pale, be-freckled flesh under his own, warm, brown fingertips.

Maverick bristled but it went unnoticed, Cassidy and Lucien were too into each other. Their PDA's were incredibly off putting. Grimacing, he turned his back on the scene and began fiddling with his components, his face flushing. Cassidy was an idiot. Lucien would wake up and realize it one day. He kept his trap shut because her voice sounded like sweet, southern rain on a hot, tin roof and her parents were loaded. He would use her any way he could, while he could. What else were women good for anyway?

* * *

The floorboards creaked under Lucien's feet as he padded down the hallway from the bathroom. Cassidy squirmed her way under the covers, reveling in the sumptuousness of their new, feather duvet. It was a hot

121

as balls New Orleans August, but the fabric felt cool against her skin. She spread her lanky body out wide, her fingertips reaching for the edges of the mattress and then further still.

"What are you doing?" Lucien laughed, standing naked in the doorway, bemused and slightly damp from the shower.

"Imagining having this bed all to myself!" Cassidy raised one eyebrow and wagged it at her partner. She couldn't help but notice how good his lean form looked in the lamp light. Suddenly, the empty bed discarded all of its previous appeal.

"Well that doesn't sound like any fun at all!" Her lover pounced, and she squealed in mock terror, pulling the covers up to her chin.

He crawled catlike across the bedding and wrested the blankets free, exposing her thin shoulders and pale moon breasts. She batted him away and pulled herself up on her elbows, her eyebrows dropping and face tightening.

"Babe. I want to get serious for a second." Her voice wavered a little.

Lucien seemed suspended above her. His taught, mahogany abs almost grazing her own milk-white chest. He sighed and sat back on his ankles, his face softening as he looked at her. He knew what was coming and he wouldn't have expected any less. Rehearsal had been tense and they'd barely spoken on the bike ride home.

"What's up, beautiful?"

Cassidy blushed. It was amazing that even after all this time he still thought she was beautiful, and she still gave a shit that he did.

"It's Maverick," Cassidy said, and swallowed

hard then continued. "Look, I know the two of you have been tight since high school, but c'mon. He's been getting worse, babe, and today, with the rats... It's bad enough having to go to that fucked up building twice a week, but to live there? It just gets weirder and weirder every time we go. Now he has a metal cage inside the metal cage? Who the hell does he think is trying to intercept his transmissions anyway? And now apparently, he's trying to torture rats with sound waves? What do you think the point of all that is? Seriously, he'll be wearing a tinfoil hat in no time."

Cassidy pushed all the remaining air out of her lungs and waited for the blowback. Instead, Lucien just sighed and sat back on the bed.

"He's always been weird Cass, but yeah... I know what you're sayin'. Ever since he moved into that place he's been... well... ever since The Storm..."

Lucien's eyes were beginning to get that far away look again, that look that chilled Cassidy to the bone. The Storm. It was always The Storm. It was as if Katrina had happened yesterday. It was always the excuse and always the way that Maverick and Lucien kept her outside their miniature cabal. There was no way for her to understand. She was an outsider. She was a carpetbagger. A Yankee.

"I get it, Lu. I get it. I'm not talking shit about him, I promise. He does scare me though, lately more than ever. It's the way he looks at me..." *Like a piece of rotten meat.* She shuddered.

"He's harmless, babe. Seriously." Lucien reached out and took her bony frame in his arms. "If I had a dollar for every guy that kicked his ass in high school."

"But those rats..." The memory of their black, mindless eyes had burned themselves into her brain.

123

"What if he pulls some weird shit like that at the show next week?" She shuddered again.

"You were there. You heard the sounds. The frequency is much too low to effect humans. It's like a dog whistle, babe. That's it. You've seen it—a dog hears something that we can't, and it goes bat shit for a second. Same thing." Lucien stroked her shoulder. How was she supposed to understand that it was all in fun? She was from Massachusetts. She didn't grow up fighting, and fishing, and hunting like good ol' Louisiana boys.

Cassidy relaxed into his body. He was always so sure, so solid. She let his caress soothe her tired muscles and awaken the coiled serpent in her belly.

"Yeah, you're probably right..." She murmured as she lay back into the pillows and pulled him toward her.

Their tongues met and mingled as the heat built in her body and she strained against him. At some point the longing was just too much and she turned her face to the side, forcing his kisses to cascade down her throat and out across her breast. He lingered there for a while, taking each nipple in turn and rolling them over his tongue, suckling until they stiffened and flushed. Cassidy kneaded the bedding with her hands, the tension inside her building to a feverish pitch. He sure knew how to drive her fucking crazy. She could feel his cock, hot and hard against her thigh as he knelt above her, toying with her, but that's not what she wanted, not yet. He was a good boy, he had patience. She on the other hand, she hated to be kept waiting.

Cassidy gyrated her hips in an ancient dance of invitation. Hers was an altar that demanded to be worshiped upon. Lucien had seen this dance performed

124

many times and had no trouble translating it's meaning. He let his tongue trail between the valley of her breasts and then out along the flat expanse of her stomach. Cassidy arched her back in anticipation. As he paused for a moment to circle her belly button, she closed her eyes tight, gripping the sheets hard between her fingers. He toyed with her only a moment more, a simple kiss on the inside of each plump thigh, before diving in.

As always, Cassidy let out a quick gasp of astonishment. She had never been with another man who could eat pussy the way Lucien did. Women yes, but that went without saying. It always made her wonder how he'd learned such an invaluable skill, certainly not at the all boys' schools he'd attended as a teenager. As he sucked on her swollen labia, his tongue darting this way and that before toying over her clitoris, she was fairly positive he hadn't fine-tuned this skill sitting up at night in his parents' house watching Sci-Fi reruns with his weirdo friend.

With her eyes tightly closed and her body spread as wide as possible, Cassidy felt her clit, now swollen and full, nearing the point of explosion. Her body rocked in time to an internal rhythm, dancing ever closer to the edge of climax. As she felt herself let go, and the wetness spread itself from between her legs out across the bed, she had no way of knowing that in that moment, both of their thoughts had been on Maverick.

* * *

There is nothing worse than silence.

The steady hum of machinery. That's what has been lost in this city of mortar and bone. The world has become so quiet, he almost can't bear to leave the confines of his home. The dry, empty hallways that must once have been buzzing with life. That emptiness, that silence... He remembers that silence. Before it happened, it was there. The Silence. No birds, no insects. It was as if all intelligent life had heard the call and then they left. Vacated. Hasta la vista. It was deafening, The Silence. In the end, it was all that remained.

Maverick tweaked the oscillator and swung the volume up to ten. Anything to drown out the pulsing, underwater drone of the blood pumping through his brain. Good. The thrumming stopped, and pure noise took over. Now he could think clearly. Fuck Cassidy. That was the first clear thought he could formulate as the drugs made their lazy way through his veins and the noise took over. *Fuck Cassidy.*

Lucien deserved better, he was the one who had always been there. In school, when Maverick had been too small to fight, Lucien was the only other kid in a black t-shirt. It didn't matter that he was from the 9th Ward. It didn't matter what all the white kids called him behind his back. No, Lucien could kick all their asses. They'd spent every spare second together since then, even sharing the same bed on those all too frequent nights when his own drunk-ass father put him out. So many nights Lucien had held him as he cried himself to sleep. So many more they held each other until... Lucien's parents always allowed him to sleep over, they didn't worry about him, they worried about girls. Lucien had laughed about it at the time. He'd laughed too until Lucien went away to school and came back with *her.*

Cassidy was nothing but a succubus. She was a

leech. She was nothing but an opportunist. Fuck her and her East Coast education. She thought she was better than them all, and what horror had she ever been through?

The monitors screamed as he twisted the dials. His mind filled with static. The walls wavered, the colors descended. He was finally floating free. As the sounds wrapped around him, he closed his eyes and began to see.

White shapes gathered in his mind. Spider-like they branched off into a single, long, discernible pattern. The wave-form emerged, shimmering in its perfection. Undulating like a serpent before him. He felt his body open. He'd only ever once been with a woman. That is what it felt like now, except less awkward. As the wave-form enveloped his mind, his hands began to work the dials. The sound screeching through the monitors now inseparable from the symbols they formed in his head. They had been made concrete, sentient. At some point he'd unbuckled his pants. His hands worked the dials. The sigil shapes glowed. Soon, there would be release.

In the center of the room, two small, white shapes shuddered in their cage. As the waves clashed against them, they seemed to cling to each other for purchase. The electricity in their tiny bodies fizzed and popped, one mounted the other in a mad and hopeless bid for salvation. As they began to copulate, they fell on each other. Teeth gnashing and eyes wide, the blood dripped onto the wood-chips. Maverick stumbled towards them, his eyes round and red. He alone witnessed how they flayed each other. How they stripped the flesh from the bones even as they remained entwined. As the female fell dead, her tiny body just little more than a few strips of flesh hanging from bone, the male kept riding her, teeth gnashing at the air until he fell upon himself, consuming his own small body in the same terrible frenzy.

Maverick carefully switched off his machines. The wave-form shimmered behind his eyes.

He'd wanted to take it for a test run, but there had only been a hand full of people scattered about the club. There was no way he was going to take any risks. His experiment wasn't ready, and even if it was, it was quite possible that if it got out, he might not be able to put it back. This sad little show was not the time or the place for the unveiling of something this immense. Maverick unplugged his modulator and wrapped it gingerly in a soft handkerchief before putting it in his backpack. He felt a twinge of guilt for bringing it all this way and then letting it languish. A soft touch shocked him out of his reverie and he spun around to meet the gaze of a big-eyed pixie with a shock of blue hair and a wide, wet mouth.

* * *

Lucien dragged the last of the gear out into the street under the gas lamp which cast a hazy circumference of light in what was otherwise desolation. The cats and rats outnumbered the people in this part of town. He had no idea why Maverick had agreed to the show. They'd be lucky if they'd made enough for a cab home. He glanced behind him through the door of the bar to see Cassidy still perched on a bar stool slamming shots. She didn't even look up. He had no idea what was wrong with her. It was like she couldn't bear to be in the same room with him. He sighed and hoisted the first speaker up into Maverick's van. Where the fuck was

Maverick anyhow? Lucien felt his back bristle and immediately spun around to find him there, lurking mere inches behind him. He jumped slightly and then broke in to nervous laughter.

"You scared the shit outta me bruv, fuck!" Lucien looked beyond his friend's blank, impassive face to the figure standing just off to the side behind him. She was a little thin thing with big, watery eyes and a shock of cobalt hair. She smiled a little half smile and nodded in his direction but said nothing.

"I'll take it from here, Lu." Maverick breezed by him, slamming the rear doors and heading toward the driver side.

"You sure you don't want help unloading?" Lucien had never seen his friend even so much as talk to a girl at a show before. He watched now with more than a little amusement as the skinny, punk chick climbed into the passenger side of the van without so much as a glance back in his direction.

"No, man, I got this. You go home. I'll see you in a couple days at practice."

Maverick pulled the door closed without waiting for a response and put the van in reverse. Lucien watched him pull away into the night, headed out deeper into the 'hood. He shook his head and smiled, well good for him, he thought. Maybe he was finally becoming a real boy.

* * *

As he hauled the final piece of equipment up the stairs and into his studio, he stifled an exhausted grunt. He could feel a damp sheen of perspiration blanketing his

129

skin, but did his best not to show his weakness. The girl, who called herself Claire sat on the edge of his unmade futon, her eyes traveling around the room. As he watched her, he couldn't help but feel the itch of irritation. She looked too damn comfortable, just sitting there, lounging about useless on his bed while he worked. He hated the way her eyes were all over his equipment. He cleared his throat and stepped in front of her and she drew her wide, hungry eyes lazily back to him.

"So this is where it all happens." She made no move to stand and instead looked him up and down appraisingly. Maverick squirmed beneath his skin.

"It's quite the set up. It must have cost a fortune." Claire shifted her weight, extending her thin legs out across the floor. Her vinyl mini dress squeaked, and she smiled what was probably intended to be an invitation.

"I don't know. I've been collecting for years." Maverick felt the heat rush to his face. He turned his back on her and crossed quickly to his gear. He flicked a switch and a deep base throb filled the room, keeping the awkward silence at bay.

"Are you going to play something for me?" Her voice was heavy with suggestion and Maverick felt the nausea growing in the pit of his stomach.

"If you like." He moved his hands over the keyboard of a big Roland synth, eliciting a ghostly dirge.

"So it's not all industrial noise with you then." Claire smiled slightly, "You really can play."

Maverick shrugged, but still wouldn't look at her. "Piano lessons since I was eight. Mom's idea, Dad thought it would make me too... feminine, but Dad wasn't there much anyway..." He trailed off. He'd never told anyone that.

"Well that's OK," Claire chuckled, "I like feminine men."

Maverick felt himself go red in the face. She was laughing at him! He knew she was. Back at the club, with Lucien out by the van... He'd seen the way his friend had looked at her and she'd pretended to ignore him! It was painfully obvious what was going on. Lucien had put her up to this. It had been a bad idea to invite her up here. Somehow or another he had to get out of this. He had to get rid of her. His hands moved on their own over the dials, tweaking the levels up.

"Why is your equipment in a metal cage." She had to raise her voice slightly to carry over the sounds being broadcast from a tower of speakers against the far wall.

"It's a Faraday cage. The metal keeps all electronic signals from escaping. My computers are not hooked up to any outside network. All information that they contain is guarded and invulnerable to cyberattack." He kept his head down as he carefully removed a silk wrapped package from his backpack and began undressing it.

"Well that's wild! What kind of information do they contain? What's so important that you'd go through all this trouble?" Claire rose from the bed with the intent to drag Maverick back to it. He was a weirdo, but that mixed with his inky black hair and hollow eyed, heroin-chic complexion gave him a certain Nick Cave sexiness. She had no doubt that once you cracked the shell, he would be up for some pretty freaky shit.

Maverick anticipated her movement and with a quickness that she hadn't expected, he came around his stacks and shut the sliding, metal gate, cutting her off.

Claire sighed and threaded her fingers through the

131

grating. She could feel the buzzing of his electronics through the metal, like a charge.

"Well that's no fun!" She exclaimed, "I thought you invited me back here because you found me attractive, but maybe I'm not your type." Claire felt a pang of spitefulness, she was never one to take rejection well. "Maybe Lucien's more your type. That's what everyone says anyway."

She regretted the words as soon as they came out of her mouth. Maverick's face fell, and a look of pain crossed his eyes before his face hardened itself back into its typical stolid mask.

"We'll have some fun. I promise." Maverick returned to his stacks and finished hooking up the last of his components. "I want to play you something, and I want you to take off your clothes."

He looked up at her briefly and for a split second, she thought she saw a glimmer there in the still, bottomless pools of his eyes. *Well good*, she thought, *this is more like it*.

The grating seemed to shimmer before her as Maverick placed his hands on the keys, his dirge transforming into a haunting melody that gained in pace and intensity. She swayed in time with the music, dancing for him alone. Her hands slid over the slippery surface of her dress and then as her fingers found the zipper, she began, slowly, to unwrap herself. Her clothing slipped to the floor as she slithered out of it. Now clad only in a pair of black lace panties and combat boots, she began to dance in earnest, reaching up at the metal mesh and pressing her small, firm breasts against it, feeling the sting of cold metal on her skin.

The music seemed to swell, increasing in urgency.

She caught his eyes and saw that he was gazing at her with a curiosity that bordered on morbid fascination. She wondered if he'd ever seen a naked woman before. It was no matter, she wanted him now so badly she could taste it and it tasted like liquid metal on her tongue. Before she could think about it, she had removed her underwear and her hands were roaming free all over her body. She reached down to touch herself between her legs and found that her pussy was already wet. The music gathered in her mind and she was cresting on a wave of it. She clawed at the gate and flattened her body to rub against it. The metal was sharp and it grated her skin, but to her it felt like a lover's caress. Her mind and body were on fire. She clawed at herself in a blind fury to satiate her desire and yet she had no idea that the taste on her tongue was her own blood.

* * *

All sound stuttered to a halt. Maverick shook his head as a sign of banishment. The body in the center of the room was no longer moving. After the frenzy, it took a surprisingly long time to die and even when he was fairly sure it was over, there had been the twitching. *That* had gone on for an uncomfortably long time. The blood that had begun to pool was now spreading out from the central mass of flesh and crawling across the floor.

He opened the gate and gingerly stepped over the body. He'd need to clean up the mess. He pulled the comforter off his futon and dragged it across the floor, being careful not to smear it through the blood. Irreverently he rolled the carcass onto it and wrapped it up tightly, even still, the blood seemed to bloom through the fabric like a series of tie-dyed roses. He felt a mild twinge of panic before he remembered seeing a blue FEMA tarp frayed and hanging from the fence behind the building. That would work well, he'd have to go down anyway to get a bucket of water.

* * *

It had been surprisingly difficult to haul the body all the way down to the van but less so to drag it over the side of the Industrial Canal. He had watched the last bit of blue being swallowed under the muddy swirls before turning back and heading up the embankment. Once back in the studio, he stripped himself nude and threw his clothing, boots and all, into the same garbage bag that held a mess of bloody rags and a little black PVC dress. He rubbed his body down with a sponge in a bucket of cold, clean water and redressed in a fresh set of clothes before setting out again to dispose of the whole shebang in one of the moldering dumpsters in the back of the industrial park. It was closing on dawn when his head finally hit his pillow and blackness descended, leading him to oblivion. His final thoughts were of Lucien, as always.

He never noticed the bits of flesh caught in the metal mesh of the grating, hanging like little scraps of ground meat.

* * *

Sunlight filters through the dirty, yellow window. In the distance, a ship's horn sends a mournful call. Cars parade their way along the I-10 expressway, causing a buzzing in the building below them. The metallic whine of the rail-yard doesn't even penetrate the mind of the sagging warehouse's sole occupant. Maverick is incognizant. He sits, cross-legged, in the middle of the room, headphones plastered to the sides of his head.

No sound escapes.

The smell of rotting flesh is beginning to blossom, it competes with the aroma of human excrement coming from a bucket against the wall. The wave-form begs to be let loose...

No sound escapes.

Maverick's fingers twitch. He longs to push the sound through the speakers, to open the windows and let it fly free, but there is no one in this desolate wasteland to hear it. The sound of the I-10 would destroy it. There is no one. No one, and of course there are still tests to be done. It's not ready, not yet.

He doesn't hear the banging on the door. The wave-form gathers in his mind and spiders outwards.

Give me life.
I was once the all.
The word.
The only.
I was once the sound of heaven itself.

The banging doesn't stop. It grows louder. There is nothing but darkness. The door finally gives. Nothing but darkness as he stumbles to his feet, vomiting a thick, clear stream of spittle onto the floor. The headphones are torn away and the world ends. All is silence, and silence is death.

* * *

"I don't care where you put it, just get it out of the way!" Lucien barks, as the opening band trundles down the hall, a guitar case slamming into his hipbone.

The crowd was tense and pensive. Somehow word had gotten out that Maverick had spent the last week under observation at Charity. Rumors were beginning to fly.

"Fuck it," thought Lucien. "Bad press is still good press, right? Wasn't that Oscar Wilde or some shit?"

Cassidy kept her eyes on Maverick as he stacked his gear onto the stage. He was a sickly shade of greige and when he passed his hands through his thick, black hair, it stood up in spikes and arcs as if it hadn't been washed in days. Ten minutes until curtain and still he'd yet to say two words to her. Instead he kept his head down, a sick, uneven smile glossing his lips. She was sure he blamed her for what happened, but they'd really had no choice. When he never answered the door for rehearsal, nor the next day, nor the next, Lucien had no choice but to kick it down. He'd been so sick when they'd found him, there was no other option but to take him to the hospital. By the time they'd gotten him there, he was unresponsive. It was insane that they'd only kept him in for a week, but without insurance, he was just another junkie with a death wish.

The Mudlark Theatre was a place that existed half in and half out of the imaginary. The scent of patchouli permeated. All the wood in the place seemed determined to reunite in the center of the room. Great swaths of tattered fabric hung hither and yon and every surface seemed hopelessly impermanent. The Mudlark

Theatre was a place that existed half in and half out of the imaginary. The show was to go on in ten minutes, whether the saints wished it or not.

The audience was surprisingly receptive. It was a decent sized crowd as far as Cassidy was concerned, and in such an out of the way venue! She slithered across the stage to Maverick's bone shaking beats and Lucien's searing guitar. The sounds that issued from her belly and up through her throat were primal, guttural and yet somehow managed to approach the angelic. As they geared up for the finale, she gripped the microphone as one might a lover and breathed,

"We are the Queen in Yellow. Thank you, this is the end..." And it was.

All went as well as could be expected until the last pounding chorus, then Cassidy felt the ground suddenly give way beneath her feet. The sound seemed to come from everywhere and nowhere at once. It was as if it were such a part of the everyday that it had always been there, just under the floorboards. She looked out over the sea of faces, aware that her set had been hijacked, her mic had gone dead. She screamed and screamed into it, hoping to drown out the music that filled her brain and curled her toes. She looked to Lucien, but he held his guitar limply at arm's length, his eyes staring into the future, confused and helpless. She looked to Maverick and he seemed to rise in the middle of the chaos, standing tall. He was the epicenter of the storm as the music swirled around him.

Cassidy tried in vain to make eye contact with someone in the crowd. She hoped that she was having some kind of psychological break, that the terror that paralyzed her lived in her mind alone. She shook her

137

head to clear her vision and swallowed the metallic taste in her mouth. It seemed that most of the crowd had taken to a trance-like swaying, then rubbing, and then to full on grinding upon each other. The music rose and fell, modulating as if in time with her heartbeat, or perhaps her heart had begun beating in time with it. Cassidy took a deep breath and tried to hold on to the sanity that was rapidly retreating as something else moved in to take its place. The wetness spread between her legs and she fought her basest instincts to strip herself bare and offer up her body to whoever was willing...

Maverick grinned as he looked out over the crowd. The wave-form gathered in his mind. It was almost time.

A charge fell over the crowd. As the sound grew and took shape, one by one they tore at their clothing and then at each others'. Before long, the room was nothing but a sea of naked flesh, rising and falling in rhythm. Fingers clawed and mouths gaped, tongues lolling desperately in mouths hungering to be filled. A petite blonde fell to the floor, rivulets of blood running down the inside of her legs, her lover, a busty redhead, followed her down, her own face a red smear. Hardened cocks searched for holes and filled them, and when that was no longer enough, they made their own, ragged and wet. The music they made was horrible, and yet it chorused perfectly with the sound still wailing from the speakers above them.

Cassidy herself could not remember how she came to be unclothed. She found herself laying on the stage, Lucien enthusiastically fucking her before an orgy of people writhing and screaming below them.

She looked to Maverick and his cold eyes burned

right though her. He undid his pants and pushed Lucien aside. Cassidy could not move as Maverick roughly penetrated her. She closed her eyes and rode a wave of terrified ecstasy before looking over her shoulder at Lucien now fucking Maverick from behind as Maverick continued his methodical thrusting. She fought the patterns forming in her brain. Soon there would be nothing left, only the sound. It wanted to consume her, to be consumed. In a haze she looked around the room. Everyone was sucking and fucking, falling upon each other in a frenzy of desire. And then there was blood.

A girl crouched in the back row. Her phone held aloft, videoing the show for Tulane radio. She dialed down her hearing aid as the feedback loop squealed through her brain. There was nothing to do but flee. She pushed through the writhing wall of bodies towards the door. In her desperation, she never thought to stop recording.

The last thing that Cassidy remembered was the blood.

The red clouded her eyes as she crawled across the stage, dragging the lifeless body of her lover behind her, his teeth still embedded in her leg. Shapes spun behind her eyes and her body screamed for release, but still she crawled. The audience had fallen in upon itself, their cries of ecstasy and horror crescendo-ed in perfect time as the music swelled. The modulation rose, and the wave form towered behind her eyes, taking shape, gaining substance.

The last thing Cassidy remembered was the blood.

Just a little farther and it would be done. She would not let it escape this room. Just a little further. As her hand closed around the cord, she pulled.

The last thing Cassidy remembered was the blood.

* * *

The media would report it differently, 25 people dead, *consumed* in a drug induced frenzy at a heavy metal show. Many more hopelessly disfigured. Bath salts, they said.

They found Maverick, or what was left of him. The pieces he'd pulled apart were scattered in strange and bloody lines. Runic offerings before a wall of dead machinery. It took two men to extricate Cassidy from the wreckage that surrounded her as she smashed and tore at the metal boxes with bloody fingers. All was cold, all was silent. In fact, one newspaper mentioned how a paramedic, visibly shaken, noted that none of the survivors, while being pulled from the carnage, ever made a single sound. Some of them screamed, but nothing came out. "It was as if all sound had been sucked from the place," he'd been quoted as saying.

There was nothing left of the modulator, nor of any of the other gear for that matter. Cassidy made sure it was all destroyed before she moved back East. She refused all interviews and has never spoken a word about what she knew really happened.

In Maverick's studio they found scraps of rotten meat that the officials determined to be human in origin and a bag of bloody rags in a dumpster. The rest of Maverick's equipment ended up in an NOPD evidence locker scheduled for incineration. Seemingly, there were no recordings found on Maverick's computer and any recordings of The Queen in Yellow's final concert have yet to surface.

Monday

Benjamin Johnson

The young man was uncertain, even as he was led by the hand down to the river.

"How long will it take?" he asked, unable to keep the anxiety, the agitation, the excitability from his voice.

Elias grinned wolfishly, his eye teeth glinting in the dark. "Not that long. You'll see."

Elias was tall and thin, his bones visibly supporting the cloth of brown skin that made up his body. He was a canvas person, a doll made of twigs; a scarecrow with curly black hair, tangled by the wings of fleeing ravens.

The other boy was Stephen. He was a little older than Elias, brand new to this sort of thing. His hair was the yellow straw of a cornfield, his eyes the dark brown of decaying stalks.

"Have you... have you brought a lot of guys out here before?" he asked.

Elias shrugged. "I guess that depends on your definition of 'a lot of guys.' By my standards, no."

"What standards are those?"

"None of your business. How about that?" Elias snapped a smile in his direction. He always snapped, always bit, never did things gently. To Stephen, it seemed as though the shadow of a laugh was dancing just behind those teeth of his, white and sharp. Either that or a howl, he could never be sure. In truth, he didn't know which one he preferred.

Twigs cracked beneath their feet as they started off the beaten path and onto a more thickly wooded one.

The path was one Stephen knew well, a path that all the kids in their little town had taken at one point or another to get down to the river, that forbidden ribbon of water with its unstable banks. No place for a child, their mothers would scold. Still, it was only children who went there in the heat of late summer, who populated the shores with beach towels and laughter, who made a game of avoiding those dirt clods that were liable to plummet from the cliff-side, taking plant, animal, or child with them.

Shrieks of laughter as swimsuits were stripped off and plunges taken purposefully, stark naked into the cold water.

Stephen had been there, had taken his own leap, had seen the beach towels and bare bottoms, striped with sand and sunscreen. That had been a long time ago though, back when things were simpler and expectations were lower and summer was summer and he was a kid.

Now he was nearing the end of high school and he and his friends were on the cusp of an uninviting adulthood that promised little more than the donning of their father's and mother's farm-hats, trading soft hands for calloused ones as they struggled to make the corn fields surrounding the town grow.

Stephen had been working towards a football scholarship that would take him far away from here. That was over now.

* * *

Elias had arrived in town at the beginning of the year, had taken to his new surroundings like a crow does to swimming. Stephen, along with the other adolescents in their grade, had thought of him as something of an oddity: to be pitied, but not approached, to be talked of, but never to him.

There was always something a little strange about Elias, something almost inhuman to the fangs in his smile, the hungry look in his eyes as he walked down the hall.

The other boys said they'd caught glimpses of him staring at them in the locker room after gym class.

Stephen doubted it. After all, they'd never noticed *him* doing it and he felt he was much less subtle than Elias might be, with his quiet wildness, his rarely spoken thoughts. So when the other boys decided they'd had enough of Elias' peculiarity, Stephen felt it only right to let him know.

"Hey, uh... Magwood," he'd said, approaching the boy with the curly hair, the wide eyes, the soft-looking lips. They were in the biology lab. Class had just ended, with only stragglers left behind to pack up books and hurry onward.

Elias had blinked at him with those big brown eyes and smiled, as he always did. Stephen felt his eyes drawn to his teeth, the pointed canines blinking out from between those pink, pink lips. Elias was as

143

tall as Stephen, but skinnier, his thin frame hidden by his rolled-up sleeves and baggy pants. His hair was dark, dark, dark and curled like a nest of vipers.

"You should be careful, Magwood. Hannigan and some of the others were saying shit about you. After school, I think they were planning on making you eat shit too. I don't want to get involved, I just… stay safe, please."

He'd grabbed his bookbag and started to walk away.

"You're Stephen, right?"

He'd stopped, given a curt nod.

"We've never spoken before," Elias continued.

"You don't really speak to anyone," Stephen replied.

Elias shrugged. "True. Though I wouldn't blame that on lack of trying."

"Just be careful, man. Please? I've got to go."

"Go where? It's lunchtime. You can spare a minute or two."

"I have an appointment at the counselor's office."

"For what?"

"Career guidance."

Elias gave something like a grimace. "Rough. I heard about the football game last week." He raised a fist. "Go Bobcats."

Stephen studied the arm attached to that fist, studied the long tendons and the lighter brown of Elias's underarm skin.

Elias grinned wider. It was the grin of someone who knew something, or possibly knew too much. It unnerved Stephen, sent spiders crawling beneath his skin.

"Thank you for the warning, Stephen," Elias had said, his voice little more than a whisper.

Stephen licked his dry, cracked lips, his eyes darting around the room. "No, uh... no problem."

He'd turned to go again, but something held him in place, some spell that transfixed him as he'd never been transfixed before. He'd turned back around and swallowed at the sight of Elias, closer than he'd been before, still showing all his teeth.

"I can repay you."

Stephen swallowed. "Excuse me?"

"For looking out for me. I can give you something I think you want."

"I don't want anything from you," Stephen said hastily and made to leave again, the spell broken, but Elias caught his hand and held on tightly and ended any struggle before it had really begun.

Elias didn't have to stand on tiptoes to reach Stephen's ear, he was so tall and gangly. His lips, those pink, pink lips, brushed up against Stephen's earlobe as he whispered to him what he thought he might want, what he could give him. The hair on the back of Stephen's neck stood on end.

Elias pulled away and finished packing up his supplies. Stephen watched him dumbly, couldn't tear his eyes from the infernal smile still stretched over the other boy's lips.

"I... I don't..."

"Think about it," Elias had said and stalked away, moving like a scarecrow possessed out into the maelstrom of the school hallway, his raven-black hair quickly disappearing from view.

* * *

The call of a coyote brought Stephen back to the present, back to the hidden trail and Elias's damp palm, sliding up against his own. He coughed, to break the silence if nothing else.

Elias gave his hand a squeeze and Stephen felt his heart rate pick up, felt blood gush though his arteries, filling his head among other things with red.

The path began to thin, dirt trailing off where others had turned back, the trees following suit with their wispy branches above.

Stephen looked wistfully to the sky, past the slender foliage of early summer, at the moon. It was bright and full tonight, dangling like a hanged man from the heavens, white as the whites of a killer's eyes, staring down at the two boys by the riverbank.

Elias stopped only when they'd reached the precipice at the water's edge. It was a long drop down to the river itself, though one could climb if they had the strength, using tangled roots and rocky outcrops as ladder rungs to the blue far below. Down the cliff face was the way of those seeking adventure or those too stupid to know better.

Stephen wondered which Elias was as his companion sank to the ground and swung two feet over the edge. Slowly, carefully, he lowered himself until his chest was pressed against the dirt of the cliff, his hands gripping two thick tree roots like thighs. "Coming?" he asked.

His teeth flashed in the dark and Stephen swallowed. As Elias clambered down, he followed not far behind, hands digging into once-familiar dirt and clay, coming back stained brown, fingernails like a nicotine addict. Down they went, towards dark water and abyss.

They climbed until they reached an outcropping of rock and soil, large enough to stand up in, as though someone had raked an ice-cream scoop across the cliff face. Younger ones commonly referred to the spot as 'the cave' though it was, in fact, no more than six feet deep, the result of many years of natural erosion.

Elias was waiting for Stephen inside, his smile lit up like the moon, even before the other's runners touched down on rock.

"Here?" Stephen asked. He hated himself for the whininess in his voice then, the fear behind that single word.

Elias didn't seem to mind. "Here," he replied his voice little more than a soft growl.

Stephen looked about at their surroundings, at the tangled brown roots growing through cracks in the cave wall. The moon was now the eye of an overprotective mother, framed by the cave mouth. Stephen had been here before, had kissed Billy Turner in this exact spot so many summers before, something the both of them had sworn never to mention again.

"Take off your clothes."

It wasn't an order so much as an instruction, a thing to be followed as assuredly as a fire evacuation plan. Elias was halfway undressed himself, his shoes discarded in a pile against the cave wall, his shirt in a tangle over his head.

Stephen looked at the other boy's brown ribs, skin stretched tight over his thin frame. He looked skeletal, delicate, like Stephen could break him with only a touch.

147

Elias caught him looking. "Don't make me ask again, football star," he said, grinning to his ears.

Stephen nodded and began to strip. He kicked his shoes off first, then shrugged off his jacket and his shirt. Then came his belt and his pants and his socks until finally he was standing there in only his thin, grey boxers.

Elias's hands were on his own waistband, but he had been caught staring too, frozen and hungry, eyes tracing patterns over Stephen's muscular body, his pale freckled skin. The two of them shared a laugh then. There was nervousness in Elias's voice and it felt good for Stephen to finally hear it, to know he wasn't the only one with doubts, with reservations, with fear.

"You going to take yours off first?" Stephen asked suddenly.

Elias stopped laughing, though his lips still twitched with the ghost of mirth. "We could do it together. On three?"

Stephen nodded. "One."

"Two. Three."

Fabric hit the floor of the cave. Stephen kicked his boxers away to lie amongst his other clothes and, for a long time, stared at the ground, counting cracks in the rock and dirt. Eventually, however, curiosity won out and he glanced up at Elias, shyly at first, then all at once.

Elias' body was scrawny and gaunt, even more so in the blue moonlight. His thin chest, his prominent ribs, his bony hips all belonged to an animal half-starved. His penis was long and semi-erect, dangling between lanky, brown legs. He was staring at Stephen, unblinking, the moon reflected in his eyes.

Stephen felt his own penis stiffen as the blood rushed down from his face and migrated south. Elias smiled when he saw it, though this smile was a softer one than his usual, a smile that said only kind things, tender things.

"Where do we start?" Stephen asked, his heart beating a tattoo against his ribcage.

"At the mouth," Elias said, "then we work our way down." He took a step forward then seemed to hesitate. He was frozen, caught in the moonlight, a statue carved from marble and hematite.

"Something wrong?" Stephen asked.

"It's… It's nothing," Elias said. "I just don't want you to feel like you have to do this with me. You don't, if you don't want to."

Something stirred in the pit of Stephen's stomach. "You've never done this before."

"I have," Elias said hastily. "It's only that… Well, I was in your shoes then. I didn't know."

The words hung in the air as he spoke them, like mist dappled with moonlight, formed from words upon words left unsaid.

Stephen shuffled his feet. "Will it hurt?"

Elias didn't answer for a while. Then: "Yes."

Stephen nodded. His feet moved almost of their own accord then, touching sole to earth as he walked across the cave floor and stood in front of Elias. He placed his hands on the other boy's bare hips.

"I trust you," he said. "Whether it hurts or not. I want this."

Elias raised his eyes to meet Stephen's. "Are you sure?"

"I'm sure. We start at the mouth?"

The gleam returned to Elias's eyes and he chuckled, low and growly. "We start at the mouth."

Stephen nodded, closed his eyes, and leaned into the kiss, memories of the other boy he'd kissed here so long ago fading from memory as his lips connected with Elias', those pink, pink lips, as his tongue tasted those white teeth, as they began to explore one another's bodies with their hands.

Warmth flooded through Stephen's entire body and his penis hardened fully, pressing up against Elias's thigh, yearning as a stake yearns to pierce a heart. His mind was fireworks on a grassy hillside, his mouth a medley of fruit and honey, his body dancing to the rhythm beat by his heart. A moan escaped his lips, answered by a soft growl from Elias.

And then, without warning, the pain began.

Elias' lips were gone, replaced by something bristling and biting. His teeth too were suddenly sharp as knives. It felt as though there were more of them too, dozens upon dozens, sinking themselves into the flesh of Stephen's mouth.

Stephen screamed as he felt skin leave skin, layers of flesh separate and fall away, lacerated by daggers in his lover's mouth.

Elias pulled away, taking part of Stephen with him. Blood spattered across Elias' chest, soaking him in a fine spray of scarlet, red rivulets mixing with sweat.

Lumps of Stephen's mouth dangled from Elias's face, between his teeth. Elias smiled at him and this time his teeth were white and red.

Stephen couldn't think, couldn't move, could only go rigid as a board and pray the pain would stop. Elias tore out his tongue, chewed it and swallowed it, bit into his throat and let scarlet juices spatter the cave walls.

Jagged teeth tore at Stephen's face, ripping cheek from bone, eye from socket, blood pouring like water down his chest. And then his chest too, clawed to pieces by nails longer than they should have been, ribcage wrenched open and his innards exposed.

Blood, bone, and bile leaked onto the cave floor. Stephen sank to his knees but the thing that was Elias kept going, biting and chewing and swallowing and kissing, consuming all that was left of him. Stephen disappeared, piece by aching piece into Elias's stomach, sliding down his throat, lumps of flesh in the gullet of the Big Bad Wolf.

And then, suddenly, it was all over. Stephen clutched what little remained of his body to himself, shivering and shaking in a mangled pool of his own organs, no longer human, simply meat.

Blood traced its way over the ground, dripping between the cracks, trailing over the cliff edge and falling down, down, down to the river below.

The thing that was Elias sat with its back to the wall, a thin stream of scarlet dribbling from the corner of its mouth. It wasn't quite Elias anymore, wasn't quite human at all. Its eyes glowed yellow. Its black, curly hair stretched down from its scalp, over its face and back and chest, tapering at a point just over its genitals. Its nose and mouth stretched, doglike from its face. Its white teeth were fangs, stained crimson.

It licked its lips with a tongue too long, licked blood and sinew from the tips of its claws.

The mass of flesh that had been Stephen writhed on the floor, mewling softly.

The thing growled and got to its feet, still human in appearance. It stepped gingerly over the mess of limbs and organs, over the remains of a human being, and stalked towards the cave's edge. It gazed out over the river, over the black and blue snake as it coiled its way between cliffs. The moon shone down on the thing and it basked in its silvery glow, opened its jaws as though trying to drink the moonlight, trying to taste it on its tongue.

Behind it, the mewling became a growl.

The thing glanced over its shoulder and snapped out a response.

The flesh pile was moving, shifting. Bits of meat splattered the ground as the pile shook, reclaimed breath making it rise and fall.

The thing stalked over to the flesh and began to pick through it, sorting it with tapered claws. It pushed aside muscle and bone and scooped pooled blood into its still thirsty mouth. And then its claws brushed what it was looking for.

Fur.

The thing that had been Stephen rose, slowly and unsteadily to its feet, bits of its old body dripping from its shoulders like candlewax, leaving ruddy brown streaks in their wake.

This second thing's eyes were now yellow. Its blonde hair grew thickly, a mantle of gold over its torso. It ran a long tongue over its teeth and found them numerous and sharp as razorblades.

The former Elias whimpered at its new companion, grazed a concerned claw over its coarse, furry cheek.

The former Stephen blinked and, with little warning, let loose a howl, low and haunting enough to frighten the dead. It crashed forward, still unsteady on both two legs and four, leaping over the edge of the cliff and plunging towards the dark water below.

The former Elias howled along and leapt as well, landing in the water like a furry cannonball, water washing away the blood from its muzzle, from its chest, from its skin.

The two creatures circled each other, splashing one another, emitting barks almost like laughter into the night. Up above the moon shone down on them, full and bright as the sun.

The Dark Gem
Lisi Damette

Jolene Harris shuffled down the wooden planks that led past the shops lining Main Street. Every step shot pain up from her knee to her side, but she knew if she didn't get to the general store before they closed, it'd be twice as bad that night. Cowboys from the B&D Ranch rode past, one even tipped his hat at her, but Jolene just concentrated on putting one foot in front of the other.

The bell over the door rang as she entered the shop. Mrs. Gurnsey greeted her from behind the counter. "Evening, Mrs. Harris. Is there anything I can get for you?"

With a wince, Jolene handed the shopkeeper her wicker basket and list. "Just these, Mrs. Gurnsey. Thank you."

As Mrs. Gurnsey filled bags with flour, salt, and sugar from the barrels behind the counter, she watched Jolene's stiff movements. With a shake of her head, she called out, "Still running into that cupboard?"

Jolene kept her gaze down. "No, ma'am. I walked into the hitching post this time." Bolts of cloth stacked to one side of the store drew Jolene's attention. Her fingers reached for one then pulled back at the last minute.

"Go on, then. That color would look lovely on you," Mrs. Gurnsey said.

Jolene shook her head. "Shouldn't want what you can't have." She shuffled back to the counter to collect her basket.

"Put it on your account?"

With a nod, Jolene picked up the basket. "Good day to you."

"Watch out for those hitching posts," she replied.

Jolene stiffened then rushed out of the store as fast as her aching body could carry her. A cart rumbled by as the door closed behind her. It stopped at one of the few empty storefronts on Main Street. The rough looking man driving the cart leapt down from the seat and stretched. A slight limp marred his stride as he headed to the back of the cart. From beneath the dusty tarps, he unloaded beautiful pieces of furniture, expertly carved, upholstered with fabric that must have cost a fortune. As he placed a settee to the side of the street, he turned and looked Jolene directly in the eyes. She stifled a squeak, rushing down the wooden sidewalk until the man was out of sight. In her haste, she missed the newly hung shingle that advertised the building as *The Dark Gem.*

* * *

Jolene sat at the scarred wooden table, staring at the full plate across from her. She had barely picked at her meager portion of food. The dim light of the room grew darker, but she didn't dare light the lamp until she heard hoof beats nearing the rickety cabin.

The hoof beats never came.

Sitting at the table in the now pitch-black cabin, feeling the cool drafts of air that seeped in through the cracks and crevices of the walls, she turned her options over and over in her mind. She could put the plate in the oven, though it was cooling and would probably make the food dry and tough which might anger Barnaby. She could relight the stove, though it would use more fuel which might anger Barnaby. She could leave it be, though it would be stone cold by the time he got home and that might anger Barnaby.

The sun rose over the hills. The beams slid across the table to where Jolene sat, her head lolling on her chest. She woke with a start, heart pounding. A quick glance around the cabin assured her that her husband hadn't returned while she slept.

After a quick wash in freezing water, she examined her bruised ribs, pleased to see the color fading. She dressed but as she plaited her hair she took the opportunity to study her face in the mirror. Even after years of marriage she still had a pretty, round, youthful face. Thoughts crept into her head. *Maybe he'll never come back. Maybe I'm free.* But free to do what? Take in sewing? Laundry? Better to push those thoughts away. The devil makes work for idle hands, they say. The day went by in a blur of housework and chores. Her eyes cut to the empty road leading to the homestead every few minutes. The sun rose high above only to fall low once more. The road remained empty.

As darkness fell, Jolene made dinner. She set the table and readied the candles to light the moment she heard Barnaby's horse approach. The minutes ticked by and she continued to sit in the darkness, dinner cooling, until she a spark of something that she hadn't felt in years flare up inside her belly—her own anger.

Despite the pain in her body, she leapt to her feet and grabbed her shawl, slamming the heavy wooden door behind her. The walk to town did nothing to cool her temper; if anything it stoked the flames she thought had long burned out. Her feet automatically took her to the one place she could count on to find Barnaby: Johnson's Saloon. Gas lamps burned bright within the building. Cheery piano music played. She pushed through the swinging doors and was shocked to find not the roaring crowd drinking, gambling, and whoring she expected but Thad Johnson morosely wiping down the bar. Only a few old-timers sat in the corner, nursing their beers. The poker and blackjack tables stood empty. Bored whores sat on the stairs that led up to their private rooms, some reading, some doing needlepoint.

Jolene nodded to Thad Johnson. He barely gave her a glance. "He's not here, Mrs. Harris."

"Do you know—," she began but one of the whores snapped, "Check that damn cat house down the street!"

"Thank you, kindly." Jolene backed out of the saloon as the whore mumbled, "Never seen so many flock to one place like that. Ain't natural."

"Probably witchcraft," another added.

"Enough of that talk," Thad said with enough edge to his voice that the women quieted at once. By then, Jolene was back on the sidewalk.

The Dark Gem's shingle wavered back and forth in the cool night breeze. Jolene made her way up the sidewalk. There were enough horses in front of the building to carry half the town away. She stopped in front of a familiar painted pony and patted its nose.

"Hey there, Percy. You need a brush and some oats?" The horse nuzzled her hand. "Don't worry. I'm going to take you home soon."

The door to the establishment opened. Music and laughter burst through the quiet night as Doc Reynolds staggered out. "Evening, Doc," Jolene called.

He didn't turn around or acknowledge her in any way, just stumbled down the road until he disappeared into the night. The Dark Gem's door closed slowly. Jolene made it up the steps and into the building before the door shut completely and she lost her nerve.

The inside of the building was like another world. Jolene expected it to be tacky, offensive even, but it was beautiful. *I bet this is how rich people live*, she thought. Gorgeous wood paneling covered the walls. Tasteful paintings of pastoral scenes dotted the paneling throughout the room. A well-stocked bar stood at one end. The rough looking man she had seen earlier stood behind it, polishing a glass. He nodded to her in greeting, neither welcoming nor threatening.

She scanned the couches but there was no sign of her errant husband. The unguarded staircase beckoned to her. A mirror caught her reflection. This fierceness welling inside of her showing her to be a stranger to herself. *Might as well get it over with. Nothing they could do to me that Barnaby hasn't already done. I survive him every day, I'll survive this.* A last glance over her shoulder assured her that the bartender's attention was elsewhere. Her foot hit the bottom step. When no one stopped her, she raced up the stairs as quick as her sore body would allow.

159

Doors lined the corridor like evenly spaced mirror images. Moans and groans escaped from behind each one. Jolene paused, trying to decipher these foreign sounds of pleasure, trying to suss out which room held Barnaby. At the fourth door she recognized the grunts from within. Kneeling in front of the door, she peered through the keyhole.

Barnaby knelt face down on a double bed. Ornate woodwork covered the bedposts his wrists were tied to. Nothing covered the young woman that knelt behind him. Long golden hair cascaded down her pert, ivory breasts. Her firm backside pumped back and forth as she impaled her rigid cock deep inside Barnaby pale, flabby ass. Barnaby's face reddened, his eyes rolled back in his head. The blonde grabbed his hips and thrust faster as his back arched. Jolene was about to turn away, disgusted not with the act but with the adultery, when a shimmer rose from her husband's body at the moment of his climax. The blonde inhaled deeply. The shimmer wavered then curled like smoke seeping up into the woman's nostrils. A flush crept across the blonde's body and she groaned in turn as the last of the shimmer disappeared inside her.

Barnaby's body fell forward limp against the bed. His eyes were glazed, unseeing. The blonde slid out of him and slinked over to her washbasin. As she crossed the room, she looked directly at the keyhole, meeting Jolene's gaze.

With a gasp, Jolene skittered away from the door. A hand fell on her shoulder. She cringed and scurried away, expecting to find the rough looking bartender raining blows down upon her. But the punches and kicks never came. She slowly opened her eyes to find the most beautiful woman she'd ever seen standing over her. Raven hair in an intricate braid coiled around her head. Silky red material dipped low to reveal her large milky white breasts, narrowed to a small waist then flared out to accentuate her rounded hips. Her hand reached for Jolene's face and again Jolene recoiled but the touch was soft. Cupping Jolene's chin in her hand, she rotated the young woman's face to examine her bruises.

"That your man in there?" the raven-haired woman asked.

Jolene nodded; a sudden flare of anger and strength hidden behind the fresh wall of fear surged forth as the beautiful woman spoke again. "You can take him home now, if you want. Delilah's done with him."

"No," Jolene said, barely above a whisper. She cleared her throat and tried again. "No. You can have him."

The raven-haired woman smiled. It reminded Jolene of a hungry beast about to feed. "I'm glad to see he hasn't beaten all the life out of you." She touched the bruise and Jolene winced. "Still fresh," the woman said. Leaning close to Jolene, she inhaled deeply. A slight tugging sensation ran through the skin of Jolene's cheek.

The dull ache of the bruising lifted away. Jolene's body felt better than it had in years. She met the woman's gaze with wide eyes. Again, the woman smiled. A rosy tint filled her cheeks. "How?" Jolene asked.

The woman met her question with another. "Will you leave him?" Jolene nodded. "Where will you go?"

"I hadn't gotten that far in my thinking yet," she admitted.

"Come with me," the woman said, taking her hand but Jolene pulled against her.

"No, ma'am. I don't have any money and I'm not doing that."

"I don't want your money and I have no intention of whoring you out, unless that's what you want." Jolene remained skeptical. The woman continued. "But you do have something I need." Again, she tried to lead Jolene away and again Jolene resisted. The woman studied Jolene once more. With a shrug she said, "I'll take your anger, your hurt. All the pain and anguish will slide off of you like water when you step from a warm bath."

"How are you gonna do that?" Jolene asked, surprised again by her own strength.

"That," the woman said, "I have to show you."

Jolene allowed the raven-haired woman to lead her down the corridor to a smaller staircase. The woman kept Jolene's hand in hers as they climbed to the top of the stairs that ended in a single door. Fishing a large ring of keys from a hidden pocket, the woman unlocked the door and escorted Jolene in.

Gas lamps flared to life. The room took up the entire top floor of The Dark Gem. The décor was even more opulent than below.

"My name is Genevieve," the woman said as she sat Jolene down on the silk covered settee before sliding down beside her.

"Nice to meet you," Jolene replied automatically. "I'm Jolene Harris."

Genevieve took Jolene's hand and kissed it. A blush colored Jolene's cheeks. Leaning close, Genevieve nuzzled Jolene's ear. The soft, cool breath tickled. A hot prickling spread down her neck. Her nipples tightened, the clef between her legs moistened.

"What are you doing?" Jolene said, even as her breath quickened. Genevieve breathed in deeply. That slight tug pulled up from Jolene's skin again. Just as suddenly as the heat spread through her body, it left, leaving her blank, like a slate that had been wiped clean. Genevieve knelt in front of Jolene. Her hands touched the hem of the rough spun, hand-sewn dress that reached to Jolene's feet. With deft fingers, she slid the dress up, exposing Jolene's ankles, knees, thighs. Jolene gasped but didn't stop her. Gently, Genevieve pried Jolene's knees apart. She leaned forward and blew cool breath through the slit in Jolene's undergarments.

Again, heat filled Jolene. Tiny tendrils of pleasure unfurled from her, up through her belly and down into her thighs. Genevieve's mouth found the skin beneath the cloth. Her tongue probed Jolene's lips, licking from top to bottom and back before darting between them to flick against the hard pebble of her clit. Jolene moaned as Genevieve's lips closed over her clit and sucked. Two fingers slid inside her. Heat built up in her core, reaching a crescendo as wave after wave of pleasure broke over her. Her hips bucked as the first orgasm she'd ever had tore through her.

Genevieve waited until the last wave subsided before pulling away. She climbed up Jolene's body then kissed her deeply.

Jolene could taste herself on the other woman's lips. It was delicious. "Did you enjoy that?" Genevieve asked, her eyes sparkling. Her hand slipped between Jolene's legs, stroking the still tender clit. Sparks of pleasure caused Jolene to tremble. "Yes," she moaned.

"Would you like to feel an even greater pleasure?"

Jolene's eyes widened. "There's more?"

With her free hand, Genevieve brushed a stray hair from Jolene's cheek. "I can make you like me. Pain, anger, lust, every strong human emotion feeds me, gives me pleasure."

"What do I have to do?"

"Give up this life."

"Done," Jolene replied without hesitation. The heat built once more in the pit of her stomach as Genevieve's hand continued to stroke her.

"Give up the sun. Your world will be the night."

"Agreed," Jolene said. Her back arched.

"You'll need a helper, a slave. Someone you can easily control." This gave Jolene pause. Genevieve continued, "Barnaby."

Jolene shook her head vehemently. "No."

"Just think, all the years of serving him, now he'll serve you." Genevieve cooed. "He'll live for your touch, beg you to take the anger and fear from him."

"He'll beg?"

"And plead...possibly cry."

The returning wave of pleasure hit her hard. She cried out as she writhed under Genevieve's touch. Genevieve thrust her open mouth against Jolene's and sucked. Something pulled deep inside of her. The pleasure left but still Genevieve sucked. Any lasting pain or soreness from the all the beatings that came before left her body but still Genevieve sucked. Spots danced in front of Jolene's eyes. Light headedness filled her. The room tilted. A bright light grew behind her vision, flashed. Then everything went black.

* * *

"Woah," Barnaby called and Percy, the painted pony, slowed to a stop. The cart rocked back as Barnaby leapt down from the driver's seat. He pulled the tarp back, exposing delicately carved furniture, ornate tables and a silk settee. He fished a long, thin box out of the cart. After unlocking the door, Barnaby carried the box into the building.

The gas lamp flickered as Barnaby adjusted the flame's strength. Satisfied, he carried the thin box up two flights of stairs and into the top floor. With the utmost gentleness, he placed the box on the floor and lifted the lid. Jolene's eyes flicked up and she narrowed her gaze at her husband. "Did you hang out the shingle?"

"Not yet," he replied. "Thought I'd bring the furniture in first."

"Hang it now," she commanded.

He rushed to accommodate her. She sat up and straightened the silky folds of her dress. Shadows crept across the floor as the last of the sun's rays disappeared on the horizon. After a leisurely stroll through the building surveying her new domain, Jolene stepped out onto the sidewalk in front of the building. Above her swung the shingle announcing *The Red Ruby* now occupied the space.

Jolene took a deep breath of the night air. The town brimmed over with anger, hate, pain, and lust; so many emotions to sate her hunger, and the hunger of the girls that would arrive the following evening. With a snap of her fingers, she signaled Barnaby to follow her in. He scrambled to comply, closing the door behind them.

165

The Christ of St. Jozef Church
Angel Leigh McCoy

My name used to be Michael Phelps, Ph.D. I was 33, and I taught Economics at the Ohio College of Mount St. Joseph. The story of my decline began when I stepped off the train in Tilburg, Netherlands, and found myself surrounded by beautiful bodies, chic haircuts, and a language in the sea of which I floundered. A Dutch peacock caught my eye. He wore purple pants so tight they sucked up into the crack of his behind creating a vertical smile. I wanted to caress that smile, tip it horizontal, but my soft abs, my unimaginative attire, and my distaste for all things unhealthy kept me isolated. I was a human desert in the center of a vast oasis.

I taxied into town. My hotel had a tactless charm, gold and green, with flowers everywhere: in the wallpaper, on the bedspread, and in the furniture's gilt embellishments. It flaunted its tastelessness with the irreverence of old age.

I hung my suits in the armoire, washed off the stink of travel, and put on my pajamas. An envelope on the bedside table awaited me, marked with my name. It bore the seal of the Order of St. Jozef. The letter instructed me to meet them in three days' time for the holy transformation. A wave of nausea surprised me, and I thought of the monk who had approached me.

167

He'd said, "Your sacrifice will secure your place at His side."

I asked, "Will it be painful?"

He replied, "Yes."

"Will it be over quickly?"

"No."

I curled up in bed and rested my head on the foreign pillow, but it took me hours to fall asleep.

Day 1

I had come to Tilburg on a pretense, an International Game Theory conference. On that first day, I shook hands and said the right things. We spoke English and Economics, two languages that, to me, were comfortable. I tried to fit in—in the company of peers. Eventually, we bid each other a good evening. My comrades left in groups, abandoning me to my fate. I wasn't surprised. My fertive efforts at extroversion made them uncomfortable. For that matter, I made myself uncomfortable.

Searching for supper, I came across a café and ducked inside. Quickly, I chose a corner booth. The café draped my shoulders with a smoky arm and, once its curious patrons had quit gawking, it whispered a welcome. I relaxed. The server spoke English. He guided me through my choice of a ham *broodje* and Coca-Cola.

The other booths held scenes from the theater of personal experience. Four friends coveted each others' opinions. A married couple worshipped the face of their baby. Teen lovers had intercourse through their eyes. And at the bar, alone, a young man slowly killed his beer.

I stayed in my cocoon and picked at the crust of my baguette, pulling it back to reveal its pulpy flesh.

Inside, the bread had knitted together in chambers. Something tiny could find a world of security in there.

"Hoi," he said, standing beside my booth. He wore jeans, tight-fitted and baby blue. His red shirt pulled my eyes up his body like a rising flush to the curve of collarbone and the contour of masculine neck. There, I found the smile and, finally, the eyes. The two were linked, without shame, the smile reaching into the eyes and making them tight and twinkling. Brown.

"Hello." I gathered my jacket up off the seat, preparing to leave.

He thought it was an invitation to sit.

"I... I was just leaving." I retreated deeper into the booth.

Seated beside me, blocking my escape, he held out his hand, "My name is Nicolaas." His English had a Dutch lilt with a hint of British pucker.

I couldn't ignore the hand. Clasping it without commitment, I nodded and replied, "Michael."

"I hope you don't mind that I come to greet you," he said. "You're American, yes?"

"Yes, that's right." I looked him directly in those big, brown eyes—big and brown like a little boy's—so unlike my own and yet so like what mine could have become.

"I visited New York last year."

"You did?"

"*Ja.*" Yes. Charming, that one word, how he said it, not like we nasal Americans do, but more like a sigh of pleasure, ahhhhhhh with a Y. "I have friends there at university."

"Which school?" I asked, making conversation.

"NYU."

"Really? Did you like it?"

169

"Oh, *ja.*" Nicolaas rested his elbow on the back of the booth. A natural animation flowed over his features as he talked. "You have so much space in America. The forests and the fields—even the places with all the houses that look alike. You drive through them, and you never find the end. It is like God's will. You never escape. I love it!" He grinned at me as if we were sharing a private joke. "You think I am crazy, *ja?*"

"No," I replied. "Why?" I meant why would I think he was crazy.

Nicolaas thought I meant why did he love it. He answered by pounding his fist against his chest, "Because it makes the heart beat faster." He paused, then with a tap-dancer shrug, he chuckled. "It helped that I had a round-trip ticket."

I laughed.

The waiter appeared table-side, and Nicolaas ordered us each a beer. He insisted—because, he said, he owed me a drink. He had a way about him that I found difficult to resist. His easy, almost lazy, discourse took center stage and left me feeling like the audience. This made it comfortable for me to accept his company. As the evening progressed, I found myself seduced into a spirited state of conversation that was due only in part to the stream of beer that crossed the table. Six weeks earlier, if someone had shown me a recording of myself that night, as I see it now in my memories, I wouldn't have recognized the lively man, me, with the changing expressions. Nicolaas had that effect on me.

At the end, we shook hands, and I wandered back to my hotel with a grin on my face. The moon adored me. The stars twinkled just for me. The people I passed saw a happy man.

The next morning, I saw a drunken man, and I regretted having made plans to meet Nicolaas for dinner.

Day 2

The second day of the Economics conference unfolded, but by afternoon, my mind was wandering to the Dutch man who had worked his way so elegantly past my defenses. For hours, against a backdrop of droning Economics theory, my thoughts tumbled until the edges had smoothed. I decided that Nicolaas and I could be friends, and that he wanted no more than that either. I chastised myself for thinking otherwise and blamed it on the beer, the foreign country, and my overactive imagination.

After the last session, I rushed back to the hotel, showered, shaved, and went to meet Nicolaas. I arrived late and had the uneasy experience of seeing him before he saw me. He was pacing slowly in front of the shwarma restaurant, a cigarette forgotten and unlit in his hand. The downturn of his mouth told me he was thinking I had stood him up. I straddled the uncomfortable line between wanting to walk away and not wanting to leave that disappointment on his face. Before I knew it, I had approached him. He saw me, and his smile pulled at the corners of *my* mouth as well. I felt my eyes twinkle, and try as I might, I couldn't get rid of the tightness in my gut. I looked away so he wouldn't see and said the most innocuous thing I could think of, "Awful weather today."

"Oh? I hadn't noticed."

The interior of the restaurant was decorated with

Middle Eastern flare, a passion-colored explosion. The discourse of the other diners sang, accompanied by plucked music. Our waiter walked us to a table in the back, as if he sensed that our rendezvous should not occur in the middle where anyone could see. I thanked him, though I doubted he understood my gratitude. A red cloth spilled across our table, lit with a globed candle. Nicolaas sat, not across from me, but beside me, just around the table's corner.

"You almost didn't come," Nicolaas said, matter-of-factly, without accusation, once he'd folded his long-fingered hands. The pallor of his skin stood out in silhouette against the tablecloth like homemade whipped cream on strawberries.

I didn't know what to say, so I said nothing. I was there, after all. I *had* come.

"I almost didn't come," Nicolaas confessed.

That surprised me. I wanted to ask why, but I didn't. I looked down at the neatly manicured curves of my own fingernails.

Nicolaas laughed. He had a laugh that made everything right. It erased the awful discomfort of moments. It pushed aside doubts and illuminated a circle where we didn't have to think about anything important. His laughter saved me.

Our conversation turned to more philosophical topics, including modernity, music, and mothers. He thrilled me with mundane stories of his childhood. At first, he did the majority of the talking, and I listened, but just like the night before, his seduction worked its leisurely magic. I emerged from my hiding place.

The food arrived in stages, like our unfolding camaraderie, without noticeable thresholds crossed. By dessert, the sweetness of it had me savoring. We took nibbles of each other, making it last. I offered him tastes of my life, my thoughts, and my feelings. He gave more generously, filling me. I set free the glutton inside.

I paid for dinner. I saw it as a perfectly friendly gesture, nothing to confess on Sunday morning. "It's the least I can do," I told him.

He replied, "You've already done more than you know."

Outside, we paused for a cigarette. That was the excuse, although I think I would have used any excuse to delay saying good-night. We laughed and talked. We blew our smoke irreverently into the face of the night. We could still do that because we hadn't crossed any lines.

I asked, "Do you have far to go?"

Nicolaas shook his head, "No. About a quarter kilometer in that direction." He pointed with his chin, lifting it toward the east.

"Would you like me to walk with you?"

"*Ja.*"

The streets of Tilburg threatened to swallow us. From the open square, we wandered into an alley lined with dark shops. The rain had stopped. The damp cobblestones felt slippery. Time slowed, and there was only Nicolaas and me.

Eventually, Nicolaas paused. "This is my home."

"Well," I replied, looking up at the apartments perched above a bakery.

"Would you like...?" Nicolaas tipped his head toward the entrance to the stairs.

"No, I..." I couldn't. "I should get to bed. I have..." After everything, I couldn't. "I have a long day ahead of me." I wanted to, but I couldn't.

173

Nicolaas smiled. Bless him, he smiled. "*Alstewbleeft*," he murmured. Thank you. Resting his hand on my arm, Nicolaas leaned toward me and pressed a kiss to my cheek.

His lips were so soft. So warm. Desire bloomed inside me. Its fruit swelled in my groin—ripe and luscious. I closed my eyes and wanted him.

Who knows what could have happened. I could have turned my head, ever so slightly. He could have... I could have... if only... but, the sound of footsteps broke into our moment. They approached with the regularity of a marching drumbeat, keeping time for the soldiers' steps. I caught sight of monk's robes and the glint of a silver cross on a woolen yoke.

"*Goede avond, heren*," the monk greeted. His tone held rebuke.

"*Goede avond, broer*," Nicolaas replied with a nod.

The monk looked me directly in the eyes. His were so blue, they verged on white. They were angels' eyes—judging eyes. Time slowed.

I nodded, but said nothing.

The moment passed, time resumed, and the monk continued on his way. I offered Nicolaas my hand, and we shook. Without another word, I turned to go.

"Michael!" Nicolaas called. "Tomorrow night, I'll be at the cafe where we met."

I didn't even look back. I hoped maybe he would think I hadn't heard. I felt like a traitor, as much to myself as to Nicolaas. The night to which he referred would be at the end of my third day in Tilburg. I had a previous engagement.

Later, in bed, I dreamed I was walking through endless alleys. Nicolaas was ahead of me. I was following him, enamored of his silhouette against the streetlights. He didn't know I was there.

A flutter of fabric in a doorway caught my eye. It was a monk. His face was shadowed by a hood. I nodded a greeting, but then my attention returned to Nicolaas.

A second monk appeared in a somber side street. He floated to the intersection, feet hidden and silenced by his long robe, then stood there and watched me go by. I didn't nod that time. Disquiet was spreading through me and hurrying me along.

Nicolaas turned a corner. I broke into a run. The uneven stones made me misstep, and I fell onto my hands and knees, tearing my pants and scraping my palms.

There were monks behind me, ahead of me, and on both sides. For months, they had been in my dreams and correspondence. They had filled my waking prayer. The promise I'd made was culminating, and for the first time, I became aware of my desire to escape it.

I stumbled to my feet and ran, my heart hammering, my breath a sharp stab in my side. I skittered around the corner and found myself in a courtyard, surrounded by modern buildings squeezed together like parishioners in pews. Old St. Jozef's Church stood at the pulpit. I came to a halt, pinned there by the imposing structure as if God himself had appeared before me. From deep in its belly came the sound of chanting, male voices all. They repeated their mantra, "Lord Jesus Christ, have mercy on me, a sinner."

Nicolaas was almost lost in the shadow of the church.

A monk near me said, "If not you, then him."

With the urgency of the damned, I screamed, "Nicolaas!" He entered the church.

Then, I was kneeling at Nicolaas's feet. He was seated on a carved and velvet-lined throne, naked. His skin reflected the candlelight, and his eyes draped me with warmth. I studied his face, beatific in its acceptance. I wanted him, and I wanted to be him.

He touched my cheek with his hand, and my gaze trailed down his bare chest and stomach, across the fleshy tumble of his sex, and along the firm thickness of thigh, down his calves, to his feet. A basin of warm water and a cloth had been provided. I started with his ankles and worked my way to his soles, washing away the dirt, forgiving him in advance.

The monks stayed at the periphery of my vision, black curtains that rippled in a draft.

Nicolaas' fingers hooked under my chin and raised my gaze to his. "*Mijn schat*, I do this for you."

Day 3

I awoke with two lingering symptoms: a shameful erection and a feeling of unease that proved much more difficult to ditch than its companion. I left my room and walked through Tilburg in a state of carefully contained agitation. I noticed other pedestrians only enough to avoid bumping into them. I didn't go to the train station, though I could have. I walked and planned, ruffled by thoughts of Nicolaas. I imagined I could meet him later and convince him to run away with me, break my contract with the Order, and beseech God to release me.

And then, there it was. St. Jozef's Church. Like a stone golem, it squatted amidst technology and technicolor media, eternal amidst the ephemeral. Saints gazed down upon me from the shelter of the arched entrance. The wooden portal had a slow, heavy swing. As I opened it, the aromas of mystic ritual and forbidden knowledge escaped. With trepidation, I stepped into the vestibule. It didn't occur to me to turn around and leave.

Pausing at the font, I dipped my fingers into the holy water. The water was cool in its stone receptacle. It clung to my skin, but refused to enter my pores. I genuflected to the distant altar before glancing around the spacious interior. I was alone. Relief threaded through me, and I relaxed. Impressive, the sanctuary was, with its gothic arches and stone pillars. Jewel-toned stained glass told the story of the Crucifixion.

Turning to the right, I began my exploration with an alcove dedicated to Jesus Christ. I got no further. Shock and horror clutched at me as I stared up at the scene framed within the alcove. A life-size, life-like Christ figure hung on a wooden cross.

His face... so real... dark eyelashes sheltering blue eyes that rolled upward and drained shimmery tears onto his pale cheeks. Brown hair, dirty and ragged. The thorns upon his head had been harvested from a real bush. They pierced his skin, and trails of blood ran down his forehead and nose. He was haggard, cheeks sunken, mouth open to reveal perfect teeth and an anguished tongue.

The creator had included every detail of him, including hair in his armpits, on his limbs, and streaming down his belly to where a pool of it could be imagined beneath the fabric covering his genitals. The angularity of his figure betrayed hunger. His knees were skinned and bloody. Purple bruises and welts from a surprising number of abuses covered his torso, arms, and legs. He was bleeding internally as well as externally.

Rarely in my life, had I ever seen anything so

deeply jarring. I found myself imagining Jesus real and alive, no longer just a storybook character who was the Son of God. Suddenly, I grasped his humanity as surely as I had always understood his divinity. Hunger and thirst, defecation and urination, sexual urges— they were no longer implausible for Jesus.

And pain. Real, gut-wrenching pain. This Christ had the nails through his hands and feet, like all those others, but here, I could see how they penetrated his flesh, pushed it aside, and invaded between the bones.

I realized my own condition; the gape of my mouth, and the unblinking paralysis of my eyes. I had to look away. A shiver coursed up my spine and clutched at the back of my neck. My stomach churned.

"Are you all right?" asked a man with a Dutch lilt to his English.

It startled me, and an instant heat rose in my cheeks. I found a monk standing there, watching me with frank evaluation. I took an involuntary step back.

He clasped his hands in front of his belly. His hair was gray, and his face was lined with age. Through thin lips, he repeated, "Sir, are you all right?"

Too loudly, I replied, "Yes." I cleared my throat and lowered my voice, "Yes, thank you. I'm fine. It's just..." It was just that horrible depiction.

"It's striking, isn't it?" the monk commented, his eyes shifting to the Crucifixion.

"It's so... real," I replied.

"Yes. I think it does an admirable job of conveying what Jesus Christ suffered for us."

I nodded.

The monk said, "Each year, thousands make pilgrimages to see the Christ of St. Jozef's Church and leave inspired to change their lives. This diorama has been here for 100 years. It is a gift from God. Your contribution to it will absolve your sins."

"My... I... I'm not ready."

"*Ja, mijn schat*," said a familiar voice. "You are ready."

I turned and found Nicolaas beside me. I gazed into his brown eyes and saw myself reflected there, with the white face of Jesus just over my shoulder. The shape of Nicolaas' beautiful body was hidden by monk's robes. My heart swelled painfully until it was beating in my neck and temples. I had no words. I knew my fate had been sealed.

I hung my head and whispered, "Your will be done, Father."

"Come," said Nicolaas, and he took my hand. "I have agreed to do this for you and for Him." He led me along under the flying arches, past colorful depictions of the life of Christ.

The other monks followed us down a stone stairwell to the basement. I stood in the center and allowed Nicolaas to remove my coat. He handed it to a monk and returned to unbutton my shirt. I watched his fingers deftly open each one and felt them brush against my skin. My thoughts went to other possibilities, and I was filled with regret.

Nicolaas completely undressed me. I stood there with only my hands to cover myself, goose bumps rising on my arms and chest. The monks lined the room and began to chant, their voices monotone.

Nicolaas took a whip from a stand and said a prayer over it. The first lash landed squarely across my back and sent me to my knees. The pain was electric, and tears filled my eyes. Two monks came forward, pulled my hair, and punched me. I felt a rib break. They continued until I got to my feet.

Between each crack of the whip, Nicolaas said, "My Lord Jesus, have mercy on me, a sinner."

If I faltered, I was beaten, so I stood as long as I could, begging God in silent prayer to carry me through the worst of it. Eventually, it stopped, and I was wrapped at the hips with a white cloth that covered me, in front and behind. My blood drained down onto it, staining it.

They brought out a cross and lay it flat. With a monk at each limb, they put me upon it. I had long since lost the strength to fight them. When the first nail went into my wrist, I screamed, and a white light blinded me.

Their chanting had grown voluminous, feverish in its call for Him to accept my sacrifice.

"Father!" I cried. "Why have you forsaken me?"

With the second nail, I saw his face in front of me. Jesus of Nazareth was smiling.

Day 4

I awoke, frozen in time. I'd never seen the sanctuary from that angle, but I recognized the gate beyond which I had stood when I'd first looked upon the Christ of St. Jozef's Church. At that moment, another man stood in that same spot, a young man with a Chicago Cubs t-shirt. He stared at me, eyes horrified, mouth gaping, and I felt a profound kinship with him.

Later, Nicolaas came to see me one last time. He knelt at the gate, tears streaming down his face, and whispered, "Please, forgive me." He didn't need to ask. I already had. I had come to Tilburg expecting to sacrifice myself, but I had never predicted that I would fall in love with my own betrayer. I could never hate him whom I loved so dearly. He too had sacrificed for God's plan.

As the first day of my hundred years on the cross unfolded, the pain dimmed to a hum in my spine, and I gazed down upon the horrified and pious faces raised up to me. I suffered for all their sins.

"It looks so real," they said, in a multitude of languages.

Eye Contact
Jeff C. Stevenson

Josh Horton never knew what hit him that morning at 10:08. He saw it coming—something big, white, fuzzy around the edges—but he never saw where it went. One minute, he was a construction flagger directing traffic on Massachusetts Route 97, the next moment he was a quadriplegic.

* * *

Steven Peabody was born three months premature in 1980. When his eyes first fluttered open, one was normal while the right eye had only developed with the sclera in place. No pupil, no iris, only the white had been formed, like the cue ball used in a game of billiards. A healthy, clear mucus membrane lubricated it. The doctor said it simply hadn't received enough oxygen during the early weeks of pregnancy. He wore an eyepatch for as long as he could remember, mainly so others were not subjected to seeing the white globe lolling about in the socket.

When he was three, he awoke in the middle of the night due to his right eye causing him discomfort. This was troubling since the nerve had never formed so it was much like an unplugged TV set; there was nothing there to obtain a signal or broadcast one. The eye itself seemed to tingle. He sat up in bed, rubbing it furiously, not certain what the strange feeling meant. He had always been able to scratch an itch before, but this seemed to be coming from deep inside his skull. The persistent tickle wouldn't stop. He was preparing to cry out for his mother when all at once, his eye came loose and plopped out of his head.

It was cool in the palm of his hand. It reminded him immediately of the texture and weight of the slime toy he had played with that afternoon. One of the neighbor boys had shown him a plastic toy trashcan. He had pried the lid off, then told Steven to touch the squishy and oozy contents. Soon they were all shrieking as they squeezed and stretched the strange concoction.

By the moonlight that shone brightly into his window, Steven gingerly turned his eye over. It was perfectly round, about the size of a hard-boiled egg, flawlessly white. He rolled it around with his index finger, wondering if he would feel anything. There was no pain or discomfort coming from the empty socket. His eyelid had simply flopped over it like a tired shade covering an open window.

The itching sensation was gone and that was a relief. The eye didn't seem at all damaged when he had grabbed it as it fell out of his head. Since there was no iris or pupil, there was no front or back as far as he could tell. It remained damp in his grasp, still lubricated, so without thinking about it too much, he placed it back into the socket. It slipped snugly into the hole with only the slightest sound, a moist plop. He blinked several times. It stayed in place.

Steven yawned. What had occurred was an odd event for anyone, let alone a three-year-old, but it wasn't at all alarming. After all, it was his eye, he was familiar with it, knew what it looked like when it was unmasked and he stared into the mirror. Long ago, his family had lost interest in it. He was a healthy child and that was all that mattered. The unsightly area was kept covered, so no one gave it much thought. He was simply the cute little boy with the eye patch.

That all changed a few years after he started school.

* * *

The first thing Steven learned in kindergarten class at Witchcraft Heights Elementary School was the morning pledge: *I am a smart, special, valuable student. I respect myself and I respect others. My words and actions are kind and honest. I accept only my best in all that I do.* For the next few years, those words kept his self-image tight and intact. The other children liked his eyepatch. They didn't really care that what it hid was considered so gross that they had to beg him to show them what it concealed.

But things changed in 1994. Steven was a freshman at Salem High School. There was no morning pledge. Maybe it was the lack of those special words repeated each day—much like a protective ritual—that allowed the events to unfold. New school, new kids, and many had no idea what to make of the kid with the eye patch. It had been accepted and barely noticed when he was at Witchcraft Heights, but at Salem High, it marked him as different.

He had always only had a small, tight circle of

185

guys he considered friends. Sometimes they were jerkoff buddies—as long as no one told—but that usually only lasted for a week or two. The school friendships were rarely carried over during the summer, which was when he found himself alone most of the time. He knew he was unlike the other kids. He was often lost in thought and would frequently wake in the middle of the night to find himself standing in front of the bedroom window, gazing out at the sleeping town. Through the tree branches, he would watch things form out of the beams of moonlight, move from limb to limb, then fade from view. Sometimes, even with his left eye closed, he could see shadowy shapes attempting to manifest themselves.

Different, he whispered to the night. *I'm different in so many ways.*

Each evening, he'd gaze at himself in the bathroom mirror. Without the eyeball in place, the right eyelid was collapsed into the socket. The flap of skin was droopy where it covered the hollow spot. He lifted it by the eyelashes to peer inside. All was dark red, a mystery he always wondered about. Why him? What was the point of having an eye you could remove? All it did was make him look freakish. *The outside of me matches how I feel most of the time on the inside*, he thought. *Different. I'm different in so many ways.*

Steven had never told anyone about the ability to remove and replace the eye. When his mother took him to the doctor, he never asked about it other than to see if it was bothering Steven in any way. "No," he had always said, anxious that the doctor would examine it too closely and it would pop out. It was his own little secret, one other precious, tiny part of his life he could keep to himself.

* * *

He ate lunch alone in the high school cafeteria. This was nothing new, it had happened dozens of times before. The trick was to keep your head down and focus on the lunch tray in front of you like its contents were the most fascinating things you had ever seen. He hadn't found a group to hang out with yet, or maybe they had not come looking for him, the guy with the eyepatch. *I have a name*, he wanted to tell everyone. Sometimes, he wanted to yell it at them.

He was so intent on spooning the pasta with meat sauce into his mouth that he didn't notice the flutter of activity that was coming and going around him. Out of the corner of his left eye, something bright was placed on the table. It was a shelled, hard-boiled egg. There were two more near it. Behind him, someone gulped back a laugh. Another egg was left next to his arm. Then three more were quickly dropped off as students rushed past, leaving their offerings gently rolling about on the table. Within seconds, more than a dozen shelled eggs littered the area. He managed to finish his lunch, throat tight with furious embarrassment, his left eye filled with tears.

Once he was in the bathroom, he slammed the stall door closed. Blessedly alone, he wept openly, chest aching with pain as he sobbed. Again, he wondered why he couldn't have been born normal like all the other kids. *Why this?* his mind screamed, fists tight, face hot. *Why do I have to look like this?*

* * *

It continued the next day. White rocks were left around his desk before the teacher arrived in the classroom. He was too embarrassed to even try to explain what the stones represented but assumed the teacher would know.

When Steven fetched his jacket from the cloakroom, ping-pong balls were in the pockets. As he opened his locker, dozens of white poker chips fell out. When he returned home one day, golf balls had been tossed on his lawn. He managed to collect them before his parents arrived from work. The silent taunting went on for two or three weeks, but soon those behind the tormenting ran out of ideas or lost interest. Steven never reported anyone, knew they simply wanted to see what his reaction would be. He had none. He simply shut down during the day, remained still and silent, but at night, he opened himself up to the peculiar dreams that billowed about like capes expanding on blustery days. Something was coming, something was going to happen.

* * *

When freshman year finally came to an end, he looked forward to a summer when he could be on his own. It was the same with his sophomore and junior years. It. was just time passing, friendless and alone. The late-night awakenings continued along with the strange visions of shadows forming, moving about. They were nothing he was able to make sense of during the day, but he had a lingering feeling of hope, that things were going to change, better days may be on the horizon.

On August 15 of 1998, he turned 18, was able to obtain an unrestricted driver's license. But he had nowhere he wanted to go, no one to take a trip with. He had spent the summer working at a home furnishing shop, long, boring hours with the temperature usually in the eighties. Time crawled by as the first day of school—September 7—crept closer along with the cooler weather. A new season, the last year of high school, and then what?

If he had only known that Ryan Conant had moved to the area over the summer, his reluctance to start twelfth grade would have evaporated.

* * *

Ryan had thick brown hair, big brown eyes, and was, for some reason, immediately attracted to Steven. He never spoke, only watched him eat lunch alone, catching his attention when Steven would take a moment to glance up. Ryan never looked away, Steven always did.

Whenever Steven glanced his way, those big brown eyes were already locked onto him. It wasn't creepy or menacing; Steven didn't feel threatened or nervous, just curious. He didn't think that he was attracted to Ryan—not in a boyfriend way—but there was something about the new kid that he was interested in. Yeah, maybe in a boyfriend way. Maybe.

One morning Ryan arrived late to school. The two-hour block had already begun promptly at 7:50 a.m.; he showed up just after nine. He whispered to the teacher, then hurried over to his desk. Steven noticed that something had happened to Ryan. His left ear was red and scratched with dried blood on the lobe, a few streaks down his neck. Ryan glanced at Steven. This time, Steven held the gaze.

Later that week, Ryan's right wrist had bruise marks on it.

* * *

Steven had an idea. It came to him, as most strange notions did, in the middle of the night. It was something he had never attempted before or even thought about, like the possibilities his unrestricted driver's license offered. He awoke with the right eye tingling a bit, indicating that it wanted to be removed. Once it was on the bedside table, the thought came to him fully formed, as if it was being read off an instruction manual. It only took a few moments for him to understand the where and the how. It wasn't until much later that he learned the why.

The next day, Steven was up just before the sun was beginning to light up the town. He quickly and quietly snuck out of the house, climbed on his old bicycle—the car would be too noisy at that hour—and rode to Ryan's home, gliding silently under the yellow glow of the street lights. He knew Ryan lived in a condo on 1 Chase Street, several blocks away. The fall morning was cold, his coat was pulled up tight as he peddled, breath white as it puffed before him. When he arrived, he dumped the bike on the sidewalk, reached into his pocket, grasped the item. Before him was a row of mailboxes. He found the one with Ryan's last name and affixed the object out of sight on the bottom of his mailbox. Seconds later Steven was headed back down the street, panting with excitement as he peddled home.

At the end of the school day, he followed Ryan home, making certain he never knew Steven was always two blocks behind him. Once Ryan had slammed the front door, Steven reached under the mailbox, felt around and grabbed the object. It felt different than it had that morning. A short piece of cold, heavy wood was now attached to it. He separated them, slipped them both into his pocket, then hurried down the street as fast as he could. After he had rounded the corner, was certain no one was looking, he deftly lifted his patch, reached into his pocket, pulled the eyeball out and placed it into the socket. He then released the patch. It snapped back into place.

Later that night, after dinner, Steven laid on the bed. He had never done this before, didn't know what to expect, just knew he was obeying the idea that had come to him the previous evening. In his hands, he held the thin woodgrain lighter that had been attached to the eyeball. He kept twisting it over and over between his fingers.

His breathing steadied out. Floaters and coils of colors formed, dissipated, reappeared, enlarged until they filled the field of vision behind his shut eyelids. Shadows appeared, as they always did. But this time, images formed. A man wearing a construction hat. A younger man. A woman.

Steven gasped, opened his eye, sat up in bed as if waking from a nightmare, heart pounding hard.

* * *

Josh Horton's life had always been one of enormous changes, usually due to his drinking or his temper and love of fighting, or his desire to control and subdue. He'd been Ryan's stepfather for under three years but had already left his marks on the 18-year-old queer and his mother. Josh couldn't help it, had never been good at self-control, or slowing down to gather his thoughts. He was never a thinker or one to ponder. He'd always been a man of action, like his father, who had taught him from a young age that you took what you wanted or you were left with nothing.

Working as part of a union crew had Josh earning some of the best money of his life; a solid, steady income. Things were lining up, situations were good, except for his home life. The wife, once so pretty and docile, had started to pester him, wanted to change him, didn't like him drinking so much or the way he treated her in bed or the way he disciplined her son. He had resorted to using some force to settle her down a bit, but then the boy had surprised him, so he needed to be dealt with, too. It was like they both wanted him to fail, a repeat performance of what had occurred in New Hampshire.

Moving to Salem was supposed to be a fresh start, a do-over for him and them. His wife's sister lived in nearby Danvers and mentioned some ongoing construction on Route 97. They could move down, rent a place for a year, no commitment. No need to put down roots, just a time to steady themselves a bit. He had agreed with her that it sounded like the right thing to do. Losing his job in New Hampshire had started the downward slide. They needed to get out of there, put some distance between that state and what had happened there.

The construction work had been as promised, but the wife and kid had started to change within a few weeks of moving to Salem. She spent too much time listening to her sister, suddenly didn't like him smoking in the house anymore. She'd hidden his smokes and favorite slim woodgrain Zippo lighter once. He taught her to never do that again.

She knew he needed the beers after work to relax, but now for some reason she was nervous about mistakes being repeated. The kid was beginning to fight back a bit, too, which made for a surprisingly enjoyable challenge, but there was usually some injuries or blood, and always some shouting and crying. The neighbors had already complained twice. It was all getting on his nerves, nudging his temper, ratcheting up his thirst.

That morning, he had gone to work a little hung over, a little fire of rage simmering because of the wife and her son. Maybe he had just been distracted thinking of ways to deal with them. He needed someone to blame for what happened. After all, the job wasn't rocket science. It was as simple and mindless as reducing the water gushing out of a facet. You just used your hands and held up a sign to slow the cars so they could safely move past the guys working on the road. Despite a shutdown of lanes, everyone would get where they needed to be. That was Josh's job that day. He just had to slow them down. The bright traffic cones were out so there was no way people couldn't see him. The crew was shy one day-glow orange vest but he was assured they'd have it for him right after lunch. No worries. Other than that, and his lighter having gone missing again, things were fine that morning. He wanted to figure out how to get his home life in order but he had all day to solve that problem.

He couldn't determine the make or model of the big white van or truck or jeep that came at him. It seemed to appear out of nowhere. That was pretty much his last thought. For a moment, it was white brilliance personified. Whatever it was, for the bare instant he saw it, he put his hand up to make it slow down and stop. He'd been doing that all morning, but whatever was driving it or moving this thing ignored the order. Instead, it sped up, bolted forward. In a flash, it was right there in front of him, pushing in closer. Josh felt his chest seize up with fear. *This can't be happening,* he thought. *It's too close.* One of the guys shouted out a warning. Then, everything went snow-blind white.

Josh was thrown 15 feet into the air and propelled about 60 feet from the point of impact. Whatever it was that hit him was estimated to be going anywhere from 80 to 100 miles per hour and then it vanished down the road. It was just there and gone. The workers had rushed to Josh's side where he lay, unconscious. By the time the ambulance arrived, no one was sure if he would even make it to the hospital. His body was so twisted and mangled, it was hard to look at. He was screaming in such pain that a few of the men thought it would be a mercy if he died before his wife and stepson saw him.

But he held on. Many hours later, when his wife and Ryan were finally able to speak to the doctor, they were told that Josh had been catastrophically injured. He had suffered a broken neck, a partially severed spinal cord, a shattered leg and elbow and severe brain injuries. He would require at least six months in the hospital.

"Of course, he'll need round-the-clock care once he's released," the doctor had finished. "We'll do our best to get him home to you, but things may change. He has a long, hard and painful journey in front of him."

When Ryan and his mother returned home, their answering machine had messages from the construction firm, the law firm that represented the company, a worker's compensation representative and the president of the local union. Before they returned any calls, mother and son fell into one another's arms, weeping in shocked gratitude.

* * *

Life situations drastically and immediately improved for Ryan and his mom. Things tend to move quickly when multi-million dollar lawsuits are in the mix. Since Josh had no deflector vest, the company was at fault, desperate to settle as soon as possible. A young woman raising a senior in high school while having to care for her permanently injured husband was going to make terrible headlines if they didn't step in with a huge amount of compassion.

The settlement was agreed upon after just three weeks of negotiations, with the insurance company initially offering $24,000,000. That award was later cut in half by a judge to about $12,000,000, which was believed to be one of the largest in Massachusetts's history. It was more than enough for Ryan and his mother to live happily ever after while Josh lived the rest of his life shut away in a care facility.

Neither the driver nor the white vehicle—or whatever it was—that had struck Josh was ever located.

* * *

Ryan was absent from school for a week due to the event. Steven found that he missed Ryan's eyes staring at him. Perhaps he was watching out for him. That would be nice, to have someone caring for him. There had always been a protective nature to Ryan—maybe it was those big brown eyes—even though they had never spoken. Steven found that he longed to see him but didn't want to stop by Ryan's house; Steven wanted Ryan to come to him when he was ready. Steven had something to show him and tell him now that he knew the why of what he had accomplished.

A week before Halloween, Ryan returned to school. He had made no inroads to acquiring friends, but the class had gone ahead and made a sympathy card. He had mumbled thanks, folded it up, shuffled to his seat, head down. During the first two-hour block, he turned around several times to glance at Steven. They never smiled at one another, but some peculiar connection had been formed, the early nudges of what was to be affection.

The day before Halloween, Ryan sat down next to Steven during lunch. They had never been so near one another. They didn't speak. Steven put down his spoon, reached into his pants' pocket, pulled out what he had been carrying ever since his last visit to Ryan's home.

With a sharp clack, he set Josh's slim woodgrain Zippo lighter on the table between them.

196

Steven watched Ryan slowly reach for it, then abruptly grab it as if it was about to escape. He examined it carefully, turned it around in his hands as if there was a secret code written on it. Finally, he returned it to the table.

Ryan looked at Steven. "Thank you."

Steven couldn't help it. He smiled. Ryan did, too.

"You're welcome," he said, the grin still stuck on his face.

"How'd you... how'd you know?" Ryan whispered. "And how'd you do it?"

Steven thought about how to explain what he himself didn't understand, but as he sorted through the words, nothing came together. He shrugged. "I saw it, I guess. I saw what was happening. Knew I had to do something. Knew I *could* do something. So, I did."

Ryan nodded slowly. His eyes suddenly welled up, he furiously wiped the tears away. "It was...horrible. What he did to us. To my Mom. To me..."

"I know." Steven wanted to touch him, comfort him, make the thoughts be forgotten. Maybe he could learn to do that.

* * *

They went out together the next night for Halloween, Ryan as a simple ghost, white sheet with eyeholes. Steven wore the slasher mask from the movie *Scream*. Salem spent the entire month in high-gear Halloween mode so every night the streets had been packed with thousands of tourists, witches, ghosts, and monsters. Crowds roamed the streets, children screamed from house to house, scary sounds

197

echoed from each stately home. For Salem, it was a night like any other in October, one that was filled with friendly terror.

Steven and Ryan still didn't need to speak much. There was comfort in the silence they shared. The affection between them was drawing them closer together. After they had traveled another block in contentment, casually weaving their way through the packed streets, Ryan suddenly asked, "What's it like to have one eye? What do you see in front of you?"

No one had ever asked Steven such a question. He took his time before answering. "I guess you could say that I see as if I am missing the right side of my face."

After a moment of thinking it over, Ryan said, "Cool." Then: "I know you're half blind, but if you were totally blind, would you know when we passed a tree or bush or car? Can you sense things around you?"

"Sure," Steven answered. "Everything makes a noise. You just have to listen."

Ryan rustled his sheet, rearranged it, reached out, slipped his hand into Steven's, pulled him over to the side street for privacy.

Kissed him.

The kiss lasted most of the night, or at least that's what it felt like to Steven. He had never been kissed before, not like that, not by a ghost.

When they finished, Ryan asked, "What you did for me, you can do for others, right?"

Steven looked around at the boisterous crowd. Briefly, some smoky shadows formed, strained to break through, manifest themselves in the midst of the evening festivities. They wanted to make themselves known. They flickered like black embers, vanished like sparks above a fire.

Steven nodded. "I think I can."

"Good," Ryan said. Maybe he was near tears again. Steven couldn't tell with the sheet covering most of his face.

Steven squeezed Ryan's hand.

* * *

Steven Peabody fell in love with Ryan Conant that Halloween night in 1998. They married in Massachusetts in 2004, raised three children, and still live in Salem.

Broken Lines of Salt and Flesh
Robert E. Furey

Dani tapped twice against the door with a single knuckle. Truth be told she hoped there'd be no answer. 'I knocked and when you didn't answer I went home!' She didn't want to be here. Her friend might be trying to help, but she just felt like ice-cream and videos would be a better salve. She raised her knuckle for one more fleeting tap.

The door swung open.

"Hey, girl, come on in!" Her friend Samantha, a kohl-eyed wiccan, seemed to love the trappings of witchcraft as a fashion guide more than anything else. Her lips were painted bruise-blue, her skin rouged to an unnatural pink, and dreamcatchers swung from her earlobes. A few too many pentagrams decorated her apartment and the scent of burnt sage hung heavy in the air. Tendrils of smoke swirled upwards from a smudge resting in a repurposed casino ashtray Samantha had stolen her last night on a waitressing job. The edge of some Las Vegas logo jutted from beneath the herb bundle.

Dani carried her heavy overnight bag to the couch and plopped down beside it. Crossing her arms and legs, she feigned feeling comfortable.

"So, girls' night in, right?" Dani said. She hoped Samantha wouldn't ask to take her out to 'meet people.'

"Well…" Samantha looked a bit mischievous, a bit excited. "I was thinking about trying something a little… different?" She puttered about, carrying dishes of powders, shifting positions of objects on the tabletop, now blowing some life back into the burning smudge.

'Something different' these days always meant some witchy option. Over the three years of their friendship, Sam's interests had gone from crystal power and aromatherapy, to ear candles and phrenology. The problem was, she never stuck with any of them long enough to really figure them out. Wicca had burst into her life several months ago and rapidly came to be the latest answer for everything, including Dani's broken heart.

Dani's boyfriend, Edward, had broken it. She'd loved him and he'd turned out to be nothing but a serial cheater. In the fallout of that one horrible night catching him in a ménage a trois in the bed they shared, Dani had not only ended it with him, but two of her friends from work, so the ménage and her job too were out of her life in a tear-drenched and heart-wrenching firestorm of betrayal. After everything, she knew she hated him, but dammit, inside, during some unwelcome moments she missed him too. And missing him made her feel worse about herself.

"Let me guess," Dani said. "A magic spell?"

Samantha stopped her frenetic puttering about the room. Facing Dani, arms akimbo, she said, "Don't be like that. Anything I do has got to be better than you sitting home alone with mountains of popcorn and way too many candy bars." She scolded Dani with her expression and held her gaze long enough that Dani looked away.

"Okay, fine. What are we doing?" She just didn't have the energy to fight. As long as she avoided actually seeing or meeting anyone she would play along. "I'm not going out, Sam. I'm not there yet."

"And that's exactly what we're working on, getting you feeling better," Samantha said, beaming again. "We'll get your spirits up and then, after that, we can talk about meeting new misters."

Dani could live with that. Anything that put it off. "Alright, what do I have to do?"

"Okay," Sam said, lacing her fingers together. "I have to do most of the work here setting up a summoning circle and stuff." She opened a book to where a beaded bookmark dangled from between the pages. "I already psychically cleared my whole apartment and set up all the charms we would ever want." Her eyes darted from a pentagram to the smoking sage bundle to the circle of sea salt spread around the inside edge of her table.

Dani smiled, sighing tolerantly. "Okay, then, what do I have to do? Just watch and feel happier?" She sat on the sofa, her legs crossed, her arms tight across her chest.

Samantha sprinkled salt runes and signs inside the circle on the table, tweaking the shapes with her fingertip as she spoke. "All you have to do is be positive. And be extra shower-fresh clean."

"That's all I have to do? Take a shower?" Dani's anxiety dissipated.

"Yup!" Samantha smiled again. "I'll finish the summoning circle by the time you're done and…"

"And summon me up a new boyfriend?" She tried to make her smile more enthusiasm-flavored, but knew it whispered more of a simmering tolerance. She just hoped Sam didn't notice.

"Not exactly," she said. "I'll be summoning a wellness spirit. Spirits don't know about love and sex; they are sexless, but know we have love and sex and kind of understand what it does to us when something goes wrong. They're curious. But it'll feel your sad and just take it away, all that mopiness, poof! Gone!" She held her book up, glancing over the pages and pointing to the tabletop. "This one means you're sad by a personal tragedy." Sam's open hand hovered above a twisted group of sea salt lines inside the larger circle.

"It's hardly a tragedy. It's just a break…"

"Personal. Tragedy," Sam said, interrupting Dani midsentence.

Dani rolled her eyes. "Fine."

Samantha worked her way around the table. Holding the book sideways she looked at the page and jabbed toward the table with one finger. "This is the invitation rune. I'm opening a portal between the physical and spiritual realms."

"Is that what it says in your book?" Dani's eyebrow arched with her question.

"Yes. That's what it says in my book. Now shush." Samantha moved to the next picture on the table, once again turning the book until now it was upside down in her hand. "This one asks for help getting rid of your issues." Twisting her book a final quarter turn to the left, she glanced from the page to the table, to the page and back to the table again, pushing salt into the fine details of the last rune. "This calls the spirit by name, crt…vw…rtng." Her forehead wrinkled as she stumbled through reading the name. "Crtvwrtng." Looking up, she said, "He's one of the nice ones that help people."

"One of the nice ones?" Dani asked. "Is that what it says in…"

"Yes! That's what it says in my book." Samantha poked and pushed the name rune a few more times before placing the book on a shelf festooned with dangling pentagrams and dreamcatchers. "Now go take a shower so you can meet…" She paused. "Cr… tvwrt… ng."

* * *

The bathroom door remained open so Samantha could direct things without leaving her conjuring circle. The table was just visible from the shower if Dani peeked around the curtain, and Sam stood with her face in the book, her lips silently working through whatever incantation she'd picked. Dani…she just enjoyed the solitude.

Water, warm and revitalizing, splashed over her face and sluiced down the length of her body. This had to be the best part of the spell. Dani shut her eyes and pulled her hair back in the spray, feeling the warmth saturating the length of it. She turned in the shower, letting the water stroke her skin while steamy air swirled about in a warm and soothing embrace. Nothing but magic about the way a shower feels.

"You know what, Sam?" Dani called from the bathroom. "If nothing else, a long shower using someone else's hot water already feels even better." Dani expected something pithy in return, but Samantha didn't respond. She pulled the curtain back and glanced into the living room. "Are you still out there?"

Samantha stood silently, leaning over her salt-circled table top. She held the book close to her face while her fingertip traced lines through the crystals. Her lips formed words too quietly to be heard. Candles flickered, amorphous shadows tossed about the walls.

Dani let her thoughts relax and wander. The stream kneaded her, like a personal masseuse, the rivulets running from her back to her bottom and down her legs with lines of caressing fingertips, the water as blithe as feathers. *So nice*, she thought. *So very nice.*

Fluid sensations coiled around her thighs and seemed to run up her leg, a hallucination all the more sensuous in its defiance of gravity. A thousand tiny fingers massaged towards her core, reawakening a yearning, kneading away the emptiness of losing Edward, remembering Eddie. They'd met the first week she came to Sin City and started her job, her a waitress and Eddie a dealer. His hands…

Dani's fingers sought their way to her mound, guiding the flow of warm waters. The pulsing tide lifted her, matching the rhythm of the shower with the thumping beat of her heart, and a swelling deep in her belly. He'd touched her this way. He'd made her feel these things.

"Dani."

She started at her name. Close to her ear, a whisper, both clear and barely there.

She spun, pulled back the shower curtain. "Eddie?" Alone in the bathroom, she'd lost her calm and felt herself getting angry. "Eddie!" she called toward the door but got no answer. Raising her voice, she yelled, "God dammit, Sam. You better not have called Ed over here."

Samantha didn't respond. She remained standing by the table staring into her book, rocking in place. Dani glared, waited a beat for an answer before muttering "I mean it" to herself and yanking the shower curtain closed.

And now she was thinking about Eddie again. So much for feeling better. Dammit, Eddie, what happened? "No, know what, Eddie? Fuck you." She whispered her own incantation.

Dani shook her head, clearing away stress as best she could. Turning up the heat just a smidge, she sighed as the shower pulsed with increased vigor against her skin. Her neck and shoulders loosened, the strain in her back washed out. She'd taken a lot of showers with her ex. The starts of many busy days started with him under the warmth and steam...

"Dammit," she whispered. "I thought this was supposed to wash away all my sad," she said to Sam but not loud enough to really be heard. Again, she peeked around the curtain, to where Sam leaned forward gripping the table's edge. She'd made a mess of her little salt circle.

Dani rolled her eyes and tugged the curtain closed again. Lifting her hair, she let the spray hit the back of her neck. Water ran down her back and past her buttocks in long streams like fingertips tracing from shoulders to thighs. Light enough to be imagination, the water stroked her skin, kneading her body with a growing confidence. Heavier pressure drew the streams into larger torrents, like tentacles twisting around her waist, winding up through her thighs.

Her eyes snapped open. The sensations were gone but the images remained. Dani's chest heaved. Tingling, centered in her belly, remained. She had allowed herself to let go a little, to relax a little. When next she closed her eyes again, releasing herself to wherever the feeling flooded in from, something solid encircled her waist. Arms, strong and heavily tattooed, Eddie's, held her in an embrace she remembered and missed.

Even in her anger, burning still, Dani felt herself where Eddie would have, just as he had done. She let the illusionary arms around her body command her, the chest she imagined pressed against her shoulders. The warm, streaming water gushed down her body in long fingers running through her sex until her pussy throbbed for Eddie. Her fingers slid through the folds for her and for the memory of him.

A whisper, near her ear, where none should be, startled her again.

"Dani."

A loud crash from the living room broke the chimera. She was alone again.

"Sam? Are you okay?" Dani called. When there was no response, she pulled back the curtain. The table lay on its side. All of Samantha's pretty salt drawings spilled over the carpet. Sam was not there. "Samantha?"

Dani moved to turn off the faucet. The curtain drew back and Samantha peered at Dani for a long moment. Her face blank, her gaze empty, empty and yet…

"Sam, what are you doing?" Dani asked as her friend pushed through the curtain and into the spray. They were close, and had seen each other naked before, but Dani's face was still flushed from her daydream and Samantha climbing into the shower unannounced was quite unwelcome. Then she saw it.

"What the fuck is that?" Dani asked, pointing at a cock hanging between Samantha's legs. Heavy and aflush, it swung freely as she stepped over the tub wall to where water began streaming along the length of it. Rows of what appeared to be 1000 tiny legs sprouted from root to lumpy head in quivering spirals coiling from base to cap. It hung there like a fat coil of centipedes.

Samantha grinned, her irises drawn back to narrow rings encircling pupils painfully dilated, pupils simultaneously malevolent and open into a terrifying emptiness. She had an open cut on the side of her head. Blood washed out of her hair under the spray, crimson to pink to gone.

Bewildered and quivering in spite of the water's heat, Dani froze. With nowhere to go in the confines of the shower, and confusion directing her actions, she blurted, "What are you doing with that?" She snatched at the cock hanging from Samantha's crotch.

Plump, and warm, and swelling in her grip, the cock was attached to Samantha, even a part of Samantha. It grew in Dani's fingers, pumping fatter with a heartbeat, writhing like a snake. The terrible rows of tiny legs frenetically clawed into her palm. Paralyzed, she couldn't let it go. She could only look again toward those terrible eyes.

Samantha's neck arched back, eyelids drooping, mouth agape. A moan rasped from her yawing lips, bubbling through water collecting in her throat. Leaning in, Samantha croaked, "You asked to forget your problems, I'm here to take care of your little Eddie problem." Samantha looked down to where Dani still gripped the swollen cock. "You like my surprise, I see." A grin stretched mirthlessly over her teeth.

Dani pulled her hand away as if suddenly burned. In scrambling retreat, she tore at the shower curtain. Slipping on the wet tub in her panic to escape, she stumbled to hands and knees. Seized high on both arms, Dani fell back, yanked roughly into Samantha's embrace. Samantha's grip dug hard into her flesh, squeezing until Dani's fingers prickled.

"Ready for me to take care of your problem?" Samantha's mouth croaked close to Dani's ear. Her voice stabbed like a visceral shot through Dani's heart.

No words formed, no scream escaped her lips, only gurgling fear weakly sputtered. She grew limp like a still living mouse dangling from the jaws of a feral cat.

Fingers clamped around the back of her neck shoved her forward, banging her head against the slick tiled stall. Samantha pushed until Dani's head turned and her cheek pressed into the wall. A heat spiked against her skin, hotter than the water.

Eddie's voice emanated from Sam's mouth. "I missed you, sugar," the grotesque partnership of Sam and Eddie said. "I want you to feel better. Don't you want to feel better?"

Dani's eyes swiveled painfully until they were looking over her shoulder into Samantha's grinning face. "Only one way for all of us to get there," Eddie's voice said from Samantha's lips. "Ready?"

The word dragged out into a growl as Samantha pressed against Dani. Samantha's fingers vised into Dani's hip, pulling her back and forcing her over. Dani clawed for balance, her fingers slipping over the wet tiles. The grip was Eddie's and for a moment she arched her back for him, like a cat in uncontrollable heat. But then those 1000 tiny legs striping that cock scrabbled against the soft skin between her thighs.

"Samantha! Sam! Don't, please…" Dani cried out. Scrambling for purchase, she tried to pull away, slipping.

She screamed with the invasion. Samantha's body pressed close against Dani until that penis snugged in, and the 1000 tiny legs set themselves firmly inside. The deeper it climbed, the firmer it set.

A hard-driven wedge of pain exploded outward from Dani's hips, rattling along her spine, torqueing the bones of her arms and legs. Her face beat against the wall for an eternity until a final wordless howl emanated from Samantha. When Samantha bellowed, she pulled away. The cock remained inside, those legs still pulling it deeper, twisting higher into Dani's abdomen.

The gripping hands at Dani's neck and thigh released. She slipped to the floor, crying soundlessly. Managing to turn herself over, Dani looked up at Samantha, the old Samantha.

"Dani…" Samantha whimpered. Her expression faded into a terrible absence before her body shriveled to dust, and pummeled by water, collected into a grey paste swirling down the drain.

Dani lay crumpled on her back. Her chest heaved, gasping for air and shivering in spite of the hot water spray. Dull waves of doubt washed over her. Questioning what she could not have seen. Even as dirty rivulets

211

drained away the piled ash where Samantha had been, until no trace remained, until only self-doubt that anything of the kind had ever happened took its place.

Seeking some reassurance, some confirmation of hallucination, Dani tried to call out, managing only a weakened cry. "Samantha? Sam?" Nothing returned but the hiss of the shower. Through the doorway, the table remained on its side, the floor with the scattered mess strewn from its fall. "Samantha?"

Deep in her belly a tickle spread, to a tugging, to a flame. Dani leaned forward, clutching at herself with both arms. Heat collected into a ball travelling down her spine and searing the insides of her hips. The heat writhed and pressed outward until, like a fast-growing mushroom, something unfurled between her legs. When finally, it hung with an unfamiliar weight between her thighs, Dani recoiled.

As the cock sprouting from her crotch quivered, a predatory shadow engulfed her inner spark. Darkness, the same terrible emptiness she'd glimpsed in Samantha's eyes, enfolded her, stifling and suffocating until an icy oblivion rushed in. Unable even to sob, her final flickers of awareness were of her body moving under another's will, stretching, expressing glee in the same rasping laughter she'd heard from Samantha's tortured lips. In a final colossal effort before she was extinguished, she croaked, "Eddie."

* * *

"Dani," he said, gesturing toward the open door of his convertible.

The night remained young. Dani had not made

him work too hard, too much impatience for that. Things would be more entertaining with fewer drinks anyway, body and mind.

She took his hand and sat on the edge of the car seat, turning forward with her knees held together. "Thank you."

He swung the door shut and leaned over the open car, leering, with a triumphant grin. "Glad you decided to talk to me, babe," he said.

While he moved around the car to the driver's side, Dani reached under her skirt and adjusted things. Her dress was very short. No need to give anything away just yet.

He slid behind the wheel and brought the car rumbling to life. Dash lights tinted his face in shine and shadow. "Back to my new place," he said. "We'll have a drink and … whatever we want."

"Well, I know what I want," Dani said. Her hand stroked his leg, leaving little in question. "And I have a surprise for you, too."

"Oh, baby, I do love surprises." His tires squealed as they pulled out into traffic and accelerated toward Eddie's place.

"Just one thing, when we get to your place, take a shower for me?" Her fingers massaged at his thigh.

Eddie flashed his teeth, side-glancing with the glow of passing traffic lights streaming over his face. "You gonna get in with me, baby?"

Dani's mouth chortled. "Oh, promise I'll get in, Eddie. Right before you're done."

The Grave of Lilith
Harry F. Rey

Jerusalem, 1982

We were meeting for our third date, Ricard and I, but
it had been over a month since we'd first met. Richard
was an archaeologist; dashing and young. Boston born
and educated, he managed to retain the look of a
British Empire builder melded with a Harvard accent
and gorgeous blond locks. He had the energy of a
prize-winning bull who'd just vanquished yet another
matador. My good friend Lilly at Yale had insisted I
become friends with Richard the moment she heard I'd
be spending a semester in Jerusalem as part of my
doctorate in biblical archaeology. She'd done the same
thing the previous year, and I could never quite shake
the feeling she'd done Richard, too. My nickname for
her was Lilith, Whore of New Haven, after all.

Richard's sexuality aside, our first date had ended
rather successfully. That is to say, in my small rented
room in the Hebrew University dorms in the Mount
Scopus area of the city, a bit of West Jerusalem nestled
in the East. We'd drunkenly ravished one another till the
early morning call to prayer could be heard across the
gold-stoned rooftops. Although in the sleepy light or

morning the lovemaking had been a bit awkward. I'd felt rather inadequate to Richard by comparison, bowled over by his prowess, and a little afraid to be honest of his forearm-sized cock swinging from his body that could have been sculpted by an old Italian master. "Ready for it?" He'd asked with a smirk from the doorframe of my little washroom. There was little I could do but turn over and moan into the pillow. I had to beg him to stop after about 30 seconds, less someone think a murder was being committed. But he seemed satisfied enough to finish off in my mouth then promptly fall asleep.

We'd chalked that one down to a bit too much wine and Arak, a local aniseed liquor that seemed to flow like water, since it accompanied every order one made at a cafe or restaurant here. So we tried once again, our second date this time taking place at a hummus restaurant just off the Via Dolorosa, that famous road to Golgotha Christ had dragged a cross up on his journey to crucifixion. As Richard had ordered us extra Pita breads with almost native-sounding Hebrew, I glanced behind him into that street of legend, imagining Jesus trotting up it and giving me a wink and a nod. We did not sleep together that day.

After that, Richard went quiet for a week. I even wrote to Lilly to tell her the whole set up had been a mistake, and I would focus my attention solely on my studies of biblical Hebrew, and failing that, pursuing one or two of the local boys who sold falafel outside the Jaffa Gate.

But then a postcard turned up in my letterbox in the dormitory hall. It had no address, so must have been hand delivered, and quite early, too, as I found it at 7:30 in the morning.

I ravished Richard's long, drawn out scrawl, reading it while I clutched my paper cup of coffee and morning cigarette as I waited for the first class to begin. His leisurely handwriting could not be more different from the curt, sharp bursts of energy he spoke in. It simply added another layer to this already fascinating man, one I'd just about given up hope on.

Dearest Jonathan. I do apologize for the lack of correspondence. I was taken quite suddenly across the Jordan due to a rather large piece of rock that needed my immediate attention. I do hope to see you this evening at the below address, at sunset. I have something rather exciting to tell you.

All my love,
Richard.

I learned nothing that day. Absolutely nothing. The lecturer could have been speaking in tongues for all I cared. Richard wanted to see me, and more than that, tell me something exciting. There was no way in hell I'd make the same mistake as last time. So I skipped class after lunch and spent the afternoon preparing myself to meet Richard. I'd show this bull of a man I was a worthy ride.

* * *

I waited at Amir's Cafe just inside the Old City walls by the Jaffa Gate, sitting alone at a table outside and watching the sun set over the Tower of David with a cup of thick Turkish coffee.

"You do know it's not really *David's* Tower, don't you?"

"Richard!" I jumped up and he clasped me in a strong handshake and a thick smile. Despite him being a shade over 30, he dressed exceedingly well, wearing a crisp white shirt, beige slacks and well-worn hiking boots. What surprised me however was the red silk ascot tucked under his open collar. And he wore the ascot entirely without irony, I assumed, Richard not seemingly one for irony. The most remarkable thing was that I could simply not imagine the outfit working without it.

Perhaps if this had been Connecticut, in the local coffee-cum-bookshop where I generally took my dates, I would have turned and ran a country mile at the sight of such attire. But given this was Israel in 1982, and the other fellows on the street were Arabs in flowing robes and headscarves or Ultra-Orthodox Jews in heavy black coats and black hats. The site of a pristine white shirt and, yes, an unironic ascot, was welcome.

"Jonathan, don't tell me you're drinking coffee at this hour without a hookah pipe?"

Oh, and he had the number one quality in men that turns me on, he seemed to be attracted to me.

"I… I'm sorry?"

Richard let out a wailing laugh, smacked me on the shoulder and we sat down, side by side at the table, facing the tower. He called over the cafe owner, presumably Amir, a grey-haired Arab man with an impressive brush of a moustache who trundled out an elaborate looking hookah pipe. As he lit the burner with a match and pushed the coal around with bare, calloused thumbs, Richard fired out a few lines of rusty-sounding Arabic. He must have tickled the man in the right way, because after a moment of sternness, his grey moustache quivered and he let out a long, smoky laugh, clapping Richard on the back and leaving one pipe between us, rather intimately so.

"What was that?" I asked in earnest as Richard took a deep suck on the pipe, the water inside the bulbous vase bubbling away as he drew a deep breath in.

"Nothing much." He huffed out smoke like an exhausted dragon and handed me the pipe. "I may have ordered us 50 more Turkish coffees, though." He bellowed out another tremendous laugh. Smoke poured from my nostrils as I choked out a giggle

"So we can be up all night." I offered with a delicate smile.

"Come now," Richard said softly, leaning over the arm of his chair and openly stroking a finger down my smooth-shaven cheek. A shock of electricity seized my body from his public touch and disarming smile. I could not want this man more. "I've something much more interesting than *shagging* to discuss."

A pit of embarrassment opened inside me. Without a doubt my cheeks turned blood-red rouge.

"Although," he added, leaning ever closer and giving me a whiff of sweat and musk, "I was rather hoping to stick it in you again, young Jonathan." I erupted into an unspeakable coughing fit that lasted all the way till old grey-mustached Amir brought us more coffee, and a large glass of water out of concern for my wellbeing.

After a time I calmed down, and we sipped our coffee and passed the hookah pipe in a smirk-filled silence. My mind filled with both the pulsating memory of his cock, and my determination to make the most of it this time. I didn't care if I had to swallow all the Tylenol I'd brought. I'd straddle this man and swing on it till the sun rose again.

"It is a beautiful city, isn't it?" he said eventually, and I agreed. Jaffa Gate, the entrance to the Old City of Jerusalem, was all the entertainment anyone needed. Groups of Hasidic Jews dressed like they lived in 18th Century Poland milled around, navigating their way through the maze of streets to their holy Western Wall. Arab traders selling carpets and chess sets alternated between yelling at tourists and each other. Christian pilgrims were stewarded around by tour guides in shorts and sandals, strapped into microphone packs as if they were performers on a great, stony stage. Armenians, Greek Orthodox, Catholics and more all passed back and forth in front of our table, as if we sat on the crossroads of history itself.

"A port city on the shore of eternity." I said, eyeing up a handsome young man rolling a cigarette near our table.

"What is?"

"Jerusalem."

"Ah." Richard said, not seeming to get the poetic reference and skipping ahead to what he wanted to say. "Come up to the north with me." Richard said. I took my eyes off the young Jewish man, whose dark skin and long sidelocks seemed like beauty from another time, and passed the hookah pipe back.

"When?" I said, blowing out a long bellow of smoke.

"Tomorrow morning. I want to dig something up."

The smile across Richards face enchanted me. If we hadn't been in the holiest city in the world I probably would have kissed him.

"I'm assuming, or hoping, someone gave you permission?"

"Yes. Well the Antiquities Authority was never the problem, they don't give a damn about all that superstitious mumbo-jumbo." The cheeks of his thin, elegant face sucked in as he smoked the hookah. "It was the Rabbinate blocking the dig all this time. But they've finally lifted their ban."

"The Rabbinate?" I asked, confused as to why the rabbis who worked for the Israeli Government would object to an archaeological excavation, or how they even could.

"They've been blocking this dig ever since Israel took the Golan in '67." He took a sip of his coffee and gazed into the early evening bustle. "Apparently the rabbis wouldn't even give their blessing to soldiers occupying the site. Anyway, I'm going up there tomorrow to scope out the dig—we can be there and back in a day. I'd thought you'd like to come."

"I mean I'd love to, of course." The thought of going off an adventure with this man, and not least, one that directly involved my field of study was beyond a bike-shaped present under the Christmas tree. Yet my lips pursed into confusion as if I'd missed out on an important detail. "Wait, what mumbo-jumbo are you talking about?"

"*Ayin Harah,*" he said in Hebrew, taking a slurp of coffee.

"The evil eye?" I responded with a cocked eyebrow and a hint of snark.

Richard sighed. "Do you believe in God?" He asked me in a tone one might invoke to deliver fatal news. I gripped the intricately detailed handle of the hookah pipe, surprised by the question.

"I'm not really sure how to answer that."

"Come on," he jutted his hand out, impatient for an answer. "You're here amongst this crowd, studying all this biblical nonsense. It's a simple question, Jonathan."

"I'm studying biblical archaeology." I said quietly. "So I know that Tower over there was not built by David, of course, but by Suleiman the Magnificent. Theology is not my area of study."

"Christ, Jonathan. Don't be so damn waspy about it."

"Well why do you care what I believe in? You're the one who called it mumbo-jumbo."

He turned to me with a flash of something in his eyes, something that looked like fear. His face had aged a decade with one look. Suddenly I did not recognize him one little bit.

"Because fear of God begets respect. And I didn't call it mumbo-jumbo. The fools at the Israel Antiquities Authority did."

"So, do you believe in God? Or this *Ayin Harrah* or whatever the dig site is cursed with?"

"I'm an archaeologist, of course I believe in things I cannot see. That's why we have to dig."

"I see." I took a long draw of the pipe. Surprisingly, the flash of anger across his face had turned me on. Now I didn't want to gently lower myself onto his erect cock and gyrate my hips up and down it. I wanted him to smack my body against the wall as he fucked the living hell out of me till I forgot my very name.

"You've heard of the *Shedim*?" he asked. I shook my head. "These are dark ones, destructive creatures who came into existence on the eve of the very last day of creation, sunset on the Sixth Day." He paused, glancing up at the sky which had turned a magnificent

222

fuchsia. "These are demons, Jonathan. Serpent-like demons with human forms and wings who abduct children from their cradles and sacrifice their tiny bodies, cracking skulls over bare rocks on the altar of the evil mistress they serve."

"Mistress?" I asked, and took a final sip of coffee, now cold.

"Lilith."

I snorted in a horribly unflattering way, cupping my hand under my mouth to stop the coffee dripping out. Richard glared at me.

"Sorry," I said, composing myself. "It's just…I know a girl, back at Yale. She introduced us, actually. I mean, she knows you." I searched his face for some sign of recognition. "I call her Lilith, you know, because she's a bit of a slut." I felt instantly disgusted with myself for saying that last part, like the slur was childish gossip, or backtalking about an ex when Richard would be inside me this night, and not her.

"Of course you know a girl like that, you're a homosexual." Richard said with a confident, matter of fact-ness that caused me to cock my head in surprise.

"And what are you?"

"It doesn't matter. But homosexuals are the henchmen of Lilith, according to the Jewish mystics."

"Oh, are we now?" I wasn't sure if I was meant to be offended, but I couldn't necessarily disagree with his statement.

"Yes. And it's why the rabbis are letting us dig there. Just us, in fact."

"What are we digging up?" I said, suddenly aware I'd made this whole adventure a *we* without even knowing what we were setting out to do.

Richard stood, stretching his arms out and yawning. "Come on then, let's get some dinner in us and then straight off to bed. I want to come at least twice before we sleep. We're setting off before sunrise, after all." He flicked out a few notes from his money clip from the table and set off to the Gate.

"Wait," I jumped up from the table and set off after him through the evening crowd as night began to descend on the city. I also wanted him to come at least twice, but I had to catch him first. "Richard!"

He threw an arm around my shoulders with a wide, tourist guide grin. "Look at these." He said, pointing to the metal *mezzuzah* covers bolted to the wall of the Jaffa Gate as we passed by. "They're made of Syrian artillery shells. Did you know?"

"Richard, what are we digging up? What could possibly be so full of evil eye in the Golan that only a couple of homosexuals would be allowed to get into, for goodness sake."

He cocked an eye at me. Most likely at the insinuation he was homosexual.

"I'm a man of the world, Jonathan. We're going to find the grave of Lilith. First wife of Adam; the other woman, as Eve might say. Mistress of the *Shedim,* friend of the homosexual."

Richard danced around the walkway along the Old City wall, enticing me to come hither. I could not say I was not enticed. I could not say his *man of the world* ways were not ones I wished to follow. I could not say what fate would befall us. He danced through the street towards my place, whistling, blond hair blowing in the evening breeze. He wore the easy confidence of a man setting out on a great adventure so well, and a man about to get laid.

* * *

We set off before sunrise in a borrowed Jeep. Richard full of energy, jabbering away as we set off into the Jordan Valley on the journey north to the Golan. I was more enchanted by the music from the Arabic radio station we picked up, the throaty, emotional wail of the male singer sounding almost like an opera. I couldn't understand the words, but the music drew more menacing as we breezed past a military checkpoint. The soldiers only focused on those going south, to Jerusalem. They didn't care for us going north, into the unknown. The idea was just to visit the site for the proposed excavation, take a few pictures, and we would be back in Jerusalem by midnight. As we drove further north, the green rocky valleys dotted with wandering sheep grew ever darker from the creep of clouds.

"A storm's coming," I said.

"Nonsense. Light rain, if anything."

Richard dismissed my worries, but he couldn't soothe the funny feeling growing in the pit of my stomach. I tried to write it off as spill over from the previous nights' activities.

I drifted into an uncomfortable sleep, pressed up against the passenger window with a bag of dusty digging tools squishing my legs together. The biblical landscape, spectacular with its ancient rocks and shepherd huts, suddenly uninteresting to me, I dreamed the strangest of dreams: of detachment. Of quite suddenly, sharply, immediately, having everything I ever loved or wanted locked away.

I awoke to the slam of a car door. We stopped at

the end of a gravel road. Beyond us, the field leading to a high, rocky hill was fenced off with barbed wire and yellow signs warning of landmines. I scratched the sleep from my eyes and looked around the silent, still landscape. The clouds had broken to a patchwork across a sunny sky. A nice day for a hike. I turned to the driver's side and saw Richard standing outside with a group of soldiers; a dozen or more Israeli teenagers in green fatigues and heavy weaponry.

He stood with his back to me as they watched him point and flail his arms across the hill, trying to convince them we had permission to get over to the other side, and into the Golan. I wondered for a moment if his life wasn't in fact a total fantasy. Perhaps he was some con man or killer, sent to sacrifice me on an ancient altar buried in the hills. I dismissed the idea from my mind, but not the uneasy feeling it left me.

Richard walked back to the jeep, rocks crunching under his boots, hands on his slim hips and sunglasses holding his billowing hair back. I jumped out of the Jeep, keen to stretch my legs, just in case I might need to run away.

"They'll let us go—"

"Thank God."

"—but only with their escort." Richard sighed, and gazed over the rolling green hills, eerily quiet for such a contested piece of land. He seemed crestfallen.

"That's not such a big deal, is it?" I said, trying to get him to see the positives. "At least they're letting us up."

Richard grabbed his camera from the car and I threw on a backpack with some water and peanuts inside. The soldiers seemed more amused by our presence than anything else. Days of guard duty on a far-off hill with only cigarettes for company must get boring. Five of them crossed over the fence with us and we walked single file along a barely visible path cut across the open field towards the hill.

Once there, we began our ascent through an untrodden gap nestled between the edges of overgrown land on either side. Only a thin strip of cloudy grey sky was visible above us for the most part.

The hill became steeper, and I struggled a bit, forgetting about trying to keep my hands or my clothes free of mud. Richard kicked down rocks and dirt as he raced ahead. At one point I was about to call out to him to slow down, but as I did the mud from his boot splattered my face. I heard a laugh from the soldier behind me.

The path grew narrower, the sight of darkness crept in. I was breathing heavily, the damp stench of sweat clinging to me. "Ouch," I called out. Something had scratched my leg, deep and hard, and still held me in its grip.

"Are you all right?" Richard asked, looking back at me for the first time on our hike. I saw my trouser leg caught in a rusty barbed wire claw from a partially hidden fence. Our little party halted, two of the soldiers lit a cigarette, clearly this meant time for a break.

The wire had ripped through the material and left a gash in my leg. I untangled myself, and saw my muddy hand and fingertips doused in fresh, red blood. Richard muttered to himself and pulled out a handkerchief from his pocket, which he passed down to me.

One of the soldiers displayed a little concern and handed me his canteen. Rolling up my trouser leg, I washed away the blood and tied the handkerchief tight. Then my eye followed the rest of the barbed wire fence up the path, past Richard and further up the hill. It had presumably been following our path from when we started, and I noticed the rusted yellow and red sign hanging there: 'Danger. Mines'.

"Richard, is this a minefield?"

"Well, over there is," he said, pointing to our left, "and I suppose over here too," now pointing to our right, where I suddenly saw another barbed wire fence, hemming us in to this little narrow path between the rocks.

"And how exactly do we know this part is safe?"

He looked down at me, grinning, and held out his hand to pull me up and get us back on our way.

"Whoever put the fence up in the first place obviously found the right path."

That didn't make me feel any safer, and as we continued on our way I endeavored to only step in Richard's muddy footprints.

Eventually we made it to the top; finally a breath of open air and a blast of wind. We were at a high point of the Golan Heights, at the corner of Syria and Lebanon. What looked like pristine rolling green hills were really fenced off minefields. The clouds we had been seeing all day were now closer. The scene looked set for a summer storm.

Richard consulted the map. "It's not too far," he said to me, and called out in Hebrew to the soldiers taking another break. The one in charge looked a bit distressed.

"Okay, we go quickly," he said in heavily accented English. The air felt too still for a warzone. The banter our soldier companions had engaged in before had dropped away to silence; a pregnant one, as we set off once again. The path led us around the edge of the mountain. My right hand was tracing along the edge of the rock wall for support, as to my left there was nothing but the sheer cliff, and an endless below.

Caught up in the view, my foot smacked what I thought was a hard rock, but I looked down and saw the unmistakable shape of a rusted red mortar shell.

"Holy shit." I jumped back, my body tensing up, waiting for an explosion. Richard looked back and shrugged, but one of the soldiers ran forward, shouting and pushing me out of the way. I felt the hand of something horrible reach inside my chest and grab onto my heart. The other three ran over and they stood around, seemingly arguing about the shell. Richard nodded along.

"It's old," he said to me, placing a supposedly reassuring hand on my shoulder, "probably from '73." He promptly walked off. I didn't know what to make of this brush with death.

The place was like a field of shells, some dead, some just waiting to explode. There had been tension in the area for months; Israeli jets bombing targets in across the border in response to sporadic rocket fire from the other side. How Richard would be able to conduct an archaeological dig under such circumstances I had no idea.

We carried on along the pathway, the plateau now just about visible. Up here it was desolate and dry, clumps of prickly grass and rocks reaching out to catch the careless walker. I got the distinct feeling few people had ventured to this hill in many years; it reminded me of an overgrown Civil War graveyard I used to visit in Tennessee.

Suddenly, the cliff disappeared behind us and we turned into open grassy land that sloped downwards, towards a shallow valley. A simple but ferocious looking fence crossed the land at the bottom of the valley. The new border. We faced down to no-man's land. A wind cut across the hill, bringing fear with it. I assumed it was a fear of more mines.

Richard ran forward like a child towards Christmas, to a ridge in the ground. The soldiers who lagged behind seemed both thoroughly bored and seriously concerned in equal measure. I half-jogged forward to greet him.

The ridge we stood on formed the upper lip of a cave—there was a drop to get down to the entrance. Richard stood with his hands on his hips, gazing down into the valley with the broadest smile. I thought he was figuring out how to get down to the cave mouth, but his eyes were drawn a bit further away, about 20 meters to the left, to a breath-taking sight. A circle of small, stumpy stones sat on the hillside just outside of the cave. It had clearly been made by man. Or at least I hoped by man.

"I found it," he said, beaming and breathless.

"Are you sure this is it?" I said, panting as well. "There are no stone circles in Jewish tradition. Or even Assyrian. What can it be?"

"The grave of Lilith."

I sniggered. I hadn't really assumed he was serious.

"It wasn't easy," Richard said, unprompted. "But

at least four separate sources place her grave right here, on the top of this hill."

"Sources?"

"Two Kabbalistic texts which back up some legends I came across while leafing through the Dead Sea Scrolls.

"Okay," I said, counting off three, "what's the fourth?"

Richard turned to face me, his eyes a deep ocean of sincerity. "From a vision." Then he leapt down off the ridge, landed with a thud on the ground and darted over to the stones.

I followed him, more carefully climbing down the side of the cave mouth, desperate to talk to him more. As I approached Richard and the stones, I glanced back at the cave's mouth. It seemed to swirl in darkness, the opening almost like a mouth devoid of teeth—a gash in the ground which looked as artificial as the stone circle in front of us or the barbed wire fence 100 meters down the hill.

I wanted to run from it, to turn and flee back where we came. I saw the soldiers standing further up, looking down on us, their weapons in hand. They did not want to approach. Despite the pleasant breeze and rolling green countryside that could have been Appalachia, I did not want to be here either. I walked farther down the hill towards Richard, but sideways. Horrified at the idea of turning my back on the cave mouth. I lifted my arms for balance as I edged towards Richard and the stone circle, suddenly conscious I might be making myself a target for a sniper's bullet from the convex of Syria and Lebanon at the bottom of the valley.

231

"Do you just want to take a few pictures and go?" I asked him, my unfounded fear making me feel slightly ashamed. He didn't pay me any attention. Instead, he was crouched over one of the stones, inside the circle.

"Jonathan, come over here," he called, pulling clumps of grass from around the knee-high rock. My stomach rolled down the hill as I swallowed to a tightening throat.

The rocks were placed in the ground at even intervals, about a foot apart. I searched my memory, scanning every lecture and ancient history book I'd read, trying to think of which culture would bury their dead in stone circles.

"Does this look like Hebrew to you?" He asked me, running his fingers along the stone's markings. I took a breath and stepped inside the circle to take a better look. The moment I did, everything went a few shades darker, like someone had pulled a blind across the sun. Even Richard looked up. The sun had disappeared behind a menacing black storm cloud from the east. I crouched down, and a wind picked up around my ears. I reached a hand out to Richard's knee to steady myself, ignore the wicked weather around us, and focus on the markings so we could get the hell away.

His hand was shaking. I looked at his eyes, but they were intently focused on the stone. Either that, they were avoiding the obvious warning signs that nature, or God, was sending.

"It doesn't look like it." I offered, focusing on it like a laser beam. I reached out to touch it too, my hand steady, but only heaven knew how. As soon as I touched the rock, my hand began to quiver like Richard's. It was freezing, like ice. Only moments ago, it had been basking in the Middle Eastern sunshine.

"I think it's cuneiform. Proto-Sumerian possibly," I said, pulling the backpack off my shoulder. I searched through it for my little notebook like a medic attending to a fatal injury. My hands shaking, and growing ever colder, I flicked to the back of the book and the crudely drawn shapes with their rough translation written beside.

Richard looked over my shoulder at it, tracing the shapes on the rock. I could see his hands had turned red from the cold, and his face had gone white.

"Hello!" The leader of the soldiers called down to us from the ridge. "We must to go."

"Just a minute!" Richard yelled back. I glanced up at them and wished I hadn't. Their guns were pointed in our direction. Perhaps not at us, but at whatever we might disturb.

"On, or in, this land. Or place..." I read out, holding the notebook against the rock for reference, "...rests, or lives..." My words trailed off.

"Unspeakable evil." Richard finished the sentence.

"Or unspeakable death." I added, for accuracy's sake.

A thumping noise erupted from the ground, vibrations buzzing up our legs. I stood and turned quickly to see the soldiers running down the hill, causing the ground to rumble.

"*Ruach ra'ah!*" One yelled, the only female of the group. She pointed her weapon at the sky. The dark clouds that had been gathering around us all day were now here, the heavens were ready to open. The wind became fiercer, billowing across the open ground and loudly proclaiming the coming storm.

The soldiers stopped at the circle's edge, fanning around and crouching, pointing their weapons into the distance.

"What did she say?" I asked Richard, suddenly noticing how difficult it was to move my frozen lips. "What's going on?"

"Evil wind." He translated.

I felt trapped inside the circle, with nowhere to turn. This was indeed a place of unspeakable evil.

I wanted to grab onto Richard, to pull him down into the grass. But he was frozen in his spot, too. His eyes were trained behind me, to the cave.

"Richard." I whispered. "We need to move."

I wanted to grab him. To yank him out of whatever stupendous slumber had taken hold of him. Grave of Lilith or not, we had to move. The commander of the soldiers yelled something out, and they sank to the ground, weapons ready. The clouds crashed into thunder. A rumble cut through the sky. A deep, roaring sound boomed from the heavens themselves. An angel of war, or death. No, two fighter jets.

Their sound-barrier breaking boom yawned into a long, low wail, a ghoulish shriek that started somewhere in the distance and rumbled through the darkened sky to reach us. Not the spirit of Lilith, but an air-raid siren yelling its warning. Louder then softer, louder then softer. War approaching.

"*Zuz!* Move!" The commander screamed at us.

All of a sudden Richard snapped back to life. His face turned from cocaine white to ruddy red. His eyes flamed into life.

"Quick," Richard yelled, "in here." The distant sound of the siren carried across on the wind. He pulled me out of the circle. Then the heavens opened. Buckets of rain fell from the sky without so much as a drop or precursory drizzle. I don't know why, but with Richard's hand gripped tightly around my arm, I could only think of him last night, moving inside me and finishing without warning, like the rain falling from the sky. He yanked at me so much it hurt. There was no choice but to go inside the cave.

* * *

For over an hour we'd waited inside the cave's mouth, big enough for us both to stand side by side without going in any further. That was fine by me. The soldiers had dispersed quite quickly after the first flurry of activity. The commander had called to us to stay put, they would come back for us, then quickly departed. We had not seen anyone since.

"There's a wind." I said, over the steady wail of the air-raid siren, still blaring through the Golan fields. Richard nodded. I wrapped myself against it, unprepared for the chill. But something caught in my mind: the wind did not come face on, from the open sky towards us, but from behind.

"Do you feel that?" I asked, turning towards the darkness and putting my hand out. "There's a wind coming from down here."

Richard turned away from the sound of warplanes

roaring through the sky and held out a hand into the darkness too.

"So it is." He agreed. We exchanged a quiet glance, neither of us wishing to say anything further, or acknowledge whatever fear we may feel. The most immediate thing we needed was shelter from the rain, and from any strafing fighters or missiles that might fly over the border from Lebanon or Syria, not so far away at the bottom of the valley.

"What's that?" I said out loud, looking back to the stone circles down the hill. One of the soldiers, a female one, had returned and was standing in the middle of the circle.

"Maybe she's coming back for us." Richard said. "Hey!" He called out. "We're over here." She didn't turn, yet she stood less than 20 meters away.

"Hey!" I tried, even louder. Despite the rain, the thundering planes, the wind and the siren, there's no way she wouldn't have heard us. The alleged grave of Lilith was not that far.

"Should we go and get her?" I said, turning to Richard. His face had gone powder white blending into the color of the clouds. "Richard?" His eyes widened, and they looked dead past me.

A gunshot cracked out, echoing around the valley and thwacking the sounds of planes and rain into background noise. I spun my head around and half-crouched, instantly thinking we were under attack. But no. I watched the soldier's lifeless body crumple into the heart of the stone circle. Her hands still clasped around the rifle, pointed upwards, to her chin.

"My God. She shot herself? Richard?" I grabbed his body and shook it, but he remained like a statue.

"Richard!" I called out at the decibel of a gunshot. "Did she shoot herself?"

His eyes stayed wide. His expression blank. Raindrops had splattered across his cheek, dampening the hair on the right side of his head. But he'd heard me, and he nodded. That bob of the head, the silent affirmative, contained more terror than I could begin to fathom. Here, this man of the world, fearless as he was forthright, smart as he was thirsty for knowledge, nodded in somber recognition at what he had just witnessed.

I reached out to the slimy edge of the cave for support and tried to make sense of it.

"Maybe," I started. "Maybe—

"Oh for fuck's sake, Jonathan," he screamed out, "she went into the middle of the stone circle and shot a rifle through her jaw!"

I said nothing else. A wave of exhaustion swept me up in its grasp. If I had been holding onto hope of being rescued, that hope now lay crumpled in a circle of stones. I slunk down the wall of the cave, dropping to the muddy ground. I rested my head against the slimy wall, closed my eyes, and resigned myself to whatever fate lay in wait.

* * *

I dreamed of the woman with flaming red hair. I saw her face as clear as Richard's huffing and puffing on top of me last night. I watched her face turn sour as she was cast out from Eden. She stood on the bare brush hill of a world unmade, looking over the thick thorny walls of paradise, as this other woman took

237

hold of her husband. Her only crime was being created in equality with man, to believe she deserved the same as a male. The Gods of Creation hated Lilith because she made man better. She made him see reason, she made him think not just with his cock but his head and his heart.

The Gods put man on earth to suffer. To fight wars and kill each other, not to thrive and prosper. Lilith stood in opposition to the cruel reality of creation. Thus, she was cast out into the barren world, and she took her solace in the world of outcasts. She became Mistress to them; a sultry red-haired goddess who stood for a world that might've been, but never would be.

My eyes opened, and I choked in a breath. The cold returned to my awakened body, the rain continued to pour outside. We'd been joined by the commander of the soldiers, who sat in the middle of the cave's entrance, talking in a low voice with Richard.

As I watched them, still with my back slumped against the cold stone, water dripping onto my head, I thought of all the men Richard represented. Those men of the world, as they had always been throughout the ages. The ones who bristled at any slight on their manhood, who would kill because of it, but who'd just as soon fuck a man when the mood took them.

The wind rushed against my cheeks, not from outside the cave, but again from inside. It swiveled and swerved around us, and it came with the faintest, haunting wail. I knew it was her. I knew my Mistress had returned.

"Jonathan, are you all right?" Richard asked as I stood. A wide, gaping smile slashed across my face.

How could I not be all right? Now I felt alive again. It felt like old times. Serving my Mistress, flying through the mud clay towns of Mesopotamia, stealing babies from cribs and stalking the men who searched into the night.

"Commander," I asked the soldier whose dark eyes now filled with fear. "Are you a homosexual?"

"I do not understand." He spun around to Richard. "What does he say?"

"Jonathan, why don't you sit back down. You're obviously not feeling very well." I heard the notes of anxious fear creep louder with every syllable from his mouth. I threw my head back and laughed. An ancient, epic laugh. Even confronted with death his concern was his masculinity, nothing else. Although that was perhaps a theory still to be tested.

"Strip, commander." I demanded. He made no move except slowly towards his handgun. He took a step back as I did forward. Richard was already flat against the wall.

"Take out your cock, because our friend Richard here is going to suck it."

"Jonathan, you've gone mad. Let me give you water."

"Do it now!" I screamed into infinity. The wind from inside and out whipped up to match the strength of my voice and the heavens themselves thundered. Both their faces collapsed; unable to turn away from what I had become. It was too late for them.

I flicked my eyes and the soldier's handgun flew from his hip holster out into the rain. His horrified face watched it disappear. A click of my fingers and his trousers dropped to the dirty ground, revealing tight white underpants almost see-through from sweat and a flash of shock across his face.

"Suck him." I said again, stepping forward. They heard the change in my voice. No longer meek little Jonathan from stuffy New England, but a powerful, ageless creature who served a terrible Mistress. Their faces finally showed some respect, but they did not move. The commander's bottom lip quivered as if he was about to burst into floods of tears to rival the pounding rain outside. Richard simply stared at me with confused fascination.

"What some men won't do to avoid being thought of as a queer." I muttered to myself. Faster than a human eye could see, my hand shot out to the soldier's balls. Through his underwear I found the heavy sac nestled under a shriveled cock, scared and cold. In one smooth motion I squeezed, twisted, and ripped them from his body.

"Arghh!" He let out a bloodcurdling scream that fell off to a whimper when he saw what I held in my bloody hands. The soldier looked down to a river of blood now flowing from the gaping wound I'd left him.

"Huh." I said, cocking my head to get a better look as he dropped involuntarily to his knees. "I guess the cock came off as well." Sure enough, I held his entire package in my hand, the little brown cock hanging on to the sac by a few sinews of skin. I turned and flung the whole thing deep into the bowels of the cave as the soldier collapsed, face first, into a pool of his own blood.

"That's for her." I told Richard with a smile and stepped over the lifeless body, blood now flowing out of the cave mouth and mixing in the wet grass. A clap of thunderous evil made him shriek out, and he tried to scramble backwards, but there was no back left. He began to mumble sounds with his quivering lips, eyes bloodshot with his nightmares come alive and skin as pale as first snow.

"W-what do you want? Please. I can give you anything. Jonathan, please."

"It's a bit late for that now, Richard. You said it yourself." I placed my bloody hand against the cave wall, trapping him and bringing our faces as close together as they had been last night. "Lilith is a friend of the homosexual. But you are no homosexual, are you?"

I licked his neck, salty with the sweat of one who feared a fate worse than death. His whole body convulsed in whimpering fear as my tongue reached up to his earlobe. The wind had died, leaving only the sound of rain lapping against the cave mouth. The darkened sky outside made this rugged patch of embattled hill-country feel like the edge of Armageddon.

The terror in Richard's once beautiful blue eyes reminded me of the stories Lilith used to tell me, tell us, her henchman, as we gathered around her bonfires that used to burn so open and brightly in the night.

"You made one mistake, Richard. Just one." I felt his hot breath against my lips. Small, tight puffs of air. I could hear his heart pounding inside him, feel his entire body convulse in petrified terror. "You thought Lilith was dead."

"Y-you… you…" He tried to mumble something, but I wasn't interested in words anymore.

"Shh." I pressed a bloody finger against his cold blue lips. "You led me back to her."

"I want to live." He finally whimpered.

I stroked his face and nodded at him with a soft smile. "I know, my sweet. I know."

Slowly, my hand worked behind his head and gripped his golden locks. Gently, but firmly, I pulled back his head, exposing his throat. My words had made him calmer.

"And you will... in time." I whispered to him. My mouth grew fuller as my teeth sprang into fangs, the ones that had served me well for millennia, and I sank them into Richard's soft open throat. I held him as his lifeblood flowed down my throat like his semen before.

It wasn't his fault, not really. He didn't know that once he'd had sex with me, or any of Lilith's many homosexual henchmen which roamed the earth, death would swiftly follow. He didn't know that when he disavowed himself, when he turned his back on admitting what was in his heart. Only those men are destined to die. The ones that hide. The ones that sneak. The ones who leave you cold and alone after digging their fill; or run out the door as soon as their loads are safely deposited in your orifices. Yes, I thought as his blood nourished my body, those ones deserve to die.

The God of Small Favours
H. P. Medina

The lower windows were unlocked, and that was potentially a problem.

Jin lowered the spyglass from his eye, frowning behind the bird-feather mask. Avocet rolled his eyes, already anticipating the problem, analysing it, and finding it undeserving of one iota of attention. He focused instead on keeping their slim little boat bobbing in the underlit waters, away from the shore and the cluster of spitting-clam eggs that could chew through their boat in as many seconds as it took to blink.

"The lower windows are unbarred," said Jin, lifting the spyglass again to ascertain that he had not, in fact, imagined the portentous opportunity dangling in front of their noses, but when he tilted his head northward, westward, and eastward, the yawning, black chasm where the windows were remained unyielding. That indicated that the windows were indeed unbarred, and as a thief, and to a lesser extent, a magician and con man, Jin did not appreciate it. His very senses were offended by the notion of an easier route, or an afternoon of curious silence, as usually it indicated that greater challenges lay ahead.

People did not leave their windows open in

Aedre, even in a new country where the police officers were part-time volunteers, former army members who missed the weight and power of authority, or nosy housewives with nothing better to do than twitch their curtains and eye up their neighbours.

"I don't like this," said Jin.

"Your feelings have been noted down, annotated, and filed away," said Avocet, struggling to keep the slim-ship above the waves, and not beneath it as it so desired to go.

Jackdaw, busy emptying his stomach over the side of the ship, looked up. "What's the matter?" he croaked, dipping his head again when the ship lurched like a drunkard feeling his way home along the cobblestones, "why are we still on this wretched vessel? Do you have something against my continued—" The ship tilted to one side, and so did Jackdaw, followed by the copious sounds of retching.

"I don't like it," insisted Jin, "I think we should head for calmer waters—"

"In Aedre?" sputtered Avocet, turning his head to where the mainland hovered, the shores perpetually wind-tumbled. "Calm waters, in Aedre? It's like asking for a rainy day in Razrosht."

Jin, who'd spent a handful of hours casing a Razrosht casino knee-deep in desert sand, yellow-fly, and snapbone birds, grimaced. He looked back at the house—the manor, really, the palace, the mansion, anything but a lowly *house*—and weighed up their options, of which there were only two: dock or flee.

Even by Aedreian standards, the house was ridiculous, an overwrought combination of styles that looked for all intents and purposes like a mad architect had drawn individual features on scraps of paper, burned them to cinders, thrown them in a hat, and then assembled a plan based on the alignments of the moon in its second phase. Turrets stood on turrets, which stood on towers, which stood on fortress walls, which stood on nothing but a sheer wall of blackglass that no well-armed battalion would be able to get through, harvested from the smooth crust of the ocean bottom.

The house itself formed part of a cliff-side, like a massive hand had chiselled in windows and doors at off-kilter angles, so that no sunlight could enter and lighten the books or the tapestries. The walls themselves weren't blackglass, they were something white—marble, probably, shipped in from Marviola, and just the logistics of shipping huge blocks of marble to a forgotten scrap-land on the lip of Aedre made Jin's head spin. If anything else, they could just dock at the pier, and chip off bits of stone; someone would pay a good sum for it.

"Fine," he said. "We'll dock. The house is probably empty, and we'll wind up torn to shreds on those rocks, and have to swim back before something in the water devours us—" Jackdaw made a sound like this was a preferable existence to the one that he was currently undertaking, "—but we'll have a good story to tell at pubs, and Empress knows, we might be able to sell the book rights to some seedy publisher with a penchant for tales of unplanned woe."

"That's the spirit," said Avocet, steering for the pier as though they hadn't spent a quarter of an hour burning coal in the middle of nowhere, with lights blinking slow and deep beneath the sea-water like giant, unwavering eyes. Jin did not question what was below them; better the knowledge unknown, as his father had said, but his father was a swindler who'd run half a dozen widows in Yamatoji out of their inheritances, so perhaps he was not the best to follow for advice.

The beach was a comma, half-buried in a paragraph of rock, and if Avocet managed to land them right without breaking them on one of the nasty little bottom-scrapers, Jin would buy him a drink at the Drunkard's Wobble.

Avocet jerked the boat hard to the right, his mask tilting nearly off his face. Something raked the boards beneath their feet, and Jackdaw narrowly missed cracking his skull open on a jutting rock and spilling all of that hard-earned brain out into the water. The boat didn't so much 'dock' as melt onto the sand near the pier, and when Jin stood up to clear the boards, he saw that the bottom of it had been chewed away as though by acid, leaving a spot very close to his foot singed. He shuddered, poking his toe into the sand beneath before he cast his glance back over the water.

Whatever had brushed up against their boat was gone, and the water was black and still as the shiny, smooth rock of the cliffs. Their way back home wasn't clear—that much was certain by the gaping hole in their boat—but they'd landed with all their extremities, and none of them worse for wear, barring Jackdaw. The tight knot of tension that had been pressing down on his stomach eased, and Jin glanced up at the house above them, feeling his anxiety melt away, replaced by the low, pre-love hum of anticipation.

It didn't look all that frightening from the shores of its own land. Ugly—by *Empress,* was it ugly—but the most ragged rocks could hide the most becoming, eye-wateringly-expensive jewel.

Something of these thoughts must have shown on his face, because Avocet laughed, and wrapped an arm around his shoulders. "Feeling better?" he asked.

"Much," said Jin, and flashed him a smile he almost—*almost*—felt. "Let's get to work."

* * *

Getting up the blackglass walls wasn't difficult, not with Jackdaw's superior strength, and his propensity for packing for every heist like they were going to wage war on the toothed land of Razrosht. Even finding a way into the house wasn't difficult, not with the unbarred, open lower windows, which led into a kitchen of some proportion, and a staggeringly obvious indication that there was no one at home, if there had been for some time judging by the amount of cobwebs draped over everything. Avocet curled his lip at that, and Jackdaw muttered darkly to himself in his native Langeillan, but Jin saw only profit.

"The house isn't destroyed," he murmured to them, in a huddle by the window they had entered. "The items look like good quality. It just means that whoever owns it isn't here for a while. We'll split up."

Avocet raised his brows, which made his mask twist on his face. "Are you certain?"

"Positive," said Jin, who'd forgotten all about the open window, the blatant twitching finger of 'come in, we're open'. A job was a job, and money was money, and he had mouths to feed, even if it was primarily his own.

Avocet left the massive kitchen first, taking a spiralling right to the other side of the house. Jackdaw, after a grimacing moment, took the left side, whisper-singing under his breath about a lass from Langeillan, and her mile-long legs.

Which left Jin the stairs, and the upper landing.

There was enough moonlight to see that the house they were in was bigger—almost significantly bigger—than the outside had shown, and that the climate was somewhere between 'freezing' and 'already frozen'. Air wisped from his mouth, and the stairs going up seemed both impossibly huge, and completely insurmountable.

Jin placed his foot on the first step. It did not creak. There were no noises—not from where Avocet had gone, nor the friendly hum of Jackdaw's Langeillan singing. There was nothing, not even the sound of his own heartbeat.

Jin did not see the shadow flickering behind him, a half-step out of his sight. He moved his hand to the left side, feeling wallpaper, smooth, cool stone beyond that; he took hold of his pocket, and pulled out the phosphorous lantern, lighting it with a flick of flint against the oil-wick. It gave off a small, green glow, just enough for him to avoid running headfirst into a massive pair of jaws.

There was no descriptor for the beast that he'd narrowly avoided decapitating himself on; one hadn't been seen on the island for over 1000 years, and the only specimen in the museum had parts of it missing, like a greater monster had bitten through chunks of it. This one was intact, and from the tip of its distended, two-pronged tail to the hand-span muzzle, it ran the length of two men. The fur was coarse and shiny somehow, ink-black, and the lolling muzzle showed two thick layers of teeth in the jaws, capped by incisors bigger than his hand. It reared, frozen in time, both of its yellow eyes on him as though it could see— but dead. Unmistakably dead.

Jin neatly stepped around it, avoiding the lambent glow of its eyes, calming his racing heart by trying to remember all he knew about the Aeneir; they were hunters; they were omnivorous; they'd disappeared more than a quarter of a century ago when something had wiped the islands clean of all life and restarted a new era of occupation. Sometimes you could see fossilized claw marks dug deep into the cliff-sides, or find skeletal remains in dens at the base of the rocks. A full specimen had been unearthed from a beach, but beyond that—

Empress, the money this would be worth to a museum! If only it wasn't twice his size, and possessed of the rather nasty habit of eyeing him up like lunch.

Jin shuddered, stepping away from it and into the first room on his left.

Initially, he thought he must have turned himself around, and found his way back down to the kitchen. It was—the same. The open window, the promise of sea beyond. The countertops, littered with the same casual mess that rich people carried with them like accents from foreign places, strange foods that become custom. The door behind him creaked shut, and Jin poked it open with the flat of his hand, looking out onto the landing, the giant beast, and then back in.

Somehow the room upstairs was identical to the one below stairs.

No, thought Jin, not identical. The room downstairs didn't have a stain on the floor, glossy and black in the moonlight, coming out from beneath a door that common sense told him to avoid at all costs. The room below hadn't had a trio of long-bladed knives sitting on the central island, gleaming with ominous intent, one still wet with liquid that Jin hoped beyond hope was jam or cream, or something else edible, something that wasn't tied to the stain on the stairs. He stepped back.

Something in the back of the room moved, with a chittering sound like a flock of birds. He froze, his back tight against the wood of the door, as the thing in the back of the room clicked past the window.

It was—or had been, at some point, he supposed—a woman, with long hair that hung down to her waist. Part of her face was gone, a fact which seemed supremely rude to Jin at the moment, if only because he could see through the gap in it, and watch the white, glossy bone of her teeth chew a raw, pulsing hunk of meat that she held in her hands.

He swallowed, reflexively pushing himself through the door, his hands shaking as he drew it gently shut behind him. The woman and her gruesome meal didn't notice; the door clicked shut, and Jin put both of his hands over his mouth, and shook, trying to stop the trembling by counting back from ten, and when that failed, counting forward from one, and when that failed, stumbling to the nearest open window, and gagging for air.

Jin couldn't stop thinking of—her? Was it her? Did it count as a 'her' when there was a wound stretched across her face that a human could not have survived? When the muscle in her cheek flopped like it wasn't attached?

They'd been wrong to come here. He'd find the others, and they'd go back, if they had to swim to shore.

Jin pulled himself back. His hands had stopped shaking, and his breathing had evened out, which was a substantial improvement. He'd just begun to question whether or not it was wise to flee when he noticed two things.

Firstly, the door to the room he'd exited quickly was open, gaping like a mouth in the wall. Jin was sure he had shut it when he'd fled.

Secondly, the beast he'd seen in the hallway was gone.

Not moved.

Not covered.

Gone. Vanished. As if it had been only the result of one too many cups of ale at the Drunkard's Wobble. Jin blinked, hoping beyond hope that it would reappear when he opened his eyes. One. Two. Three.

Please reappear, he thought.

Jin opened his eyes.

It did.

Jaw-first in front of his face.

When he'd stood in front of it, he'd missed several details about it; how the teeth were pinked like they were permanently stained, how the jaw hung wide enough to completely swallow a man's upper torso without a hitch. He'd missed the slick, wet shine of claws sharp enough to rend metal and make confetti of the boat they'd stupidly docked on the sand He'd missed the eyes, yellowed like egg yolk, gleaming in a tangle of fur that looked more like hair than any noticeable mammal.

Hot breath stroked across his face, meat-stinking.

Jin took a step back, his brain trying to consolidate whether throwing himself down the flight of stairs to his right would give him a better chance at survival than the barren, black-walled landscape to his left. Almost as though sensing it, the beast coiled itself to the right of him, blocking his access to the staircase.

"Nice beast," whispered Jin, reaching behind him to feel along the wall. The creature's tail whipped behind it, denting—if he wasn't mistaken—the balustrade. "Lovely beast. Nice—" his fist closed around the neck of a delicate-looking antique vase, and before Jin could analyse the problematic approach to his escape, he'd hefted it at the beast's triangular head, turned tail, and ran through the open doorway to his left, leaving it slamming behind him. A roar like a tonne of stone falling down a cliffside following him, accented shortly afterwards by the tap-tap-tap of claws on hardwood.

Jin cursed his choices, chiefly those that had landed him directly in this situation: hurtling into the unknown dark of a house with questionable approaches to personal aesthetic and animal training. He cursed Avocet, and his ready assurance that there was nothing to worry about. He cursed that he hadn't been clever enough—as the leader—to outwit them.

Mostly, he cursed the fact that he'd been born human, not cat, and could no longer see in the dark than he could hover above the floor like a bird.

Jin slammed through another door, shoulder-first. The room pulsed with breath, a few degrees cooler than the hallway, and he took the confused pause behind him to shove an antique armoire of some heft in front of the door. That rending howl echoed again, rattling the windows in the room which he stood. Jin pressed his shoulders back against the armoire, as though his significantly lighter body would keep the door shut where the furniture couldn't, but it seemed like the monster beyond the door had decided to seek easier prey.

Empress. *Avocet.* Jackdaw. He had to save them, somehow.

As Jin's eyes adjusted to the gloom, he could make out a little more of his newfound shelter. The walls were dark, velvety-looking in the sprinkle of moonlight that poked in through the curtains. What furniture there was looked like it had travelled here from the time-stopped region of Southern Velier; he could see the typical rose embellishments along the sides, and the peculiar staining that could have been paint, could have been otherwise. Jewels spilled along the top of a dressing table, capped by three tall mirrors that reflected Jin. They drew his eye as nothing else did in the room, not even the cabinet heaped with golden, gleaming artefacts.

The portion of his brain that was not strictly attached to this situation calculated the cost of all that casual finery. The rest of it screamed in unending, rattling terror, peppered with *Avocet Jackdaw Avocet Jackdaw.*

Jin took a step away from the armoire. It held, and so he took another step, moving to the dressing table, where the fat jewels, each the size of his coiled fist, sat on a mirrored surface. He could hear his breathing, pained and quick, the rattle of his heartbeat, but the magnetic pull of shiny things, distracted enough that he missed the subtle creak of wood behind him, the pair of black-eyed twins that pulled out of the shadows by the door and watched him over his shoulder, one at either side.

He'd never seen pearls that could grow big enough to swamp a man's palm, or rubies that shifted and glowed in the light like they were full of gold. He held a sapphire up to the window, watching the moonlight move through it, and then set it reluctantly down for a peridot, smooth as bone and the colour of frozen grass. It vibrated faintly in his palm, and Jin lifted it to his ear to hear the note it was singing.

At which point his eyes lifted to the mirror, and saw the twins standing behind him.

"Hello," said the one on his right. The eyes were like pitch, fringed with white eyelashes, an arch of black brows. It spoke with a smile on its face that never moved one inch, and there seemed to be a flickering, discordant disharmony around its edges, like a photograph which had been taken when the subject moved. Looking at the face for too long made a headache build behind his eyes, and Jin would have dropped his gaze if he wasn't rooted to the floor.

"Hello," echoed the one on his left, the same exact features bar a scar that twisted alongside the corners of a full, black-stained mouth.

Jin dropped the peridot. It clanged onto his toe, which smarted, but took the breath out of him enough to cut off the scream building in his throat.

They had no eyes. *They had no eyes.*

"H—H—" Jin said.

The twins took it as a greeting worthy of their attention.

"How did you get in here?" said the one.

"How did you get past the guard?" said the other Guard.

Oh, Empress, those teeth. Why did humans need wolf teeth?

"I—I'm—" A guest, he thought, hysterically, a plumber, a teacher, none of which was plausible to state at whatever hour of the night it was, but marginally better than admitting he'd come here to steal, "I'm—a—"

"Guest?" suggested the one, grinning, and oh Empress, he could see something red and shining in its gums and Jin did really think he might be sick.

"A plumber?" suggested the other, with the smooth, pouring voice of a singer.

"A teacher?" they both said, and Jin took a step back and slammed the small of his back into an open drawer.

"How interesting!" said the one, and reached out with a hand so pale and smooth, it glowed in the moonlight. "Tell us all about it?"

Jin didn't want that hand to touch him, but it seemed marginally better than hitting the floor in his attempt to get away, and so he closed his eyes as much as he dared, held his breath, and waited for the contact of skin to skin.

At which point the moon hovered behind a cloud, leaving him in darkness, with the sound of his own breathing echoing in his head, and no sight of the—of the twins, whatever twins they might be—until the cloud shifted, and there was light, and Jin's mouth dropped open.

He was in a different room, and the twins were not there, or perhaps they were, but he'd seen wrong.

They weren't twins, not exactly: one had brown hair, the other black hair, one had blue eyes, and the other green. They had pupils, which was a strange thing to notice, but this had been a strange night, and so Jin was prepared to forgive himself. There were no scars at the corners of mouths. The moonlight showed him that they did not have carnivore teeth, but human teeth, normal and small, behind perfect, soft lips.

Just a normal couple.

Behind him, the mirror showed the truth: black eyes, and teeth like sharks, but Jin was not facing the mirror.

"Did we frighten you?" said the blue-eyed one, a gentleman with heartbreaking beauty, the delicate set of his jaw just lightly darkened with fuzz. His voice was like a raindrop, rising and falling, and when he touched his cheek, Jin thought that he might have done a number of unspeakable things to hear him speak to him again.

"We didn't mean to," said the green-eyed one, a woman who Jin swore he'd dreamt of once, when he'd been youthful and uncomfortable with hormones, attracted to everyone who shone him a simple smile. "We're on our honeymoon, and, well—" she laughed, like a fork striking a glass, and Jin would've knelt in worship if he'd had the strength in his legs to do so.

"We couldn't sleep," said the young man, mischievous with intent, and it was then that Jin noticed that he was naked. Gods would've wept to have his body, carved out of limestone, and smoother than the Marviola marble that bracketed the outside of the house. His cock was curved up against his belly, shiny at the head.

A sweet, perfumed scent came off the pair of them, and a shuddering heat spread through his belly, down to regions best left forgotten on heists. Jin closed his hands into fists.

Look behind you, said his brain, which he ignored.

"I—I'm sorry to interrupt." His voice sounded hoarse, his breathing rocked by the thunderous warmth pulsing through his cock, "I didn't—"

"Nevermind that," said the woman, and she was nude too, her breasts golden in the light, nipples pink and puckered, "you're here now."

"We've been waiting for someone like you for a long time."

They reached for him in tandem, and the explosion of heat in his stomach left him breathless, squirming underneath the kisses peppered on his throat, his jaw. His brain wanted to tell him something important, something worrying, but Jin batted off the concerns, and gave himself to the kisses, to the one mouth scraping his nerves, and the other low on his belly, arrowing down to—

"That's quite enough," said a soft, deep voice. "I'll thank you not to eat the locals."

But it was so good, and his body was so warm, and Jin made soft, protesting sounds when the mouth travelling on his belly stopped. Somewhere in the distance, a hissing repartee echoed, and his maligned brain had a message of some urgency rattling around, but Jin could not grasp it—the room was so warm, and so beautiful, so—

A sharp, cold-snap backhand knocked him out of the stunned fugue of desert sands and doubled delights. A gentleman stood behind him, as tall as the room was high, wearing a discordantly short nightshirt and lopsided nightcap.

The beautiful couple was gone, in their place two piles of ash that smelled faintly of honeysuckle and jasmine.

"Succubi," said the gentleman, and turned on his heel. "If you'll follow me, then."

"But I—" except he was gone immediately, leaving him in a room whose walls vibrated and pulsed with breath, and against his better judgement, and in keeping with his survival instinct, Jin fled after him.

He lost track of the doors and the corridors that the gentleman pulled him through. When they'd seen the house outside, Jin was sure there hadn't been half as many corridors, hallways, and passages that there was now, and he didn't wish to question whether he had found his end at the jaws of that slavering beast, and was now wandering the twilit nightmare realm ghosts went when they were locked out of eternal rest.

When he had followed his guide for more than a full five minutes, they stopped.

His guide clicked his tongue, something forgotten in their headlong rush, and ushered him inside a sitting room. A four-poster bed hovered in the back, and a fire lit two armchairs cuddled around a wrought-iron grate. There were no windows, but the walls were covered floor to ceiling in empty frames and the room sparkled with firelight reflecting off their glass.

"You'll have a drink," said the gentleman, settling down his candle. In his other hand, there appeared a bottle.

It was perhaps testament to the path of the night he'd had that Jin didn't blink, merely nodded, and collapsed in one of the armchairs by the fire.

Out of the corner of his eye, he watched his saviour. All he had ascertained of him in the other room was that he was tall and had shapely legs, and in the increased light of this bedroom, Jin could see that had not been an exaggeration.

Then it turned, and something tired and hoarse in the back of Jin's head threw its hands up in disgust.

Its eyes were blank and pupilless, ice-floe white, and the parted set of his mouth meant that Jin could see the fangs behind his lips.

"What are you?" asked Jin, more exhausted than frightened.

The entity shrugged, and poured him a glass of very fine, aged wine. "Nothing you have to worry about," he said—it said?—lightly, dropping down into the accompanying seat by the fire. "I don't tend to eat the locals."

"I'm hardly local," Jin muttered, unable to resist the correction, against his better sense. He took the glass of offered wine and swirled it. Small golden lights danced in the red. "And I think I'm owed some answers, aren't I?"

"Humans are so very precocious," said the entity. "You barge into my house, upset my house-mates, and *you* demand answers." There was something in his voice that reminded Jin of snake-scales slithering on hot stone, and he shook the image of Razrosht out of his head. Focus. He took a sip of the wine, swallowing it down without tasting it, eager for the melting pleasure of light intoxication.

"I apologise," he said. "I've had a very taxing evening."

"I'm sure," said the entity, and Jin could not see his mouth, but he had a feeling it was smiling. "You're very lucky you didn't end up digested by the succubi.

Or eaten by Heisser—the creature you spotted walking around in the dark. He has a taste for flesh."

"And what is your taste for?" asked Jin, casual as he could. The threat of devouring seemed lesser now, and his curiosity far outweighed his self-preservation.

"Pleasure," said the entity, and shrugged his shoulders, "but I found your compatriots lacking in that department. I've deposited them outside before they could attract any more attention with their screaming."

"They're well?" asked Jin warily.

"More or less," said the entity. "Perhaps nursing lifelong terrors for shadowy spaces, but well enough. Whole, at least, which is more than can be said for you." He crossed one long and elegant leg over the other, which exposed a length of thigh more beautifully carved than statuary. "The succubi devoured your fear."

Succubi. Plural. Jin's brain churned through a convincing mock-up of the evening's events, culminating in the room that shifted and swayed in his memory. A curious emptiness hovered at the forefront of his mind.

"Surely that isn't a problem?"

The entity laughed. "You'd think, but a creature without fear is a stupid creature. It charges headlong into danger and stays there even when all its senses are screaming at it to flee. Succubi work that way, weakening their prey by making themselves beautiful, then by making their prey weak. Consider yourself lucky that I came along."

Jin laughed, low and smoky. "You haven't given me any indication to think that you won't do the same," he told him. He was feeling overfull on the wine, overfull on the evening's pleasure—on the entity's voice, his charm, the way he sat and how the fire played over copper-gleam skin. "But, thank you," he added, with a degree of sincerity that he did feel, "I was very in over my head."

"There's just the matter of repayment, of course," said the entity. "I don't do things for cheap."

"Of course," Jin sighed, resting his head back. "I suppose you'll hand me to the police."

"I can hardly walk into a police station looking like this, can I?" said the entity, and Jin made an assenting noise. "No. I'll let you go loose, of course, with something to barter for your trouble. What I would ask instead is for a kiss..." Its voice softened, and it looked aside, stating stiffly, "...it does not have to be on my face. I've been told my face is disconcerting." As if anticipating Jin's next question, he stated, "It has—been a while. For me."

"Most creatures of your appearance have eyes," said Jin, agreeably. He turned the offer over in his head, trying to see where the catch was—for there was always a catch. "You won't try and entrap me?" he said.

"No."

"You won't try and devour me at all?"

"No."

"All you want is a kiss, and it can be anywhere? Even on your hand?"

"As I've stated. You have my word."

Privately Jin thought that the word of a creature he did not recognise meant very little to him, but the core of truth in the entity's words resounded to him—though he did not think they would have if the beasts below hadn't eaten his fear—and he set his wine-glass down, moving a little closer. After all, he could understand loneliness; he'd come to this island with nothing and no one. Who would it harm?

It was very disconcerting looking at eyes which had no pupils, and therefore could not be said to be looking at you.

He pressed a kiss to the corner of its mouth. A soft, indistinct noise, a gasp hastily clutched back, blurred against his mouth. Jin reached up, tangling his fingers in the pitch-dark hair (it was as soft as it looked), and deepened the kiss against the corner of that mouth, flicking his tongue into the groove of its lower lip. The entity arched up to meet him, and one hand found its way to the small of his back, where it lay, faintly hot.

Heat swirled around Jin's head. The earlier, aching want had been nothing; now it swamped him, dragging him down under a wave of madness that wanted only *flesh* and *skin* and *contact.*

"Do you have a name?" said Jin.

It started, and said, "I don't—understand what my name would—"

"I like to know the names of creatures I bed," said Jin, and tugged it up.

For a moment, the shadows beyond it shifted, and Jin's brain warned him again *run, run, run.* He thought of the shrines in the city, dedicated to gods that had fallen from their pantheon, to creatures older than written record, known only as snatches of song; he thought of all the things he'd seen tonight. Everything in him should have been terrified; but the desert-heat of the entity's mouth on his kept him there, anchored to the floor, staring up at its face.

"Deo," said the entity. "Call me Deo." And it fell on him like a starveling wolf.

They hit the floor hard, Jin's back first, his head thumping off plush carpet. His mouth stung with kisses, too many of them to keep track of; his fingers couldn't find anything to hold onto, sliding off of Deo's nightshirt. For all its length, he was narrow, a dream of a dancer, all leg and golden skin, and Jin ripped at its clothing without stopping to think that he would need them to get out of here.

Deo laughed, long and low. It sounded decades older than he was, and so lonely, it stung.

Jin raked his nails along Deo's back, finally ridding him of the nightshirt, then pushed him down, straddling his long thighs, wanting to look at it—him. A him, Jin saw, the fuzzy edges of him sharpening for details he had omitted; a face made to start wars: delicate, soft-jawed beauty framed by a knot of hair that curled around the back of a swan-slender neck. He had a mouth for kissing, the lower lip slightly fuller than the upper one, and there was a dip of light in the centre of it that Jin wanted to sample.

Deo's hair had come loose, spread out onto the carpet like a length of black water, moving faintly as Deo tilted his head. His skin was flushed, those white eyes watching him, watching every movement of him, as Jin dragged his gaze down, over his flat chest, over the peaked nipples and the sharp decline of his stomach, to the long, thick cock pulsing over Deo's stomach. Thrill rocked low in Jin's belly, and he reached down to wrap his hand around Deo's cock, rubbing his thumb against the wet slit. When he pulled his thumb away, a thick, glossy line of pre-come followed him, and it snapped with a noise that Jin felt all the way down in his stomach.

That was when he noticed the glyphs, the markings, pearlescent on that copper skin, catching the firelight—but it seemed so inopportune to notice them now that Jin put them aside, scraped himself down, and swallowed the throbbing cock in his hand right down to the hilt.

Underneath him, Deo's body jumped, and took to wracking shudders. Jin ran his tongue up along the shaft, tracing a pulsing vein at the base with the tip of his tongue until he reached the slit again, and could taste his cock to his content. It wasn't normal, that sweetness; Jin knew it wasn't normal. But like the glyphs, he put it out of his mind, sinking down on his cock again until it pounded in Jin's throat with a hammer-beat. Up again, and then down, and Jin could feel the pulse-pulse-pulse of blood in it, and from his dipped-down position on the floor, he could see, also, how Deo's head was thrown back, twisting on the carpet.

Jin grinned. He hummed, deep into his throat, and was rewarded with a shout, near-feral; a snarl of fingers in his hair, too many to take note of, burying at the base of his skull and pushing him down. He went, humming again, feeling his own cock ache and twitch against his stomach.

It seemed like the room rocked with them, shifted with them. There were shadows on the walls, and they seemed to have eyes, but nothing beyond this was noteworthy, was necessary. Jin's fingers found a crooked hip-bone; clung to it; Jin's mouth found its way down to the swollen, heavy balls beneath his mouth, his tongue to the gap between them. Deo's sharp panting echoed like breaking glass, and all Jin could do was relish it, relish how every noise seemed to send a flutter of heat through him.

And then the room switched, and Jin was on his back, and Deo was above him, and had changed.

There were horns, antlers, really, black and spiralling from his forehead, and his face had melted of all human features. The mouth was gone, and the face was a shadow, and those white eyes watched him with a fascinated gleam. The rest of him was hard muscle and silky skin, and all Jin could think of was the legends of the beasts that had been on Aedre before time had erased them, of the missing colonies, and the gods they worshipped.

But Deo lowered his face to his, and there was a mouth somewhere, for there were kisses.

And there were hands.

Everywhere.

Touching him everywhere: there was a hand on his cock, pumping him furiously; a hand rolling his balls, making him keen; there was a hand with two slick, impossibly long fingers curling into him, finding a spot inside his body that made stars pop on his eyelids, and his eyes roll back white in his head; there were hands playing with his nipples, pinching, twitching, rolling. Jin couldn't keep track of all the hands on him—swore that Deo had only had two when they started—but there were so many more now to contend with.

He came, hard, creaming against his belly, against his chest, and still it did not end. The fingers in him twisted, and found a new spot to torment, and the stars turned to galaxies on his eyelids. The hand around his cock was joined by a mouth, wet and hot, sliding down until the tightness around him was around all of him.

Jin couldn't open his eyes, didn't dare open his eyes. He didn't think it would warrant looking at what had happened to Deo, what he'd become.

He came again, breath sobbing in his throat, from the mouth around his cock, and the flicker of a tongue against his slit, quick enough to make his eyes cross. It didn't seem like his body had tired at all from the pleasure; every moment he came was chased by another, quicker, hotter, a desire so unshakably deep that Jin could do nothing but give into it.

The fingers inside him crooked again, and Jin mewled, high and keening, thought he heard something else answer him. Pleasure roared in his head, and Jin let it suffuse every inch of him. Deo laughed.

Jin opened his eyes.

There was a shrine in Aedre dedicated to a god with no name, a being of the fabric of society. He had white eyes, and an affinity with foxes, and attracting his attention was impossible and undesirable, but his worshipers were ardent followers of the faith. Jin had heard they plucked their eyes out to see him better, that they cut their throats to mimic his sacrificial bindings, that they listened for the sound of his song on the water.

How wrong they were. How wrong.

The god with no name was more than what they dreamed of, beautiful, but not in any way that humans could comprehend. It was the beauty of sunlight on bone, the beauty of shadows through the slats of trees, of still water before a storm. It was the beauty of a creature seen only rarely, a monster that slipped through the waves around a boat, leaving ripples in its wake; it was beauty that language had not been made to describe.

Jin's brain jumbled the images: the white eyes, the shadowy face, the horns spiralling into antlers. There were gleaming lights around Deo's head, and his hair had turned to flexing darkness, and Jin could see the glyphs on his skin glowing, glowing. Jin could see him, and Deo watched his recollection, smiling a smile that was there, somehow, on his not-human face, in the tilt of his not-human head.

Wings spread from behind his back, six of them, crow wings with plush feathers.

Jin was moving. Deo was lifting him, looking to him as he positioned him back on the armchair, held aloft on cushions, tilting his head questioningly as he lined himself up. That thick cock Jin had witnessed before seemed bigger still; Jin's stomach curled with both anticipation and nervousness.

"Gently," he told him, but his voice was a whisper in a roar, and he wasn't sure Deo heard it.

But oh—oh.

Oh, he did.

There was pain, there was always pain for this, but it was muted by the sudden pleasure of a mouth at his neck, nibbling at his throat where Jin had always been susceptible. Jin whined, clawing for his back, finding only wings, and felt every long, hot inch of Deo sliding into him.

There was a hand around his cock again, two hands, three. His cock seemed to curve, impossibly, to rub against his prostate on every slide out and every slide in, and three orgasms in, Jin's body didn't seem to want to dwindle.

Another burst of pleasure made him cry out, sticky heat swamping his stomach. Then another, and another, and another—each one linking to the last, leaving him shaking and breathless, smothered in wings and heat.

Jin kept his eyes open this time, wanted to see Deo's face—Deo's face.

There was another smouldering flicker, heat on heat. Jin tensed, feeling that heat building, building, building—

When it took him, Jin wasn't even partially ready. Pleasure ruined him, leaving him limp and shrieking, writhing and twisting, every inch of him battered by sensation: a mouth sliding on his cock, a cock brushing up against his prostate, hands playing with his nipples, a mouth on his neck, a kiss to his mouth, until it took him over again, and again, until he finally passed out.

* * *

When Jin woke, he woke on the shore, in a nest made of sand and bird twigs, with a bag by his side.

He woke slowly, stretching, the sunlight stinging his eyes. Next to him, Avocet was muttering something incomprehensible—*look at him, what do you think is wrong with him?*—and Jackdaw had taken up a length of swearing so intricate that Jin hesitated to interrupt him. Every inch of him ached, and shivery, trembling pleasure warmed every one of his cells.

He sat up. Avocet looked like he'd been crying and was narrowly avoiding hitting him. "Where the hell have you been?" he said, hauling him to his feet, sending Jin's body tumbling over and over in shuddery want. "We've been looking for you all night, and you just—fell asleep on the beach? And where did you get those?"

"What?" said Jin, intelligently, looking down at the bag between them.

It was full of the jewels he'd spied—

Abruptly, Jin turned his head and looked up at the windows, but there was no figure watching them sit there. There was, however, a note at the top of the bag, which he plucked under the guise of shifting through the gleaming jewels.

"I—found them," said Jin, unconvincingly.

Avocet said nothing. He shook his head, as if the story was entirely too much for him to withstand, and said, "We're heading back. We found a boat."

As they walked towards the boat, Jin lingered to unfold the note. Written on it was:

Visit me again, will you?

Followed by a glyph that Jin had seen carved into the posts of the god with no name.

Jin grinned. His body throbbed, part pleasure, part ache.

Avocet called behind him, "What the hell are you smiling for? Hurry up!"

Quickening his pace, Jin tucked the note into his pocket for safekeeping, and didn't look back at the house until he was safely in the boat, now patchworked together using what Jin thought was a table-leg from the house. He considered asking them where they'd found it—if they'd heard anything incriminating in there—but decided not to. Instead, Jin turned his head for one last look at the house, and at the windows in the upper-floor, and could have sworn he'd spied a pair of white-gold eyes, staring down at him, and an invisible smile on a face without a mouth.

About the Editor

Andrew Robertson is an award-winning queer writer, editor and journalist. He has published articles in *Xtra!, fab magazine, ICON, Gasoline, Samaritan Magazine, neksis, Viberater* and *Shameless*. His fiction has appeared in literary magazines and quarterlies such as *Stitched Smile Publications Magazine Vol 1, Deadman's Tome, Sirens Call, Undertow, katalogue, Feeling Better Yet?,* and in anthologies including *Alice Unbound: Beyond Wonderland, Gone with the Dead, Group Hex Vol. 1* and *Vol. 2, A Tribute Anthology to Deadworld, Cuarenta y Nueve, First Hand Accounts, Happy MILF Day, Happy DILF Day,* and *Abandon.* A lifelong fan of horror, he is the founder and sometimes co-host of The Great Lakes Horror Company Podcast, official podcast to Library of the Damned, and a member of the Horror Writer's Association.

About the Authors

Valerie Alexander lives in L.A. Her stories have been published in a number of sci-fi, horror and speculative anthologies and magazines. Visit her on Twitter at @Vaxder or valeriealexander.org.

Derek Clendening is an author and artist living in Fort Erie, Ontario. His work has appeared in such anthologies as *Blood Lite 2,* and *Group Hex Vol. 2*. He is an Active member of the Horror Writers Association.

Lisi Damette is the dark persona of a writer with a near jet-black soul. She currently resides in the Pacific Northwest, nestled in a warm cabin under tall pine trees. You can reach her on twitter @Lisi_Damette

Spinster Eskie is a resident of California and has an M.Ed in creative arts education. With a background in women's studies, her focus as a writer is to expose the female experience through unsettling tales that highlight the dilemmas of misogyny and oppression. By combining the genres of feminist theory, dark comedy, horror, and science-fiction, she aims to not only disturb readers, but deliver a message that is informative and thought provoking. In 2005 Eskie's play, *Tell Me About*

Love, was featured in the Provincetown Playwright Festival. She has been featured in various online magazines such as *Deadman's Tome, Bad Moon Rising,* and *69 Flavors of Paranoia*. Eskie has a number of short stories published by Pill Hill Press, Post-Mortem Press, Scary Tales Publications, Cruentus Libri Press, and many others.

Robert E. Furey is a freelance writer and editor of *Hard Universe* living in Central Pennsylvania. In addition to his day job as university professor and forensic entomologist, he is a graduate of the Clarion West writer's program in Seattle, and attended the Speculative Fiction Writers Workshop and Science Fiction and Fantasy Novel Writing Workshop, both at the University of Kansas. His fiction has appeared in several science fiction anthologies and magazines. Rob has been a regular contributor to the *Internet Review of Science Fiction* and *Aeon Magazine* with fiction-related articles, and had his work published by Baen Books. He currently lives in a 200-year-old house with his wife, daughter, and stepson, one dog, two cats, and a demonically possessed macaw. This is Rob's first pure horror story.

Sèphera Girón is the award-winning author of over 20 published horror novels and dozens of short stories. Her books from Leisure and Samhain Horror have been reissued by various publishers while she's busy penning new tales. She has stories in *Group Hex 1, Group Hex 2, Abandon, Amazing Monster Tales No. 1, Creatures in Canada—A Darkling Around the World Anthology, The Pulp Horror Book of Phobias* and more. She is working on the next book in her *Witch Upon a Star* erotic horror series from Riverdale Avenue Books. Sèphera currently lives in Toronto. sepheragiron.ca

Kimberly Gondrella was born in Ottawa Canada but spent her formative years as a Toronto club kid. She has worked as a designer, burlesque dancer and purveyor of voodoo trinkets. She currently resides in New Orleans where, when she isn't busy writing, she is the Head Milliner at a famous French Quarter hat shop. She has just completed her first novel and yes, there will be vampires.

Benjamin Johnson is a 20-something hailing from Saskatoon, Saskatchewan, Canada. He has been writing for most of his life and has a particular interest in crafting stories centered around LGBT+ themes, particularly those with horror and fantasy elements. He and his husband, Mitchell, are both members of the Penultimates, a Saskatoon-based writing group. This is his first published piece.

Lindsay King-Miller's writing has appeared in *Glamour Magazine, The Guardian, Them.us, Vice.com*, and numerous other publications. She lives in Denver with her partner, their daughter, and two very spoiled cats. She is the author of *Ask A Queer Chick: A Guide to Sex, Love, and Life for Girls who Dig Girls* (Plume, 2016). You can follow her on Twitter @askaqueerchick.

Angel Leigh McCoy wears several hats in her daily journey: writer, editor, game designer, and audiobook narrator. She once spent a month in the Netherlands, which is when this story was inspired, researched, and written. The Christ figure she found in Tilburg is something to behold. Angel is an active member of, and webmaster for, the Horror Writers Association. She has published more than 20 short stories in anthologies and magazines, and spent a decade writing narrative for a little game called *Guild Wars 2*. She is the founder and CEO of Games Omniverse (gamesomniverse.com), an indie game design team currently working their butts off on a story-rich video game called *Danika Dire and the Wretched Wake*. angelmccoy.com

H.P. Medina is a pastel-colored entity of questionable origin residing in the sun-scorched land of Malta. They enjoy long walks by the beach, thinking about writing, reading about writing, and, occasionally, writing. They are usually accompanied by a dark void of a cat named Cookie, who criticizes everything in deep, gravelly mews.

H.P. Medina deals in fantastical fiction of any shape, size, and color, with the only stipulation that very few deaths actually stick. *The God of Small Favours* is their first foray into horror, as they have previously only published historical or historical-adjacent romances. Despite a morbid attraction to all things brutal, H.P. Medina favors happy endings, both literal and metaphorical.

Harry F. Rey is an author and lover of gay themed stories with a powerful punch. He is the author of the royal romance series *The Line of Succession* published by Deep Desires Press and the queer space opera novels *The Galactic Captains* published by Nine Star Press. His other works include *The Cruising Chronicles* short

stories, and *The Road Home: A Decade of Gay Poetry.*
harryfredrey.wixsite.com/harryfrey

Julianne Snow is the author of the *Days with the Undead* series and *Glimpses of the Undead* as well as the co-author of *The Carnival 13* and *Dragons of Faith.* Writing in the realms of speculative fiction, Julianne has roots that go deep into horror and is a member of the Horror Writers Association. With pieces of short fiction in various publications, Julianne always has a few surprises up her sleeves. juliannesnow.com

Jeff C. Stevenson is a professional member of Pen America, an active member of the Horror Writers Association, and a finalist for the Best Published Midsouth Science Fiction and Fantasy Darrell Award. Jeff has published more than 50 dark fiction stories and has been included in anthologies alongside Clive Barker, Ramsey Campbell, Richard Chizmar, Jack Ketchum, Brian Lumley, Adam Nevill, Graham Masterton, Edgar Allan Poe and Algernon Blackwood. Jeff is the author of the Amazon #1 bestselling *Fortney Road: The True Story of Life, Death, and Deception in a Christian Cult.* His first novel, the supernatural mystery, *The Children of Hydesville*, was published in July 2018 by Hellbound Books, who will also publish his suspense thriller, *I'll Come Back to Get You* in late 2018. Jeff also writes mainstream fiction under the pen name of Mary Saliger. Twitter: @JeffCStevenson

Jim Towns is an award-winning filmmaker, artist and writer. He lives in San Pedro CA with his wife and two mysterious cats.

Other Riverdale Avenue Books Afraid Titles You Might Enjoy

A Tribute Anthology to Deadworld and Comic Publisher Gary Reed
Edited by Lori Perkins

Still Hungry For Your Love
Edited by Lori Perkins

Women Who Love Monsters
Edited by Lori Perkins

Gone with the Dead: A Horror Romance Anthology
Edited by Lori Perkins

The Morris-Jumel Mansion Anthology of Paranormal Fiction
Edited by Camilla Saly-Monzingo

12498170R00157

Made in the USA
Lexington, KY
22 October 2018